W9-BQY-318

WAKING ROMEO

WAKING ROMEO
KATHRYN BARKER

FLATIRON BOOKS
NEW YORK

WAKING ROMEO. Copyright © 2021 by Kathryn Barker. All rights reserved. Printed in the United States of America. For information, address Flatiron Books, 120 Broadway, New York, NY 10271.

www.flatironbooks.com

Library of Congress Cataloging-in-Publication Data

Names: Barker, Kathryn, author.
Title: Waking Romeo / Kathryn Barker.
Description: First U.S. edition. | New York : Flatiron Books, 2022.
Identifiers: LCCN 2021037757 | ISBN 9781250174109 (hardcover) |
    ISBN 9781250174116 (ebook)
Subjects: CYAC: Time travel—Fiction. | Love—Fiction. | LCGFT: Novels.
Classification: LCC PZ7.1.B370776 Wak 2022 | DDC [Fic]—dc23
LC record available at https://lccn.loc.gov/2021037757

Our books may be purchased in bulk for promotional, educational, or business use. Please contact your local bookseller or the Macmillan Corporate and Premium Sales Department at 1-800-221-7945, extension 5442, or by email at MacmillanSpecialMarkets@macmillan.com.

Originally published in Australia in 2021 by Allen & Unwin

First U.S. Edition: 2022

10 9 8 7 6 5 4 3 2 1

For Wyatt and Orson.
I traveled across universes just to meet you.
Getting to be your mum is the most infinite gift
that I could ever imagine.

And for Danny (my Ellis), Amisha, and Ayan—
what magic to have found you.

"...no Traveler returns."

William Shakespeare

ACT I

1

Jules

2083

I'm sitting in the chapel for school assembly when Headmistress Cisco says, "And now we'll hear a special tribute from Rosaline." *Crap.* There's at least a few of these a year and I systematically avoid them all, but today's is unexpected.

Rosaline takes the stage, all pretty, blond, and clean. She gives an exaggerated sniff, though not until everyone's quiet, so as not to waste it. Even from here I can see that her big blue eyes have just the right amount of wet—enough to prove she's still grieving after all this time, yet not so much that it smudges her coveted mascara.

"It's been two years," she says softly, then gives a dramatic pause. *It hasn't been two years, you self-aggrandizing cow. It's been one year, eleven months, and thirty days.* If it *had* been two years, I would have played hooky, because Rosaline always pulls this assembly love-fest rubbish on significant milestones. The girl really does live for such stuff. I don't know how she managed to spin it the way she did, but serious props for a job well done. Nobody remembers the pesky little detail about how she dumped him and broke his heart. *Hell* no. In the retelling, she was his one great love and I was just the little skank who killed him. Well, *mostly* killed him, if you're getting all technical.

Rosaline keeps talking—it's a daisy chain of clichés, ready for the choking. I tune her out. I know what she's saying because she's said it all before, many times. Depending on how many tears she can muster, she might even get a standing ovation. Wouldn't that be the icing on the cake for our dear little darling? One of her friends will have been briefed to help her off the stage, like she's some delicate flower ready to crumple. Her mum—Headmistress Cisco—will nod ever so solemnly, but the stink of pride will still leak through. Afterward, a teacher will bookend it all with a call to arms about watching out for "signs of mental illness among your peers." That last part's for me.

Because it turns out my story wasn't a love story after all. If I'd died, then it might have been, but I didn't die. Not unless you count the nerve-dead arm.

Rosaline's building up to her can't-talk-through-the-tears bit now. She's paced herself nicely. The trick is not getting too worked up until you've finished with all the sentimental nonsense. Over the years she's become quite the expert, but what she's gained in precision she's lost in spontaneity. She's formulaic. I know from experience that she'll slot in the thinly veiled jibe at me right after she's regained her composure. I guess she figures that's the perfect spot for contrast and damage.

The audience will oblige her, and suddenly all eyes will be

on the cause of the problem. Finding me in the mishmash of homemade uniforms isn't exactly tricky. Most of the blazers might have worn out a generation back, but people still make an effort. They've found replacement clothes in the school colors, more or less. They don't wear combat boots or black hoodies, for example. Nope, that special privilege is mine, all mine. It's out of necessity, really. Hoodies are hard to come by regardless of color, and I need the pouch up front. Without something to tuck my arm into, it kind of hangs there, getting caught on stuff. *Genuine health risk,* I tell them. *Honestly.*

From behind a wall of dark fringe, I see that Romeo's besties have spied me. Laurence is keeping it simple with a fairly standard glare. Paris has gone one better, mouthing "crazy" at me from across the chapel.

"In my heart of hearts, I know . . . ," Rosaline continues, bringing it home on the closing stretch. And I decide, stuff it—I don't have to be here. With that, I get up and walk out the back door. It makes a loud clang, which isn't ideal. I've probably just helped Rosaline give her best tribute ever. If she timed it right, she could have had me brazenly, heartlessly, callously leaving the chapel right when she was tearing up the most.

Stepping outside, I'm smothered by the quiet. There was this famous quote: "*When a man is tired of London, he is tired of life.*" Now the poor old place is as dead as my arm, all sleeping and still. There are no planes in the sky or sounds of trains in the background. There's no hubbub or buzz or din of commuter traffic, like I've read about in books.

And it's not just the silence, either—the vista's equally wasted. Everywhere I look, there's nothing but yesteryear gloom. Crumbling mansions covered in bird poo, invaded by overgrown grass.

Rust and cracks and fallen-down heaps; things that will never work again. Not that we let that stop us. *Hell* no. We fill dark fridges with canned food, hang corpse TVs on walls, and wipe down can't-be-used microwaves. We cover our coffee tables in glossy magazines that advertise a world long gone and talk about things like "tech" in the present tense. It's a performance, except without an audience . . . or a point.

In the distance, I can see the skyline of the city, and even that's muted—like a theater set covered in dust. I've lived here my whole life, but I'll never get used to the ghost-town feeling. It's like being a tourist—squatting in a world that was built in the past, and peaked there. *Died* there, even. And yet here we are playing house, pretending there's a pulse.

I walk down Johnson Street, following the faded white line that I'm told was for cars, back when cars were still a thing. I always take Johnson because Johnson's always empty, probably on account of the rooster.

It's not really a rooster—it's a time-travel pod melded to an elm tree. But when pods appear from the past in places that aren't empty? It can make for some serious weirdness. The one on Johnson is this mess of metal and tree trunk that kind of resembles a giant head. That's not the rooster part. I guess the Traveler who was inside at the time got rearranged so bad that their bones jutted out the top. It looks like that thing on the top of a rooster's head.

Well, I assume it does, from what I've read. I've never actually seen a rooster.

Johnson Street isn't unique or anything. There are melded pods throughout the Settlement, same as everywhere. Dead time travelers are kind of a fixture these days the whole world over. But *living* Travelers? Nobody's seen one in years. They used to arrive from the past all the time, steal our food, then leave again. Not anymore, though. I guess most of them have already jumped past this swan song moment. Gone for a better future that clearly isn't there.

Here at the Settlement, we don't believe in leaving. That's kind of the whole point. We're the descendants of the ones who said, *Enough is enough. The rampant time travel has got to stop. We have to stay put, to live off what's left.*

Not traveling in time is everything we stand for. But if there was a pod that could send me *back* in time instead of just forward? I'd take it. I'd rewind the clock. Back, back, back—all the way to the moment that Romeo and I tried to kill ourselves. Because all that *"O happy dagger"* palaver?

Turns out: a mistake.

Three blocks from the school, I pass Laertes, the legendary health club. Our ancestors were smart—while others jumped, they stockpiled. Good old Laertes was secretly stuffed to the brim. Women's loos with boxes of batteries, men's with cans of gasoline. The massive pool got drained, then piled high with clothes and shoes—every size, every season, tags still on. Gym, yoga studio, reception, juice bar, locker room, sauna . . . linens, toiletries, dried food, bottled water, intimates, medicine. And the ten double-height squash courts? Stacked—floor to ceiling—with canned food.

Of course, the loot was all divided up well before my time. Now we keep supplies in our homes, for safety. The Capulets are pretty well-off, by general standards. We still have four whole rooms stacked high with all the good stuff. Back when I was a kid, it was five rooms, but hey—in life, things dwindle.

Skipping assembly means I'm too early for hospital visiting hours, so I decide to walk to the Wall. Not exactly "appropriate behavior," but Mum's given up on all that fanfare with me. And Dad? He's hardly even worth a mention. If I'd died according to plan, I'd be accorded perfect daughter status, I'm sure of it. I'd be the pretty, romantic little thing who was deeply about the long hair and the floaty dresses and the *love, love, LOVE*. Now? I guess I'm just not much of a poster child for all things sunshine anymore.

I don't pass a single person the whole way to the Wall. That's not surprising—we're warned against coming out here. The Travelers are dangerous, they tell us. They're desperate and ruthless and cowardly and whatever else bad you can think of. Kinder words than I've heard used on me, quite frankly.

I don't come this far out for cheap thrills in hopes of glimpsing one of the mythical Travelers, like my cousin Tybalt and I used to as kids. No, I come here for the letters. There are hundreds of them, wrapped in plastic, tucked into the Wall. Although it's more of a fence, really—"wall" implies something beyond barbed wire stuffed with old correspondence. "Wall" makes you think "solid"—the type of thing that could protect you from guns and such, if the Travelers actually had them. Which I'm told they generally don't. I guess when the Travelers imagined their glorious future, they didn't have "pressing need for firearms" in mind. Or maybe it was more pragmatic than that. With just one small pod to jump through time in, perhaps they had to pare back to the important stuff. Things like money and jewelry and lipstick and trinkets and shoes.

Walking slowly, I lightly run my good hand along the envelopes—pale skin against all those dark fates. I tell myself that I like the quiet out here, though in truth it's the letters. I guess I enjoy the company of so much star-crossed, horribly-gone-wrong love. Does that make me a bad person? Is it strange that the place where I feel most like myself is so full of gloom?

I'm ashamed to admit it, but there was a time when I read the letters. Hell, I devoured them—as many as I could. Letters from parents and children and lovers and friends, separated by decades or longer. Instructions and rendezvous points and apologies from all the ones who just couldn't wait. It didn't make me feel any better, and I'd never read them now, but at the time? Well, grief can do strange things to your way of being.

The one that stuck with me the most was written by a man. I can't remember his name. He jumped here from 2023, the very first year that the pods went to market—over four decades before I was born. People tended to be cautious back then— five years, ten years, something modest. Not him. He went a full forty years, nice and even. It wasn't for any of the shallow reasons either. Not for idle curiosity or to "look decades younger than the people you hate." He went forward to go back. He was just so damn sure that, given enough time, they'd make a machine that could do it. I mean, it was obvious, right? If you could go forward in time, why *not* backward? Why the hell not?

He'd had a daughter, you see, and there was this one particular Sunday swim that needed to not happen. That's all he wanted. That's all it was for. The bit that really got me about the letter was how it wasn't addressed to anyone. I guess when he arrived here and realized he could never go back, that it would never be possible . . . well, there wasn't anyone it *could* be for. Everyone he'd ever known was literally just a thing of the past.

It's like this the whole world over. Once the pods went to market, almost everyone upped stumps. Only, with no one staying put, the future was a mess. So people jumped again, with faith that things would right themselves in time. But because no one stayed, the future was worse. So they jumped again . . . and again . . . and again, getting more and more desperate. By the time they slowed down, it was all too late—the Fall had happened. The eight billion people who had once lived together on Earth were spread out over the rest of time. Or, as the theory goes, collecting at the *end* of it. The population left behind in any particular year was minuscule. Cities went to ancient ruin in the minutes that it took to jump once, then twice, three times for good measure.

London's no exception. As far as we know, ours is the last remaining Settlement . . . and it's far from impressive. We're keeping up appearances, more or less, but only one in twenty houses is lived in. We'll run out of people eventually. Or supplies. Or both.

O Romeo, Romeo—why did you leave me to deal with this shit on my own?

....

2

Ellis
WASTELAND

"This is how it ended," I deadpan.

"Cut," says Iggy, lowering the camera. "It's about the emotion, Ellis. *The drama.* We're looking for *gravitas.*" He gestures loosely at the apocalyptic wasteland around us.

Iggy scavenged a VHS video recorder from the 1980s last week, and it is his new favorite toy. Yesterday he filmed a one-man reenactment of something called *Monty Python.* Today, it is to be a documentary. He would like me to set the scene with "*a powerful and dramatic lead-in about how the world ended.*" I am ... disinclined.

"Once more from the top, with feeling," says Iggy, hitting the RECORD button again.

"This is how it ended," I say again in an even more perfunctory tone.

Iggy sighs. Then, changing tack: "How about we start with introductions then, shall we? First up we have Beth, seventeen years old and straight out of the 1950s." He zooms in on Beth as she hits another golf ball into the wasteland. Half Japanese, half Chinese, flawless complexion—the camera loves her.

"Make sure you get my good side, darling," she says without breaking her swing.

"Please note how Beth's ensemble really complements the backdrop. Nothing says end-of-days quite like a full skirt, twin-set, and saddle shoes, am I right?"

Beth gives the camera a cheeky wink, then tees up another ball.

"Next we have Henry, also seventeen, born in . . . 1789?"

"1798," corrects Henry through a clothespin in his mouth as he hangs out the washing.

"As you can see," Iggy continues, "Henry still dresses in the Georgian fashion of his day, despite the post-apocalyptic climate. So tell us, Henry, what's it like lounging around here at the close of time, perpetually drenched in sweat?"

"Necessitates rather a lot of laundry," says Henry with a good-natured smile. Henry is well over six feet tall and solidly built. Moreover, his red hair is teamed with freckled skin, meaning he burns easily. The climate here in the wasteland suits him poorly.

"Now me," says Iggy, reaching up and carefully patting his hair—bright purple—to check that his mohawk is in order.

Then, turning the video camera on himself: "Ignatius Jones. Born in 1966. Currently sixteen years old and quite possibly the best-dressed trans punk *on the entire planet.*"

Given that Beth, Henry, and I have no interest in competing

for that mantle, Iggy is probably right. As far as we know, the four of us are the only humans left living in this wretched, far-flung era. That is precisely why Frogs chose it. Statistically, there is, apparently, "*A considerably lower probability of Deadenders inadvertently impacting the timeline if they remain appreciably separate.*"

Translation—less chance of us botching the world if we are never truly a part of it.

"And last but not least, Ellis," says Iggy, zooming in on me as I practice letting out the clutch in time with shifting gears. "Born in the 1800s, currently nineteen years old, with very little to be said in terms of fashion."

Then he adds, "Sweet ride, by the way."

Iggy is being sarcastic. When Frogs announced that I would have to learn to drive for a future mission, we had a problem. There are no cars out here in the wasteland, and Frogs cannot move objects in time and space—only people and what they are carrying. Steering wheel, rearview mirror, pedals, and a gear box—we had to break them down and transport them here from the past, one painstaking piece at a time.

My so-called "car" is a few spare parts rigged up to a small plastic chair.

"If only someone had let me sit behind the wheel *of the bus,*" I gripe, not for the first time.

IF THIS BUS ENDS UP IN THE WRONG SPOT, EVEN BY A FRACTION . . .

". . . then we are all at risk of being obliterated by arriving pods," I say, finishing Frogs's sentence for him. It is a well-worn spiel. "I was not going to *drive* it. I just object to this ridiculous plastic chair arrangement."

"The young man attempting to drive a piece of furniture is the *original* Deadender," says Iggy in a stage whisper.

He means that I was the first. I recruited the others at Frogs's behest, pulling them out of the timeline the moment they were slated to die, and—with step-by-step instructions from our resident AI—managed to revive them. I have been living on this bus—in this wasteland—with Frogs since I was thirteen years old.

"Now, Ellis," continues Iggy, "as the founding member of our illustrious collective, are you *sure* you don't want to do *the powerful and dramatic lead-in about how the world ended?*"

"Quite sure."

Iggy shrugs. "Well, can't say I didn't offer." Then, in a *very* dramatic voice, he booms, "This . . . *is how it ended.*"

With that, Iggy takes a sweeping shot of the wasteland. There is the occasional scrap of rubble to suggest that this place used to be a suburb of London, but the old city is mostly eroded. Now all you see are monstrous clumps of melded-together pods—millions of them, as far as the doomsday horizon.

"Darling, that's terribly glum," says Beth as she whacks another golf ball into the nothingness. "Can't you manage something a *little* more cheery?"

Iggy hits PAUSE on the video recorder, considers it for a moment, then announces, "War correspondent . . . who's just been kicked in the jollies."

He adopts a strained, high-pitched voice that is, admittedly, rather comical. "This is Ignatius Jones reporting on the fall of human civilization. With robotic construction and decentralized mini factories, the pods were relatively cheap, easily accessible, and extremely well-advertised. By 2030, almost everyone had become a Traveler. But the pods could only move forward in time, never back. This . . . *is how it ended.*"

Iggy takes one last panoramic shot of the wasteland and its eternal carnage of melded-together pods. Then he adds, "It's like this because the Travelers just kept on going."

And *that* is the truth. The worse it became, the quicker they were to jump. Fifty years, then a hundred years, then two hundred years—burning through the future in a matter of days, if not hours.

Until they ran out of time . . . and space.

At first, only a few pods reappeared in the same place, at the same moment. Then more. The larger the mess of metal and bones grew, the less clear earth remained. Everything snowballed. The carnage advanced like a beast, swallowing Travelers the moment they reappeared.

Until this: the wasteland.

"Folks—you're witnessing a graveyard. Millions of dead Travelers. *Billions.* And it's growing bigger by the minute . . ." Iggy zooms in on a nearby clump of melded pods that's emitting a dull light and a terrible grinding sound.

Another Traveler, being absorbed as we speak.

"Hasta la vista, world," says Iggy more quietly, in his normal voice. Then he turns his camera to the bus. "So now, this is home."

Other than pods, the bus is essentially the only thing out here. It's a double-decker, surrounded by sundry items that give it a motor home feel: the fold-out clothesline, a few camping chairs, a garish 1970s beach umbrella for shade. Weirdly domestic items against the wasteland. Downstairs, the bus has been gutted and fitted out as living quarters—bunks, generator, tiny kitchen, ugly couch, television, videocassette recorder, curios from across the ages.

Home sweet home. Except, of course, that it is not. None of us truly have a home anymore. Or a place in time. Staring at the bus, Iggy looks sad for a moment, which is not like him. Then he clears his throat and puffs out his chest, like he is ever so proper.

"We're not Travelers. We're something different. Something *secret*," he says, switching to an aristocratic accent that is totally at odds with his ripped jeans, mohawk, and piercings. "We call ourselves Deadenders. We can only recruit people who were 'dead ends' in terms of the timeline. People who died and whose bodies were never found. Sometimes we can pull them out at the last moment and try to revive them without creating any ripple effects."

"Makes for a smashing first day on the job, let me assure you," pipes up Beth.

I pulled Beth out of a plane wreck seconds before an explosion that left no human remains. Her first day as a Deadender was ... traumatic. The same can be said of us all.

"Beats the alternative," says Henry, who was lost at sea in 1812.

"*Travelers use pods*," says Iggy in a loud voice, clearly trying to stamp out the interruptions. "Pods can only move forward in time. Deadenders, on the other hand, use *these*." He zooms in on the high-tech cuff around his wrist. "It can move us in time *and* in space. It can also send us *back*, as well as forward. As you can see, our technology is different."

SUPERIOR

"Our jumps—"

DEMONSTRABLY SUPERIOR

"Our jumps arc—"

ALMOST EMBARRASSINGLY SO

"—are programmed by an AI called Frogs, *who is prone to interrupting*," finishes Iggy, zooming in on the top level of the bus, where the circuitry that constitutes Frogs is contained.

BUT YOU ALL ADORE ME. DON'T YOU, MY LITTLE FLOCK?

Every day Frogs comes up with a new collective noun for humans. A *flock* of humans. An *unkindness* of humans. A murder, a nest, a plague, a *pod*. He finds it hilarious that people used those words to describe *other* animals.

"If you say so, my little toaster," replies Iggy. His game is to confuse Frogs with domestic appliances. They both secretly love it.

"Personally, I'd adore you even more if you stretched to air conditioning," says Henry, gazing up at the sky somewhat vaguely. Henry has never quite grasped that Frogs is a disembodied voice, speaking directly into our heads through the embedded comms; that when he talks there is nowhere to "look," exactly.

LESS SAVING OF WORLD, MORE TEMPERATURE CONTROL. WILL DO. DEAD CERTAINTY

Frogs has been experimenting with sarcasm. "Dead certainty" is what he says when something is decidedly *not* assured.

"Don't forget my 3-wood, darling," says Beth, running with the joke. "If we're listing off druthers, then I could definitely use one."

"Excuse me, but I'm trying to document the downfall of human civilization," says Iggy gravely. "Your irreverence is undermining the tone."

Beth laughs. "Humblest apologies, darling."

"Thank you. I feel like all undermining-of-tone should be done exclusively by me," says Iggy, affecting an air of mock offense. Then, zooming in on me for another close-up, he says, "So tell us, Ellis. What does it feel like being the inaugural member of a secret band of time travelers trying to save the world?"

I glance at myself in the makeshift rearview mirror—dark skin covered in a sheen of sweat, rather average home-job haircut, a not-altogether-clean black T-shirt.

"It feels incredible," I deadpan. "Wildest dreams come true, et cetera, et cetera."

KNOW WHAT WOULD MAKE IT EVEN MORE PEACHY?

Frogs means another mission.

I look at my watch—it is time.

"Finally getting it over with?" says Henry.

"Appears so," I grumble. Stepping out of the makeshift car, I pull the crumpled piece of paper out of my jeans pocket and check the details one last time.

Frogs assigned me this particular mission two months ago, and it has been a thorn in my side ever since. The job is to travel to a few decades post-Fall and synthesize a drug called Cat-9. Now, I might have been a Deadender for more than half a decade, but I was still born in 1818. Call it parochialism, but volatile drugs produced by high-tech gadgets are not exactly my specialty. It has taken me two whole months of studying salvaged manuals—and a lot of direct help from Frogs—to ready myself. Beth would have had it sorted in a matter of days, yet Frogs insisted that it had to be me.

I take a few steps away from my "car" to a patch of earth that is clear of everything except cracks. Iggy turns his video camera on me and, in that overly dramatic voice again, says, "Counting down now, folks. *Five. Four . . .*"

And I am gone.

* * *

I reappear in a high-tech laboratory that is covered in dust. This is 2056—thirty-three years after pods became a consumer item. The exodus for the future has largely already happened. Glancing out the window, I spy a huge gold skyscraper, shining like a tribute to human progress. Except it is fool's gold— London has already fallen.

LAST DESK ON THE LEFT

Frogs, speaking directly into my head through the comms.

I head for the desk. There is indeed a small silver case of Category drugs, just like the one that we scavenged for me to practice on. I open the case and chew my lip in concentration. I might have spent months perfecting how to make Cat-9, but it is still bloody complicated.

I am about to start when I hear footsteps. That cannot be right—the city is mostly abandoned. The chances of someone being here, now . . .

"Frogs?" I whisper.

SOMEONE'S COMING

The Deadenders must be kept secret—that is the cardinal

rule. If someone sees me, the ripple effects could be catastrophic.

"What do I do?" I whisper. The footsteps—they are running toward me now.

HURRY?

Shite. Making Cat-9 is *not* the kind of thing you rush. With shaky hands, I pick up the syringe—

NO, WAIT. THIS BUILDING—IT COLLAPSES TODAY ANYWAY. THE DRUGS DON'T MATTER

"What?" I blurt out, far too loud. Dialing down to a whisper, I add a hurried, "Then what was the point? Why make me do all that preparation work to produce Cat-9?"

I MADE AN ERROR

Frogs, the most intelligent machine ever built, who calculates complex probabilities in nanoseconds and singlehandedly moves people through time and space, simply made a *mistake*? I carefully put the drugs back down and take a step away from the table.

I am rattled. "You do not *make* errors."

The footsteps are almost upon me.

"Frogs? What the blazes—"

....

3

Jules

2083

I keep walking the Wall, running my hand along the deserted love letters. A few hundred words later, I'm level with the Supermarket.

After the Fall, you couldn't keep food in a supermarket—that was the first place hungry Travelers checked, they tell me. So our ancestors stashed books there instead. Chaucer under pet food, Greek myths in the dairy aisle, fairy tales in the frozen food section. And right at the very back, on a shelf once reserved for crisps, the encyclopedias.

Whenever Tybalt or I had a little-kid question ("What's a cow?" "What's an island?" "Are dolphins and dragons both made-up?"), Dad would wink at us and say, "Crisps?" Then, hand in hand, the three of us would head down to the Supermarket, all the way to the very back aisle. Damn, I loved those encyclopedias, with their faded gold covers and never-ending answers.

Dad would show us the pictures first because they were Tybalt's favorite. Then we would lie on the floor, shut our eyes, and imagine it all while Dad read: a boat, a desert, a duck, ice cream, icebergs, airplanes, tigers, telephones. Things we didn't have on our side of the Wall. Things we'd never seen and would never see . . . and which probably didn't even exist in the world anymore.

Today I keep walking, right past the Supermarket and its carefully sorted flavors. I don't stop until I get to the old theater, which is right up against the wire. It's technically still this side of the Wall, and therefore part of our known universe— only just, though. The poor thing's right on the very edge of being an outcast.

I'm the only one who still visits the theater. Every day I waltz right in, straight past the dusty ticket booth, and quietly make my way from one side to the other. Not across the stage, like some wannabe actor. I walk across one of the rows, where the audience once sat.

Stepping inside now, it's like a different landscape of colors—all rich but muted. Though the smell is what *really* gets you. Years of damp have given the velvet and the carpet a covering of green, thick as a second skin. The mold of form smells alien.

My eyes fly down to the stage, with its huge unfinished bird. Poor old bird. It's only half painted on; the rest of the backdrop's still white. I guess that's as far as they got before people started escaping to the future instead of to the theater.

Walking down the side aisle, I choose a row of seats at

random—"E" this time. Then I look up at the ceiling. It's covered in a mural of an angel, with a constellation of holes where the sky peeks through. The missing pieces are down here in the rubble with me, like some heavy metaphor. They *"droppeth as the gentle rain from heaven upon the place beneath"* à la Shakespeare? They crash to earth like a wounded . . . something? Nope, still can't find the words. But the words don't matter. The important part is *the show's not over*. Random chunks of ceiling still fall from time to time.

If one hits you in the head, it'll kill you cold.

I stand at the threshold, thinking about action versus inaction—it's kind of this theme I've got going. And then I move. I walk straight across Row E, underneath the Russian roulette roof. I don't hurry. I go at a steady pace, letting the forces above do their best or their worst, or their vicious in-between.

Yet again, I get to the other side, not a single scratch on me. Then I turn back and stare at Row L, Seat 26. The place where my cousin lay for a day and a night—one whole rotation of the planet—while we searched for him. Until Aunt Miranda, for some reason, insisted that we check here, the old theater, of all places.

Talk about a dramatic ending.

In my story, Tybalt's death had purpose. I made it the key to everything—the first tragedy that sparked all disaster to follow. There was a funny comfort in that. Maybe I should have brought him back to life on the page, but I dreaded the pretending. Instead, his death was the sinking pebble with ripple effects aplenty. It had reach. It had *consequence*. It wasn't just some random thing that could have been avoided.

I look back up at the crumbling angel, like it was some kind of contest between us just now—her versus me, me versus fate.

And then I leave.

I follow the Wall a bit more, trying to ignore the stink of what's on the other side. It's for safety, they tell us. Lobbing all our rubbish over the fence creates a buffer, which helps keep the Travelers and feral animals at bay. All that broken glass and sharp metal edges—waist-high in places—creates an effective deterrent. Really, I suspect it's more about practical matters. I mean, we've got to dump our rubbish somewhere, right?

My eyes settle on a faded label for "peaches in natural juices." *Peaches, pears, beef jerky, chicken soup, cured ham, tuna, salmon.* I've eaten them all out of packets and cans, but I've never seen a fruit tree or a cow or a hen or a pig or a fish. Or the ocean, for that matter.

Beyond the peaches and other empties, there's probably a mountain of dead batteries. Beyond the batteries, I'm guessing chocolate wrappers and drums of gasoline—both went fast, they tell me. I like to picture it like rings around a tree stump. A circle of rubbish, marking the passage of our years; a line for every time we moved the Wall in closer.

I asked Mum about the rubbish-dumping once, back when I was little. She said, "It's an imperfect solution in an imperfect world." Such a great answer. I mean, with words like that, you can justify anything.

It's still too early for hospital visiting hours, so I sit by the old fountain. I get my notebook out of my backpack—I figure I'll work on my story, which is my usual move. I've been at it for almost two years now, but the damn thing's still not finished. Frankly, I blame the language.

Writing what really happened with Romeo and me was all a bit close to the bone, so I changed things around a little. I set it way back in the past, with lots of silly clothes and frilly honor. Then, to top it all off, I wrote it in iambic pentameter. Why? Because when it comes to William Shakespeare, I'm a tragic. Seriously—I'm the ultimate fan. Even as a kid, I couldn't get enough of his plays—the irony of all those timeless themes when time is precisely what broke us. I guess a homage to him seemed only fitting. Not that Shakespeare ever wrote about stuff like teenage love, Montagues versus Capulets, or any of my other real-life dramas. And yet, fool that I am, I mimicked the Bard.

I'm a masochist, apparently.

Getting the language right is ridiculously tricky. I don't know why I even bother sometimes—it's not like anyone will ever read it. Frankly, *The Love Story of Juliet & Romeo* is a non-event to everyone except me these days. But I'm writing it anyway. I guess it's kind of like my own home-brand therapy. Piecing together, then reworking the moments that led up to what happened helps. The haters can reduce what we had to the folly of youth, but I know better. That's not my story. That's not how it *actually* went down.

I flick all the way to the end—there are dozens of pages headed with ACT VI, where everything's crossed out. Okay, so maybe the language isn't the *only* problem. Truth be told, I can't quite figure out how to end it. I won't give up, though. I refuse to give up on my story of true love. So I turn to the next blank page and write a new heading: ACT VI again.

As I'm deciding what's next, there's a flash. White light, followed by afterimage colors. It's one of those things I've been told about so much that I know what it is right off the bat, even though it's totally new to me.

Like first love, really.

I squeeze my eyes shut, waiting for the burn-bright lights to fade. When I open them again, there it is, resting on the grass just across from me. It seems strange that, in a world brought down by pods, I've never actually seen a working one. They used to pop up all the time, apparently. Not *now,* though.

I get to my feet and walk closer. The pod's smaller than I'd imagined—smaller than it looks on the vintage posters, that's for sure. But what really gets me is the metal. I've never seen anything so shiny and new—there's not a speck of rust on it, no signs of patchwork, slapdash repair. It's almost impossible to remember that this is from our past, not our future. That the peak of human progress is behind us.

I take a step closer, which is maybe a teensy bit reckless. Pods arriving this side of the Wall aren't *totally* unheard of. A generation back, it used to happen from time to time, and I know the drill. I know the "never approach" and "Travelers are dangerous" and "quarantine" warnings. And yet . . . I find that I'm curious about the person inside. What do they look like? What *is* the look of a person who had a crummy life and then found the perfect means to escape it? Are they smiling? Are they still sad? Has time healed all wounds, like it's meant to?

I need to know the answer.

I need to see for myself.

....

4

Ellis

WASTELAND

"... *two, one.*" Iggy finishes his countdown.

I am back in the wasteland.

From the perspective of Iggy, Henry, and Beth, I was gone for exactly one second. I open my mouth to explain about the so-called error, but David Bowie's "Life on Mars" starts blasting through the speakers on the bus.

"Frogs, are you truly giving us a new mission?" says Henry as he pins his britches on the line. "Ellis only just returned."

"Darling, can't it wait?" Beth whacks another golf ball, then switches to the plastic skipping rope that we use for endurance training.

AFRAID NOT

"Frogs, we live in a bus that's parked two thousand years after all life basically ended," says Iggy. "The fact that everything's already happened kind of takes the *rush* out of it, wouldn't you say?"

HANDS UP IF YOU'RE CALLING THE SHOTS?

"You don't *have* hands," Iggy points out.

DOESN'T THAT MAKE IT EVEN FUNNIER? HUH. I THOUGHT THAT MADE IT EVEN FUNNIER . . .

"So much for my Hollywood debut." Iggy switches off the video recorder.

Something is not right. Something is *definitely* not right.

"Frogs—" I start, and "Life on Mars"—the song that Frogs plays whenever we have a new mission—turns up a notch in volume. Now is not the moment for discussion, apparently. Though very soon it sure as shite *will* be.

The four of us dutifully trudge into the bus and gather around the low-tech printer that is spitting out words one line at a time. Frogs could just tell us our missions, of course, but the quirky AI has a love of all things retrospective. He is currently enamored with the 1980s, hence the dot-matrix theatrics.

My eyes fall to the chalkboard that hangs above his main console. It shows the likelihood of the Fall, expressed as a percentage. Frogs thought it would be useful for motivation. So that we—the Deadenders—could see how all the tiny tweaks and changes that we make to the timeline are having a positive impact. Today's number is ninety-four. There is currently a 94 percent chance that the world will end, courtesy of pods.

When I was recruited, the number was 100.

While we wait, I help myself to a millennium-old muesli bar. It was aboard a dinghy destined to sink, which is why we could pull it from the timeline without impact. The packaging is sodden, but I have not yet eaten today and am suddenly starving.

"And the winner is . . ." Beth picks up the sheet of paper that is covered in streaky printing. Concern crosses her face. "It's for Ellis. *Again.*"

I stop as I am about to take my first bite and manage an ineloquent, "Huh?"

The stakes are high whenever we tweak the timeline—one mistake and we could accidentally change the fate of *the entire world.* Ergo, it can be stressful. Frogs has instructed us to take it in turns. He *always* insists we take turns . . .

"Two in a row for Ellis," says Henry, sounding worried. "How about letting me have a go, hey Frogsie, old boy?"

NO, IT NEEDS TO BE ELLIS

"Come on Frogs, it's only a wake-up call," says Iggy.

Beth chimes in: "Waking someone a few minutes ahead of schedule is a fairly basic tweak, darling. A loud noise should do it. Let Henry take it. Let *me* take it."

IT NEEDS TO BE ELLIS

Beth reluctantly hands over the printout.

"Year: *2083.* Location: *London.* Mission: *Wake Romeo,*" I read aloud. "Hold on. It says here that I am due to jump in *less than three minutes.* I shall not have enough time to prepare."

Silence.

"Frogs, we spend weeks preparing for even the tiniest change to the timeline," Iggy reminds him. "*Months,* sometimes. Not being seen is everything. That takes planning. *Planning takes more than three minutes.*"

"One wrong move could be disastrous," adds Beth. "The

ripple effects could change everything. *That's* what you and El-lis taught us."

Still no answer.

"It is fine. Merely a wake-up call, remember?" I say, pocketing my breakfast and trying to affect a casual air. "Besides, I shall have Frogs in my ear the whole time, providing instruction. Be back before you have boiled the kettle."

GREAT. BECAUSE IT'S NOW LESS THAN TWO MINUTES AND COUNTING

I decamp the bus and walk a few meters into the wasteland, *out of hearing distance*. All of this is anything but fine.

"Private line?" I say in a calm, measured voice when I am far enough from the bus that the others will not hear me.

WE'RE PRIVATE

"What the blazes is going on!" I shout, letting loose.

THIS MISSION IS IMPORTANT, ELLIS

"I have been a Deadender for six years, Frogs. For *six years* you have drilled into me that *every* mission is important. That even the smallest mistake could change the entire course of history."

TRUE. SO LET'S BUMP THIS ONE UP TO REALLY IMPORTANT

"Why? What is so special about waking up some chap?"

HE'S NOT JUST SOME CHAP. ROMEO IS HIS FATHER

"Whose father?"

THE MAN WITH THE MISMATCHED EYES

"What?"

ROMEO AND SOME GIRL CALLED JULIET—THEY'RE DESTINED TO HAVE A SON. AND THEIR SON WILL BE THE MAN WITH THE MISMATCHED EYES. THAT'S ALL I KNOW

"So?"

SO? THEIR SON BUILT ME, ELLIS. AND I'M THE ONLY THING THAT CAN SEND PEOPLE BACK IN TIME, AS WELL AS FORWARD. IF YOU DON'T WAKE ROMEO, I'LL NEVER EXIST. THE DEADENDERS WILL NEVER EXIST. THERE WILL NEVER BE A CHANCE OF FIXING WHAT HAPPENED WHEN PODS WENT TO MARKET. INCIDENTALLY, YOU'LL BE DEAD, HUNDREDS OF YEARS IN THE PAST

"All right, then—*really* important. Tell me—"

FOUR STEPS TO YOUR LEFT

I move without a second thought. A moment later, there is a bright flash and a pod arrives exactly where I was standing. The man inside observes the wasteland and promptly panics. He hits a red button, and the pod disappears once more. Off to the future, again—not that there is anything *left* of it.

"Tell me precisely what I need to do," I say, barely even pausing in the conversation.

THAT'S THE PROBLEM. I DON'T KNOW. SOMETHING WEIRD IS GOING ON WITH THIS MISSION. SOMETHING . . . UNSTABLE

"Then how about we wait *until you have sorted that out!*" I raise my voice again.

CAN'T. THE DIE IS CAST. THIS IS OUR WINDOW. IT HAS TO BE NOW

I hear a loud beeping sound in my head, only that is impossible. There are never any background noises when Frogs talks to us directly through the comms.

"But—"

DO TRY TO BE CAREFUL. AND DON'T FORGET THAT TIME CAN BREAK. IF ANYTHING GOES WRONG, THERE'S A

RATHER HIGH CHANCE I WON'T EXIST ANYMORE TO COR-
RECT IT

"But—"

I do not get to finish my sentence. There is the all-too-familiar stomach-dropping-out sensation, then I am gone.

* * *

When I reappear, the first thing I notice is there is no bedroom, no bed, no sleeping body to simply "wake." I am not even indoors—I am standing in a wide, deserted street, where anyone could see me. The second thing I notice is that there is a late-model pod cooling down on the grass just up ahead . . . and some reckless girl is walking toward it.

"You jumped me out into the open," I whisper to Frogs. "There is *a girl* here." Frogs always sends us to discreet locations—pantries, alleyways. Places where no one will see us "magically" appear without the help of a pod and start rumors swirling. This is not right.

MUST BE A MISTAKE

Another one?

"She is about to get herself killed," I hiss.

The idea that Deadenders should never be seen is ingrained in me so hard that, for a moment, I am struck immobile. I simply stare at the girl and do naught. Her back is to me, yet I see her tuck a pencil into her pocket. Instantly, I am reminded of Emily. Of the moors and the windswept girl who sewed a secret pouch into her tunic just so she could always carry a pencil. The way she was forever jotting down tiny thoughts about big ideas, or vice versa . . .

At first, I do not even realize that I am moving. I have fantasized about saving Emily so many times that some echo of instinct must have possessed me. I move silently—thanks to years of being practically invisible, the girl hears nothing. She does not even know that I am there until I grab her by the hood and yank her backward. An inch or two closer and the pod's defense systems would have killed us both.

What I just did, what I have just done—it is as bad as it gets. This goes far beyond a small mistake or some mild interference.

I take a few steps back, away from the girl. I run my hand across my head, trying to gather my thoughts. "Frogs, I have made a terrible blunder. For a moment, I thought—"

"Hey, what the hell was that for?" snaps the girl.

"Frogs, I saved a life that was not meant to be saved," I whisper quickly, keeping my back to her. "What is the damage to the timeline?"

No answer, which is unlike Frogs. Something must have happened to the comms. I put my hand to my ear, though it is a pointless gesture. The transmitter chip was injected—his voice is heard *inside* my head.

"*I said*, what the hell was that for?" repeats the girl.

I slowly turn to face her. We Deadenders were taught that saving the wrong life can change everything. It can *ruin* everything, distorting the world in a billion untold ways. If I was going to commit such a cardinal sin, I might at least have done it for the right girl.

There is another blinding flash of light and the pod is gone. Whoever was inside has decided to drop in on a different future, no doubt scared off by what they saw here. Lord knows what ripple effects that will have in and of itself.

"Well?" says the girl, clearly awaiting an answer.

"That was a late-model pod," I explain eventually. "Late-model pods all have automatic defense systems. If you had touched it, you would be dead." *Like you were meant to be.*

On the bright side, that tidbit of information shuts her up. The downside is I still have no inkling what to say *next*. For years, the Deadenders have played it safe, with naught but the tiniest of changes. Minuscule adjustments on the fringes of what went wrong, because anything big was simply too risky. I stare at the girl. Could saving her life have done it? Has it changed things so profoundly that the Deadenders no longer exist?

The cuff is still around my wrist, so I suppose that is something. I stare at the thin band of circuitry, which is what allows Frogs to move us in time and space. Then I subtly pocket it to avoid any questions. Deadender technology has never existed in the world at large. Nobody outside of the bus knows that traveling in time without a pod is possible. They definitely do not know that traveling *back* in time is possible.

"Um . . . what pleasant weather we are having?" I offer stiffly. Small talk was never my forte, though I imagine that a suspicious absence of small talk could be even worse. I have to be as forgettable as possible, then leave.

As I prepare for a polite yet speedy exit, I spy a notebook lying on the grass. The cover reads, "*The Love Story of Juliet & Romeo.*" Juliet. Romeo. Not exactly common names.

"Who is Romeo?"

The girl snatches the notebook, shoving it into a nearby

backpack, and stares at me. Eventually she says, "Just a boy who needs a doctor."

"You know him? You can take me to him?" I ask.

"Maybe. Why?"

"I believe I can help."

"You're . . . you're a *doctor?*" she says, clearly confused.

"Yes. Sure. *I am a doctor,*" I agree. Anything to move this along. "If you take me to Romeo, I can administer . . . doctoring."

There is a pause while the girl considers me.

"I don't recognize you," she says at last. "You're a Traveler."

"Yes, a Traveler," I lie. The Deadenders are a *very* well-kept secret.

"Did you know whoever was in that pod?" she says.

"No."

"We haven't seen a Traveler in years. Now a pod shows up and then you show up? Two Travelers at the exact same time, but you don't know each other? That seems like a pretty big coincidence."

Yes. Yes, it does.

"Can you take me to Romeo?" I say, opting to ignore how this whole situation feels wrong. The mission was to "wake Romeo." Once it's done, the comms systems will surely come online again, and I will return to the bus. *I hope.*

The girl hesitates a moment, then says, "Yes."

"Good." As an afterthought, I add, "My name is Ellis."

"Jules."

The notebook with the names on the cover. "Jules. *Juliet?*"

"Nobody calls me that anymore."

Shite. *Shite, shite, shite.*

The man with the mismatched eyes—Frogs said that his parents were Romeo *and Juliet.* I have been interacting with the *mother*, creating Lord only knows how many unscripted changes. This is . . . not good.

This is *very* not good.

....

5

Jules
2083

I take us back along Angel Street so that Ellis won't be seen. Nobody lives on Angel anymore, and the streets on either side are empty too. Our Settlement's shrinking; those who are left all moved in closer. I guess people prefer being right near the withering heart of things.

At first Ellis watches his feet as we walk, like he's carefully weighing every single step. It's almost three whole blocks before he finally looks up and starts to walk normally. Now that he's looking, he's *really* looking. The overgrown weeds, the falling-down houses, the rusted-dead cars, even the overcast sky—it's as if all of it has his wonder and attention. But there's one thing he pointedly won't look at. Me.

I look at him, though. Dark skin, brown eyes, short black hair, tall, strong. Yep, basically physically perfect. I'll bet he's from that point in time when everyone was an "ideal." That era when they cut and starved until every "flaw" was a thing of the past. Ellis has probably never even *seen* imperfection in real life, until now. Until me.

He must have noticed my dead arm, given how he's a doctor.

And sure, some kids—like Paris and his goons—find it worthy of a solid tease. But Ellis's reaction? Making a deliberate point of not looking my way, even a little? That's a whole other level. Still, I've learned the hard way that the best you can do is shut up, take it, and quietly hate them. So I do all three. I don't bother with small talk and neither does Ellis. We both stay silent the whole way, which suits me just fine.

"This is it," I say, coming to a stop in front of the hospital. It's a crumbling Georgian two-story, covered in graffiti. The only thing that sets it apart from the other houses is the reclaimed neon light that reads "Emergency." Not that the light works anymore. Or that we'd waste a generator on it, even if it did.

"It's been a long time since our Settlement has seen a real, live Traveler," I say. "I'm not too clear on the precise details of what's next, but I'm pretty sure it involves quarantine."

The comment just hangs there.

The truth is, I have *no idea* what would happen if I got busted waltzing a Traveler straight into our only hospital. Would it end up being that one poor choice too many? Being a Capulet still counts for something, though favors come to an end eventually, and more than a few have been wasted on me already.

It's not too late, of course—I could still hand Ellis in, down at the police station. Mrs. Queen is always there, manning the front desk, pretending that justice still rates a mention. Just like Mr. Bernado keeps the post office spick-and-span for no apparent reason. I could easily abandon my plan to help Romeo and do the very thing that my mother craves of me so badly—to *act responsibly*.

But really, I'm just going through the motions. Pretending to weigh my options, unlike the last time. I was always doing this. Even if the rumors are true and Ellis does carry some revolting bygone disease that we've got no cure for. Even if I'm putting everyone at risk. Yes, when it comes to one versus many, I choose the One.

Because love is everything.

I take a deep breath and say, "Let me do the talking."

He responds with a snort. "Gladly."

Then I lead Ellis straight through the front door, as though it's any other day. If the nurses are surprised to see me here so early—and with a boy, no less—they choose not to show it. They simply nod and mutter, "Hi, Jules," as they go about their business. I'm not sure whether I should ask permission to see Romeo outside visiting hours, or if it's better to act like I'm entitled and walk right on in. I go with option B, and no one stops me.

Romeo's room is the last on the right, which used to be the parlor.

The moment I see him lying on the bed, I get chills—happens every time. I suppose that would sound romantic if they were good chills—the sweet *there's the love of my life* goose bumps variety. But they're not. They're more your *tiny bit weirded out* kind. Problem is, whenever I see Romeo, I swear it's like going back in time. The way he lies there in his death-counterfeiting sleep, as if the world is standing still for him alone? The way that, while time doth waste me, he gets a leave pass?

It's goddamn spooky.

I suppose he's aged—technically, he must have, though *I* sure can't see it. To me, he looks exactly like he did the day that everything went wrong. Fair skin, blond hair, pretty eyes eternally closed—yep, he's your regular sleeping beauty. Except, of course, without the storybook ending.

And it's not just on the outside either. On the inside, I'm sure he's every bit the same too. He doesn't have that not-a-kid-anymore slump like me, on account of all the crap that's happened. He hasn't gotten older by experience like I have. For him, every experience came to a grinding halt at age seventeen, and he's been like this ever since—blissfully ignorant. Life might have gotten *me* all wonky, yet he's still perfect and true.

It must be like that for the Travelers, I guess. I heard a story once of a man who jumped. He was only gone a moment, but when he opened the pod's hatch, his wife was an old woman, still waiting. For him it was a blink; for her it was a lifetime. It's that way for Romeo and me—him standing still while I inch by slowly. And besides—if he ever does open his eyes, it might as well have been time travel. I mean, he'll be arriving years later, with a very changed girl by his side. Jules instead of Juliet, no improvement with age.

I go to my usual seat and take his hand, like always. I give it three little squeezes, which is this thing I do. Only, after that . . . what next? Normally, I just sit here in silence and work on my story. Fixing up scenes, tweaking the blank verse to get it sounding all Shakespearian, dreaming up sweet things to have him say to me. I don't actually talk to him though, not out loud. I suppose that's strange—to make a deliberate point of saying nothing. But I have my reasons.

"What happened?" asks Ellis, checking his watch, like he's got somewhere better to be.

And boy, what a question. *Love* happened. Feuding parents happened. The drama and excitement of being warned to stay away. Misunderstandings, a lost note, drugs—*everything* happened. The whole goddamn spectrum of human emotions in a whirlwind of love and hate and sleep-deprived mix-ups. Though Ellis doesn't need to know all that—he doesn't care about our story any more than the rest of them do. He simply needs the cold, hard medical facts.

"Poison," I say. Only, the moment I do, I realize that it sounds like a domestic error. A case of poor labeling. A "pass the orange juice . . . oh shit, that's the arsenic" comic mistake. I feel the need to clarify.

"It was drugs, but the combination he took *amounted* to poison. He never woke up," I add, just in case that part wasn't obvious. A line from Shakespeare pops into my head: *If you poison us, do we not die?*

Turns out, not always.

O Romeo, poor Romeo—so much is in the timing. If you'd lived in the past with all of their whizbang medical marvels, you probably would have pulled through fine. In the fast-decaying future, chances are you'd have died that night and put an end to our story. But no—you're here in the now, poor sod, and the now has left you in limbo. *Like me.*

"This is Ellis," I say to Romeo, pushing through how fake it feels to talk as if he can hear me. "He's a doctor, and he's here to help."

I give Romeo's hand another little squeeze. And actually, talking to him doesn't seem *that* weird after all. I'm a bit self-conscious, sure, though it's doable. It makes me wonder ... should I have been talking to him all along? All those visits, day in and day out, should I have filled them with something other than silence?

But no, that was never really an option. If I'd started talking, then sooner or later I would have felt obliged to tell him the one thing that I *wasn't* saying. I'd have blurted out the secret that Mum and Dad and Aunt Miranda and I have been keeping. And if I had?

Well, the boy only gets one visitor. It wouldn't have been fair to take that away just because I couldn't bring myself to face him.

....

6

Ellis
2083

"Wake Romeo"—those were my instructions. That rather implies waking him from *sleep*, in my opinion. I knew there were complications, of course. Knew from the moment Jules said that he required a doctor. But . . . a *coma*? Really?

Juliet and Romeo—they are meant to be together. They are meant to have a son; them having a son is downright crucial. That outcome tends not to happen so well when the fellow is catatonic. *You were not being dramatic, Frogs, when you insisted that this mission was important.*

"I suppose there is naught chance he is simply sleeping?" I ask.

"Is that a joke?"

"Not a very funny one," I mutter.

Romeo is hooked up to a drip and some basic monitors

running off a generator. That is the extent of it. There are none of the golden-age gadgets that were produced right before the Fall. Right before people were so bloody clever that they created a one-way time machine, and it all went colossally tragic.

"How long has he been like this?" I say, trying to sound sufficiently medical.

"Two years," says Jules, without missing a beat. "Two years tomorrow."

This makes no sense. There must be *something* I can do, or why would Frogs send me back here?

I make a show of holding her beau's wrist, like I have seen the doctors do on Iggy's VHS collection, and then check a few more things in a medical-type fashion. Though, truly, there is not much more that I can pretend to do. As such, I decide to put an end to the idea that I will be waking Romeo any time soon. I clear my throat and try to sound a shade more mature than my nineteen years.

"Unfortunately, when the patient is in a coma—"

"I thought that technically it *wasn't* a coma," Jules interrupts. "One of the nurses said it was probably cerebral catatonia. Is that not right?"

Holy. *Shite.* I have had some rather shocking moments in my life thus far. I have been yanked back from the brink of death to bounce through time, and on one occasion I had to pick Winston Churchill's pocket. Life has thrown me some definite surprises. And yet, despite all that, this moment is still rating. I might not have much in the way of genuine medical knowledge. I might not know how to treat a burst appendix or gangrene or do anything *properly* useful. But cerebral catatonia?

My last mission—the one where Frogs made a mistake. Because of it, I am quite the expert when it comes to Cat-9. And you *need* to be an expert. The end result might be a syringe full of goo, but the simplicity is deceptive. The Category drugs were only ever produced right before the Fall, at the height of human evolution. Appearances aside, they are about as sophisticated—and complex—as it gets. They remain active for less than an hour, and achieving the right molecular structure involves a very complicated little device that is an absolute bastard to use. Without some serious training, you would never even manage to turn one on, much less produce the right Category goo. Of course, Cat-9 does not do much in particular. It is extremely specialized, really. In fact, the only thing it is actually any good at is *relieving cerebral catatonia.*

Now, I am not a natural when it comes to calculating probabilities, though I do have some experience. With my life of late, it is rather a given. The probability of starting a widespread plague if you sneeze in 1746. The probability that governments will topple if you put a penny in the path of the wrong man in a gray hat. The probability of it being a coincidence that I know how to synthesize the very specialized drug that will wake Romeo? I am no expert, but I believe it is low. Very low. Infinitesimally small. As in, *would never happen naturally, not in a million years* league of tiny.

Something suspicious is definitely afoot. I am not sure what, yet one thing is clear.

"I can wake Romeo."

....

7

Jules

2083

"Sorry, what?" I must have heard wrong.

"I can wake Romeo," says Ellis again. "But you will need to give me your Category drugs."

And with that, I realize ... *I've been conned.*

"You filthy coward!" I don't even bother to keep my voice down. "You pretended you could help him just to get your hands on some Categories!"

"You assume me a thief because I am Black? How delightful," he says, unamused.

"That's not what I meant," I protest.

"The drugs are not for me," he continues. "Doctor, remember? I can use the Categories to make Cat-9 and wake him."

"Nobody knows how to do that anymore."

"And yet, by a remarkable coincidence, I do."

The way Ellis is staring at me right now, totally unapol-ogetic? I don't think that he's lying. And because of that, a sinking feeling creeps in.

"We don't have any Category drugs," I say, hoping to put a quick end to the conversation.

"I mean no offense," he says, "but you do not look like an expert."

"We don't have any left, all right?"

"So you are a doctor too, then?" says Ellis. "Or perhaps you are a clairvoyant and that is how you know that there are none, without even checking?"

"I know because they used the last of it on me, okay?" I snap.

And there it is, one of the many awful truths: *They used the last of it on me.* Romeo's family and my family were pretty equal when it came to getting their way. Except there was only one stretcher and they brought me to the hospital first. And I was bleeding. And when the nurses injected me with Fex-amene, the nerves in my arm started dying, so they had to do something. They gave me the Dithrocyn, except that stopped my heart. So they gave me what little was left of the Category drugs in a last-ditch, cross-your-fingers moment.

The fact that I survived the stab wound was reasonably for-tuitous. The fact that I survived Category drugs in their raw state, administered without an expert? *That* was the miracle. The one in a trillion chance. By the time Romeo arrived at the hospital, all they had left were prayers.

"Lucky you," says Ellis. Only, how he says it? I can't quite tell whether he actually thinks that or not. Does he honestly believe that gobbling up the drugs that might have saved my husband counts as a plus?

I wonder if the Montagues know. I wonder if someone told them that all the drugs were lavished on little old me. Maybe that's part of why they hate me with such passion. Maybe they really do think that, in a way, I took their son from them. I can understand why that would make you bitter.

"There must be more somewhere, then," says Ellis.

"Why?"

"There just must be, all right?" He walks across the room and stares out the window. His gaze settles on the sycamore tree that's growing outside. The poor thing's all crooked on account of some unlucky Traveler. I guess a pod reappeared right where the tree was and got absorbed. The metal and bones are still there, bulging like a cancer.

"Think, think, think," Ellis mutters to himself, as he stares at the tree. He does genuinely seem to care about Romeo's fate, which is mildly shocking. After so long being the only one, it's strange to have company. I guess it must be that Hippocratic oath thing.

Ellis absently runs his hand down one of the velvet curtains. It's threadbare now and a long way from lovely, yet something about it seems to catch his attention.

"Where is the real hospital?" he says, examining the fabric more closely.

"You're in it," I say. Given all the medical equipment, I'd have thought that much was obvious, especially to a doctor.

"No, this is a grand house being used as a hospital. Where is the *actual* hospital?"

"You mean the one from before the Fall? We abandoned it years ago. It's beyond the Wall." I remember the first of many times that we moved the Wall in closer, making our world that little bit more . . . compact.

"If the drugs are not here, then they must be there," says Ellis, as if that settles the matter.

"Why? What makes you so sure that what you need even *exists* anymore?" I ask, despite the fact that I should probably be sounding a lot less defeatist. I can't help it—I don't understand how he could possibly think he'll find what he needs just because he needs it. Life doesn't simply deliver you what you want, as you like it.

Ellis turns to face me, and for a moment, I think he's going to give me a little pep talk about having faith and staying positive.

Instead, he gives a not-quite-amused snort and says, "Call it a strong hunch. We will need a reliable map," he adds, "and it is winter, so I will require a coat."

This is all moving way too fast. The best I can come up with is, "A coat? What, crossing the Wall to track down cutting-edge drugs is no big deal, but you need to be cozy?"

"Walking around in winter wearing only a T-shirt and jeans tends to attract attention," he says slowly, as if talking to a child. "You mentioned quarantine. I would rather *not*."

"Oh. Right." *Good point.* Now that I'm so close to waking Romeo, the last thing I need is Ellis getting detained for being a Traveler.

There's an antique chest of drawers in the room, filled with Romeo's clothes. They're not "we expect him to wake up" outfits—quite the opposite. They're his coma attire. Every day he's bathed and dressed and laid on the bed like he really is just

sleeping. That kind of special attention isn't offered to everyone, though he *is* a Montague, after all. His parents might not
visit except on birthdays and Christmas, but they still know
how to elicit good service.

I rummage through the drawers. I can only find a sweater—
it's pastel green, to highlight the eyes that don't open. I throw it
at Ellis, and he pulls it on over his head.

The moment I see him in it, I wish he'd take it off. It's like
some kind of mean parody—a cruel joke, and Romeo's the butt
of it. The sweater doesn't even come close to fitting Ellis. While
he is probably the same age as Romeo, more or less, he's bigger,
taller.

"Give it back, you're wrecking it," I bark.

Ellis sighs. "I suppose I shall have to brave the cold, then."

Only, as he takes the sweater off, his T-shirt rides up. I can't
help it—despite my efforts to project pissed off, I blush. The
truth is, I haven't had much experience with boys, despite what
the toilet walls promise. Hell, just because you make out with a
boy at a party, get married, have sex, and then try to kill yourself
all in the space of a few weeks, where do they get off assuming?

"Can I have a moment alone with him?" I say, mostly to
hide that I'm still blushing. Ellis nods and leaves quietly. Once
he's out of the room, I feel instantly awkward. Like I should be
saying something to Romeo again, even though that's never been
our thing. If this was my story instead of my life, it would be easy.
Juliet would simply recite a flawless sonnet about parting being
such sweet sorrow. She'd say it all, with layer after layer of delicate
meaning. She'd get the timing right and the lines right and she'd
deliver a damn near perfect performance.

Instead, I take Romeo's hand and think about where I'm

going. There was a time when "beyond the Wall" was the stuff of nightmares. When Tybalt and I were kids and told scary stories, that was always the setting. Most folks still think there are Travelers lurking around out there, posing a threat. Personally, I think there's something *far* worse out there. But I'll go anyway, for Romeo. And the fact that I didn't even think twice? It's proof that what we had—what we *have*—is real. That it was a marriage of true minds, just like Shakespeare would have wanted.

* * *

After the hospital, I guide us through the back alleys for as long as I can. It's only when we reach Elsinore Road that I realize there's a problem: Ellis. I can't very well take him inside my house while I get the map, and I can't just let him wait outside either. Our street is one of the nicest, so, unlike everywhere else, there are no empty houses here. Ironically enough, this is one of the few parts of the whole Settlement where you generally *will* be seen.

There is one place, of course—a place where Ellis could wait without being observed. Mum only has one big rule: *Nobody enters the crypt.* She tells people it's a respect thing, but I know better. She's worried what people will find there, that our family secret will be exposed. I have my own good reasons for avoiding the place, though this is clearly no time to be precious.

And so I lead Ellis through the side gate toward the back garden. From the street, our house looks almost immaculate. It's not until you venture behind the façade that you see the *real* story. The broken windows with no new glass to replace them, the peeling walls that will never see new paint. It's like there's a plague on the house, eating away its dignity. All that's left is the front that's there for show.

When we get to the back garden, I head down the stone path. Every step feels like a nasty little time machine, throwing me back two years. Well, two years tomorrow. Oh, how I hate this place. The roses used to grow from either side in the shape of a heart, meeting in the middle. Now they're wild and prone to vicious scratching. It feels like they're closing in on me, that everything's getting darker, smaller.

"Keep heading that way," I say when I can't bring myself to go any closer. "There's a crypt at the end. It's off-limits, so no one will see you in there. I'll be back soon."

"Tottering off to the big house while I am left out here in the cold?" says Ellis, as though the whole thing's mildly amusing. "How original."

It's clearly some kind of private joke, but the idea of joking now? Joking *here*?

"Stop being such an . . . an *annoyance*," I say.

Ellis chuckles. "Sweetheart, I have been called a blackguard, a devil, a brute, a thief, and a fiend—you will have to try harder than that."

"I am *not* your sweetheart." Beyond that, I don't bother. I just turn and walk away as fast as I can without running. I need to put distance between me and what's at the end of that grim rose path. Between me and the place that represents so much more than the transgressions people know about.

I shouldn't complain, I guess. Every secret has to be buried somewhere, and a crypt is surely as good a spot as any.

8

Ellis

2083

Once Jules leaves, I meander along the garden path. My stomach is rumbling, though I dare not eat the muesli bar in my pocket. It is all that I have by way of food, and there is no way of telling how long I shall be stuck here.

Instead, I focus on the lush vegetation. *My Lord,* it smells good. Out where the bus exists, you can never escape the putrid smell of rot. Here, I can smell grass and trees—I can even feel an actual breeze. It occurs to me: *We should have done this more often.* Frogs should have sent us back to simply sit, unobserved, discreetly soaking up life from time to time. Whenever it all became too much and Henry started obsessively cleaning, or Beth resumed her target practice, or Iggy started making documentaries that naught but us would ever see, or when I ended up staring aimlessly into the wasteland . . . then Frogs should have sent us to simply sit beneath a tree. It would have helped, I think. The fate of all life on earth can be a bit much to process on a daily basis. But a tree? Now a *tree* you can fight for.

Turning a corner, I very nearly step on a snail—I smile and pointedly avoid it. Life is everywhere here. Emily would love this place.

Emily. It is hard enough not thinking about her when I am on a dilapidated bus with zero reminders, but here in this ramshackle garden that is wild and bursting with green . . . I find myself gazing at a thorny rosebush, and in my mind it is 1829 again. Emily and I are both eleven years old, out on the moors in spring, amid the bluebells. She reaches into the secret pocket of her tunic and produces a small bundle wrapped in oilcloth. Inside is a piece of wood, hanging from a ribbon of leather. Emily made it herself as a gift for me. I have never been given a gift before. On the underside are letters that she carved into the wood. Emily knows that I cannot read, so she tells me what it says: *Askim.* It is the final word that my mother spoke, right before abandoning me on the streets of London Town. Askim—I know very well what it means, yet Emily says it anyway. With tears in her soft gray eyes, she whispers, "It means . . . *my love.*"

My poor, darling Emily. Everyone has their regrets, and she is mine. I have imagined a thousand versions of my life where one small change would have delivered our happy ending. A tiny deviation that meant we were never on the cliff by the ocean that day. That she was not left alone in the world, wondering if I even truly cared. I know better now, of course. After so many years in this wretched business of time, I know the risks, the variables. So really, the only way I could be sure that I would do her no harm is if we never met at all.

And *that* is what I would wish for.

The cruel irony is that particular remedy was within my reach the whole time. I am one of only four people *on the planet* with the means to make it happen, yet I still could not save her from me. According to Frogs, there are things that are strictly off-limits. There are things that you simply *never* do. You do not manipulate the timeline for your own personal ends. You do not alter the fate of billions merely to play matchmaker. At least, those used to be the rules. Apparently, they do not apply to Juliet and her Romeo.

Juliet and Romeo—what a load of bollocks. They do not even *sound* like an especially memorable couple. Their son might be something special, yet the two of *them* strike me as—

The crypt suddenly comes into view. The word CAPULET is carved into the stone above the door.

Holy. *Shite.*

I have been here before.

Pausing, I let the hugeness sink in. And then I enter the crypt. When my eyes adjust to the darkness, I see that the tombs have all been pushed to the edges, creating a large open space in the middle. There is no doubting that it is the same place, though. It was my very first tweak to the timeline—a practice run, according to Frogs. A note had been placed in a dark room, and my job was to retrieve it without creating any ripples. It was completely routine—all merely part of the Deadender training.

I try to recall the mission exactly. I remember having to count my steps—more than there would be now, for my legs were so much shorter. I remember the note—it smelled like perfume and had two tiny hearts on the front. I do not remember the year that I traveled to, though this place is definitely the same. *It cannot be a coincidence.*

This crypt and me knowing how to make Cat-9 ... there is more to this mission than Frogs divulged. Yet thanks to the comms being down, I cannot very well ask him.

However, I know one thing definitively. Whatever Frogs is really up to, it all started before these past few hours. Lord, it has been taking place since the very beginning, when I was first recruited. My life has been manipulated for *years* to accommodate Jules and her love story. Frogs has been playing a very long game indeed, and I am squarely in the middle of it. Call me a cynic, but I am guessing that note with the hearts was not truly "just an exercise." In fact, I am guessing it was rather the opposite of not important. Which means a lot of things. Top of the list is a fairly profound error on my part. I had always assumed that, because Frogs is a machine, he cannot lie.

Clearly, I was mistaken.

. . . .

9

Jules

2083

I stand outside the front door, listening. Mum's entertaining—
there's no mistaking her "we have company" titter. Of her many
laughs, it's always the fakest.

I close the door behind me as quietly as possible. On unlucky occasions, Mum thinks it's a good idea to invite me in to
say hello to her friends. Only it's not really a "hello" any more
than they're really "friends." It's more like show and tell—to
remind her social set that the Montagues weren't the only ones
who lost out big that fateful night.

Then, of course, there's the whole responsibility thing.
Mum is downright obsessed with getting me to prove myself. To demonstrate that I've *grown up* and *turned over a new
leaf* and *changed my ways* and *learned my lesson*. It's as though
getting me to show the world that I'm no longer flaky and

unstable is her whole life's mission. As a general rule, I try to avoid her.

I'm almost at the stairs when I hear, "Juliet, is that you?"

The "Juliet" always gets me—throwing me back to a different time and place. *The earlier version of me.* It's Aunt Miranda—she's the only one in the world who still calls me by my full name.

"Hi," I say, peering around the doorframe of the sitting room. It's just the two of them, talking, their dark heads close together.

"Come sit with us," says Aunt Miranda, patting the seat next to her. She's wearing the same warm smile that I grew up loving, but now there's sadness mixed in too. Seeing me makes it harder. I'm the reminder that once there were three of us—Tybalt and me as the knights, her as the dragon. Tybalt and me scraping knees, her with the kisses. I'm the reminder that someone is gone.

"Homework, sorry," I say, though everyone knows that homework these days ... well, it's *ages* beyond pointless.

"Just for a minute?" Aunt Miranda looks wistful. She wants to hug me, I can tell. She wants to put her arms around me and squeeze a fraction too tight, just like old times. She wants me to know that she still loves me, even though I'm the wrong child. It's been years now, and she never gives up. Honestly, I can't understand how she does it. How does she stay positive when her son is dead? How does she get up in the morning and slap on a *smile*? Isn't it torture? Day after goddamn day, isn't it breaking her heart?

"Sorry, I'm really tired," I say, even though it's only afternoon.

"I think I'll take some food up to my room and have an early night."

"Shouldn't you be at school?" Mum asks as I'm leaving.

"You know, I just wasn't *feeling it* today," I say, channeling my inner petulant teen.

Mum sighs, like she does so often. "Jules, you—"

"—have to grow up and take responsibility," I finish for her. "Heard it all before, Mum."

As I walk away, I hear her mutter, "You haven't heard a thing."

I ignore her.

I don't go to my room like I said I would—I go straight to Dad's museum. It's not really a museum, of course—that's simply what we've always called it. Mum hates this corner of the house. In a Settlement that's hell-bent on living in the past, I guess it's ironic that the *distant* past is somehow out of favor. That it's considered "poor taste" to dwell on it. To have a whole room dedicated to artifacts from across the centuries. Antique trinkets and treasures left behind by the Travelers, or brought here with them. I guess Dad was always a bit eccentric, even before what happened.

Our Settlement isn't big on the written word. The school has a few textbooks, and vintage magazines are always a hit. But books in general? They kind of got quarantined down at the Supermarket. After that, I guess folks forgot they weren't *actually* contagious. Dad has books, though—his own little private collection. We "borrowed" them from the Supermarket together over the years—one by one, stuffed up our sweaters, giggling all the way home.

I head for the far wall, which has always been my favorite. The top shelf is filled with bound copies of Shakespeare's plays—*Macbeth, Othello, King Lear,* and more—all thirty-five of them. Given my fangirl obsession, our shoplifting days were mostly Bard-related.

I focus on the next shelf down, which is dedicated to practical matters.

I run my finger along the spines and stop when I get to a small book that's tucked between two larger volumes. I pull it out—*A to Z of London, Street and Atlas Index.* It was published way back in 1990, so it's nearly a hundred years out of date, but it'll do.

I turn to leave—that's when I see him. He's lurking in the doorway, watching me. I can't see his mouth beneath the scratchy beard, so there's no telling what expression he's wearing, if any.

There was a time when I'd have been grounded for coming in here without asking. A time when he'd have holed me up for a solid hour while he delivered some measured lecture. But now? We've hardly heard his voice in years. He simply floats through the house like a ghost, clutching his Bible, muttering his mantra.

Mum's managed to spin it that he somehow found God and took a vow of almost-silence. Total rubbish, of course, though Mum's got a real talent for the truth and how to stretch it. She's right up there with our dear little Rosaline on *that* front. As for the idea of *having faith*? Nobody worships God anymore; we just worship the past.

"Hell is . . . ," says Dad, which is all he ever says. This clichéd biblical question that rattles around in his head all day. Poor sod, he really can't get things clear in his head.

I guess Lady Macbeth was right—*hell is murky*.

Dad is staring at the map that I'm holding, though good-ness knows what he makes of it. Much like the other man in my life, I don't have a clue what goes on in his mind. All I know is that, unlike Romeo, I can't stand being around him. It's the guilt of the matter. Romeo's sad state might be half my fault, but Dad's? Well, that's *all* on me. I was there the exact moment he cracked. Who knew that just one little secret could break him?

Somewhere off in the distance, the faulty clock tower war-bles through its thirteen chimes. Unlucky thirteen—that seems like a suitable moment to make my exit.

When I get to my bedroom, I don't bother locking it—me hiding out in here is practically the norm, and nobody ever checks on me. They won't notice I'm gone, provided I'm back by morning. I contemplate leaving a note just in case that *doesn't* happen. But no—the last time I left a note, it ended badly.

I've never been beyond the Wall, so I don't quite know what to expect. It doesn't seem like the kind of place for a school skirt, though, so I wriggle out of mine. Somewhere in the pro-cess, my arm slips out of its pocket. It looks pink—like it's alive, just snoozing. O Romeo, my Romeo—can you believe the irony? The ridiculous parallels?

My gaze sinks all the way down to my fingers, stopping at the band of gold. I've never taken it off—the ring has been there the whole time, although nobody sees it. I always tuck that hand into a pocket, stuffed safely away from prying eyes. It seemed kind of poignant before—a wedding ring on a sleep-ing hand, joining me with my sleeping husband. If Romeo really does wake, though, I guess it will be different. My arm won't be some special link between us anymore, a connection. It won't be something for me to focus on when I'm sick with guilt that I came out of it *mostly* unscathed. No, it'll just be ... again, different.

I pull on a pair of jeans, which is tricky business one-handed. It's all about the loose fit, baby. Once they're on, I tuck my hand into the pocket of the hoodie, out of sight again.

Generally speaking, I don't do mirrors. But today, with the prospect of Romeo waking? Sadist that I am, I have to look. Not much—I don't check my face or go in for a proper once-over. I focus only on the fabric of the hoodie, on the patch of black near where my heart is.

The original knife wound was small, apparently, though the attempts to save me were messy. The scar that's left is like a fat purple worm stuck beneath my skin, pulling and pucker-ing. Who knew that grand gestures of love could leave you so strangely lopsided?

It sounds ridiculous, but I don't really know if Romeo's seen me naked. We only slept together that one time and it was dark and cold, so there were plenty of blankets. Maybe he didn't see me at all. I wish I knew. In the grand scheme of true love, I know it shouldn't matter ... and yet I can't help it. Now that there's even a chance he might wake, I'm worried. Right from the start, Romeo bombed me with love—petards of affection, blowing my praise at the moon. He was always comparing me to a summer's day or linking love to beauty. I didn't care back then because I thought I fit the bill, but now?

I don't know—I just hope that true love can admit imped-iments.

After grabbing my backpack, I step out onto the balcony.

Looking down, I can't help picturing that scene from my story. The one with Romeo beneath my window, full period costume, gazing up at me with total adoration. *But soft! What light through yonder window breaks? It is the east, and Juliet is the sun.* Those weren't his exact words, of course. It's what he meant, though, more or less. Basically speaking.

I throw the backpack onto the grass below. I try not to think about falling as I step onto the ledge, preparing to climb down after it. This house has seven bedrooms, and mine is the smallest. The benefit is that it's on the top west-side story, which allows you to sneak out without being seen. There was a brief point in time when I took advantage of that fact, but not for years now. Not since I lost my claim to two good arms, among other things.

I grip the latticework. I climbed down here plenty, during the Romeo saga. Climbed far higher and worse, back when I was a kid. Only now, with my arm and the different balance? No, I don't think I can do this—not anymore.

Instead, I creep downstairs, go out the side door, then make my way around. Once I've retrieved the backpack, I head for the garden shed and rummage around until I find a rusty pair of bolt cutters. As I stash them in my backpack, I remember the other time I filled this bag with more than just schoolbooks. The time when Romeo and I planned to run away, without a single thought as to the where or the how of it. Our parents had forbidden us from being together, so we were leaving—simple as that.

Then we chose the *other* way out.

As I walk back down the garden path, my feet stop short. I hover like there's an invisible force holding me back, urging me to stay away. This is the closest I've come to the crypt since the night that Romeo and I almost died in it. Maybe this is the closest anyone's been, other than Mum. She might have her strict "off-limits" rule, yet I'm no fool. I've seen her sneak inside its stone walls once a year like clockwork to pay her respects. I've been tempted to call her on it, though I never have. The place might not be completely off-limits, at least where Mum's concerned, but some topics are.

"Ellis? Ellis?" I whisper-shout for him to come outside.

He emerges from the crypt and gives me a weird stare before clocking the jeans.

"You stopped to change your clothes?"

Only, the way he says it, like he just assumes I'm vain, à la Rosaline?

"A girl's always got to look her best," I say, batting my eyelids, flashing a vapid smile.

Ellis ignores me and says, "What does 'Capulet' mean?"

Here, that name needs no explaining. We were one of the original founding families—the ones who created the Settlement, all those generations back. Who convinced others to reject the pods and their grass-is-greener promise. To stay put, to live in the now, not for the future. To just say no to time travel. Before I was born, the name Capulet was as good as royalty, they tell me. Then, in my generation, it became synonymous with the feud—Capulets versus Montagues. And, more lately? *That family with the broken daughter.*

"It's just a name," I say, turning my back on him.

....

10

Ellis

2083

"So, this Romeo of yours," I say, coming to the point as we walk through the Settlement. "Poison? Drugs? What happened exactly?"

Jules shrugs uncomfortably. "He was heartbroken."

The implication sinks in. "He attempted *to take his own life?*"

Jules pointedly turns to face me.

"He couldn't bear the whips and scorns of time, so he took the easy way out," she says in a put-on voice, with a tight smile. "Satisfied?"

"Suicide is never so simple, and it is sure as shite not *taking the easy way out,*" I say, annoyed by her glibness.

Jules appears struck by my words, though she covers it quickly. "Like you can talk."

"Excuse me? You do not know a *bloody thing* about my life."

"Running away from your problems? Taking the easy option, instead of putting the work in? Ah, hello? You chose to be a time traveler!"

Chose to be a time traveler? One moment I was drowning at the bottom of those cliffs in 1831. The next I was soaking wet in the end-of-days wasteland.

I stare at Jules. At this snotty girl, whose son was the one who fished me out of the ocean and recruited me in the first place. Who jumped me to the wasteland, then left me in hell with naught but a talking bus. This girl who is receiving all manner of intervention to fix *her* love story, like nobody ever did for mine.

"That is it exactly, sweetheart," I say, owning the bitterness. "*Chose* to be a time traveler. Just could not wait to leave today behind. Feeling that again, quite frankly."

"I am *not* your sweetheart."

Jules fumes, which gives me no small satisfaction. But as we walk along in silence, the memory from before will not leave me alone. It is 1831—Emily and I are both thirteen years old, on the cliff, in the rain. As thunder claps, she says that she loves me. Yet I cannot say it back. Instead, I take the ribbon of leather from around my neck and hand it to her. I let the little piece of wood speak for me: *Askim.* My love. Emily looks at me, her expression unreadable. She leans in to kiss me, but I get spooked, I step backward . . .

It was not until I read Emily's heartbreak book that something terrible occurred to me. On the cliff that day—what if Emily thought I was handing her love back? What if she thought that, when I stepped away from the kiss, I was rejecting her twofold? *What if she died, years later, believing I never loved her?*

"Stop dawdling," I snap at Jules, to distract myself from the thought of it. Jules dutifully picks up the pace, though I glare at her regardless. *Juliet Capulet.* I cannot go back and fix my own love story, yet going back to fix *hers* is apparently now my sole purpose. I have to live with *my* mistakes while she gets the special treatment, without so much as a thank-you.

I am liking this mission—and this girl—less and less by the minute.

* * *

I check my watch once again. We have been walking through the Settlement, taking only the back streets, for a while now. I am busy worrying about the fate of my friends—not to mention the world—when Jules mutters, "Shit." I glance around, expecting signs of danger. All I see is a small posse of lads on bicycles, heading our way.

"It's Paris and Laurence," she says. "Plus a few extras."

"Beg pardon?"

"Hide," says Jules. I must not react fast enough, because she shoves me behind a bush. "*Hide!*"

The boys do not stop when they see Jules—they all start pedaling faster, aiming straight at her. She does not try to scurry out of their way or otherwise avoid them. Instead, she stands perfectly still as one by one they swerve at the last possible moment. I get the sense that this game of risk has happened before.

The boys circle back for a second pass. I move to reveal myself, but Jules whispers, "Stay down!"

"Crazy *freak!*" calls one of the riders, while another swings his arm from side to side for some reason. It is bullying behavior, designed to provoke. Yet Jules does not lose her cool or take the bait—she holds fast, giving them naught.

As I watch events unfold before me, a scene from my own past takes over. In my mind, it is 1823. I am five years old, in a dingy back alley of London. I am frozen in fear as my would-be attackers sneer their disgust at the hue of my skin. They circle me. They close in on me . . .

"You can come out now," says Jules, jolting me back from my memories.

The boys on bicycles are down the road and around the corner.

"Are you all right?" I ask, rubbing my side. Even after so many years, the wound that I suffered that day still pains me, especially if I think on it.

"Right as rain," says Jules.

"Who were they? Why did they do that?" I ask.

With no explanation, Jules resumes walking.

I have to say, I am slightly intrigued. Jules is not akin to Emily, with her soft gray eyes and otherworldly calm. Jules is . . . I am not sure, exactly. Perhaps the girl with the fate of the world on her shoulders has more to her than I first imagined.

We eventually arrive at a large fence with envelopes and letters stuffed into the wire. Piled *behind* the wire is refuse—cans, jars, plastic, and the like. This must be what Jules meant when she said "wall," though it is a fairly poor description. The leaning heap of rusted wire that I am looking at would not keep anyone out *or* in, not if they had half a mind to do otherwise. The garbage beyond—with its broken glass and sharp metal—probably poses a more genuine inhibitor. Either that, or the smell.

"You just toss your rubbish over the fence?" I ask, suitably appalled.

"It's an imperfect solution in an imperfect world," says Jules, somewhat glibly. Then, without another word, she leads us to a section of fence with a lesser amount of rubbish packed behind it.

"The bolt cutters are in there," she says, dropping her backpack on the ground at my feet.

Now, I might have been born at a time when chivalry was thriving, but I have never liked the women who simply expect it. Besides, Jules seems far from helpless. She handled herself very adequately back there with the lads on bicycles.

"I will get right onto that then, shall I?" I say. Jules merely stands there, hands in pockets. Perhaps I had this girl pegged right the first time.

I am sorely tempted to point out that she can bloody well cut the wire herself, yet I decide against it. *More flies with honey, honey,* as Beth would say. And it is true—things will definitely go more smoothly if I can manage to avoid making sarcastic comments. For once, I bite my tongue.

"You need to make the hole bigger," says Jules when I am finished.

I take a deep breath, willing myself to conceal how she is irritating me, and keep snipping.

When the hole is cut to her satisfaction, I try to hand the bolt cutters to Jules. She says, "In my backpack, please."

In a moment of petulance, I dump them at her feet. She glares at me, then squats. She puts the bolt cutters into the backpack with her right hand and then uses it together with her teeth to close the zipper. Her left hand stays in her pocket the entire time.

I remember the lad on the bicycle, swinging his arm. Understanding dawns. "You cannot move your arm."

Jules rolls her eyes. "Brilliant diagnosis. I thought you'd realized that earlier, given how you're a doctor and all." She continues struggling to zip up the backpack with only one hand and her teeth at her disposal. I feel like a cad.

"I sincerely apologize. Here, let me—"

"Don't. I don't need your help," she snaps at me.

"As you wish."

Jules finishes zipping the backpack up, slings it over her shoulder, and we set off. Jules goes first, though she hesitates right before crossing the threshold—like there is significance to the moment.

"Surely you have gone past this fence before?" I ask.

"Of course." She strides on through.

Beyond the fence, we are enveloped by rubbish—predominantly empty cans. It would be a challenge to traverse but for the haphazard nature of the dumping. While sections indeed reach our waists or higher, there are gaps in the waste too. It allows us to pick a meandering path, like explorers through a labyrinth of filth.

"Goddamn flies," mutters Jules, spitting one out of her mouth with a splutter.

"Flies are important," I say absently. *Everything is connected*—that is what Frogs always said during his lessons on the world and its different eras. If only he had stretched to a few more lessons on *what is truly going on with this mission.*

Jules takes a deep breath and holds it. A moment later I do likewise, for the stench is appalling.

Once we have cleared the debris, I observe the city just off in the distance—it is gray and still as a grave. Nature is thriving, pushing up through the gaps, but everything man-made has the bleached-bones look of something dead a long time. All the metal is rusty; all things once smooth are now cracked. The London of this era has been left to rot and ruin—there is none of the verve that I remember from my day. None of the bustle, busy life, and human color. Though what you truly notice is the silence. It blankets the city even thicker than the rubble and the dust.

And yet ... I must confess I rather like it here, in this time and place. It is as though my former haunts—London and the moors—have formed a most unlikely union. The result is an almost changing of the guard—wildness blooming on the carcass of "before." I notice an owl nestled in a drain pipe; on sagging wires, a raven and a dove. I see a little briar rose eclipsing a wheel, and a family of mice turning a letterbox into their home. The natural world, reclaiming its kingdom.

"Times change," I say, marveling at how the old is being repurposed.

"Time *broke*," says Jules, bluntly.

Time broke—that is almost what Frogs used to say, though he never used the past tense. He would warn us, *Time can break* ...

I say a silent prayer that his words were not prophetic.

A handful of minutes later, as we are passing an overgrown playground, I hear Beth yell, "Ellis!"

The embedded chip must be working again. I drop behind and whisper "Beth?" softly enough that Jules cannot hear me.

"The comms aren't working!" says Beth, even louder.

I do not understand. And then I see them—Henry, Iggy, and Beth are *here*. Now. They are out in the open, running toward me.

Something is *very* wrong.

When they reach us, Henry thrusts a new Deadender cuff at me and says, "It's programmed. Hurry, put it on."

Beth takes advantage of Jules's complete surprise and clamps a Deadender cuff around her wrist too.

"Beth, you cannot give *her* a—"

"Get it off!" yells Jules. "Get this thing off me!"

A bullet whistles past my right ear. The shooter is a man in a World War II uniform, complete with a gas mask that is hiding his face. Though his gun—the *power* of it—is anything but old-fashioned. We are too far away for certainty, but I would bet on my Deadender training that it is a twenty-second century handgun—silent and very deadly.

The next bullet smashes a window just to our left.

We run for shelter behind a nearby derelict pharmacy. Jules breaks away and dashes to the other side of the street, hiding behind a dusty ice-cream shop. I am about to chase after her when Henry grabs my arm and stops me.

"It matters not where she runs to," he says. "She is wearing the cuff—she will jump with us."

I notice that Iggy is holding Beth's purse. Inside, it is full of hacked-off circuitry.

"You ready?" he says to the contents of Beth's purse.

CREEDENCE

Frogs—his circuitry is fried.

"One last jump. Come on, buddy, you can do it," encourages Iggy.

Another bullet screeches by, even closer . . .

* * *

. . . Then my stomach bottoms out and the pharmacy is gone. We have jumped in space to a ransacked department store. Traveled in time as well, I would wager.

"Quick, hand him over." Beth reaches for Frogs. "We have to destroy the mainframe before the man in the gas mask can follow us."

"What the blazes is going on?" I shout.

"Wait!" says Henry. "Where is she? Where did she go?"

Jules. She is not here.

Somehow, she did not jump with us.

ACT II

....

11

Jules
2083

I smash the device against the back wall of the ice-cream shop a second time. While I can't get it off one-handed, at least the little green light on the band has gone out. I have no idea what those Travelers put on me, but I *definitely* don't want it.

I'm about to smash it a third time for good measure when Ellis grabs me by the wrist and whispers, "You have broken it already."

Wait—wasn't he on the other side of the street with the others?

Ellis does the gesture for "quiet." Fair call, given that *someone is trying to kill us*. He takes me by the upper arm and tugs. We run, block after block, until we get to a decrepit-looking Chinese restaurant.

"In here." He leads me through the front doors.

"Who were those Travelers?" I say as soon as we're inside. "And why did they put this thing on me?" I can't ask about the man with the gun. The uniform, the gas mask—the fact that I've seen them before . . .

"They are not Travelers," says Ellis. "Neither am I. We are Deadenders. The cuffs are how we travel backward and forward in time."

Back in time? And without a pod, no less?

"You know," I say, "I'm kind of not in the mood for bullshit when I'm *being shot at*. Can we be serious, please?"

"Trust me," says Ellis.

Not bloody likely.

With that, he presses some hidden latch and the cuff-thingy clicks straight off my wrist. He's not wearing his any-more either.

"I am reconnecting the causal loop, all right? The *causal loop* was broken. That is why you failed to jump with the rest of us."

"Sure. The *causal loop* is why I didn't jump in time without a pod." That, and *the laws of physics*.

Ellis finishes fixing the device and puts it on the table next to me. I notice for the first time that his fingers are stained with green paint.

"All you have to do is click it around your wrist and you will travel back in time," he explains.

"You can never go back," I say, point blank.

He stares at me. *Really* stares.

"Ellis, you're acting pretty weird," I say, when it gets too much.

"Heathcliff," he says quietly. "My Christian name is Heath-cliff. Ellis is my last name."

I shrug. Ellis doesn't go by his actual name, just like I don't anymore either. "Hey, what's in a name?"

It's kind of a joke with myself, because I put that line in my play. *What's in a name? A rose by any other name would smell as sweet.*

Ellis smiles. I scrutinize his face, trying to work out what game he's playing. I don't remember him having stubble before. Huh. I guess I'm too used to staring at Romeo's face, always smooth as a baby.

"Jules, I need you to know—" he breaks off, looking down, confused.

He's staring at the ring on my finger. My hand must have fallen out of my pocket when we were running.

"You . . . you are *married*?" says Ellis.

"So?" I reply, defensive.

"I just . . . the ring. I did not notice it before."

"My hand's been in my pocket the whole time, genius."

"Yes, of course," he stammers. "I just did not realize you were already married."

"Look, whatever you've got to say about us being too young, I've heard it all before."

"I was not going to say you are too young," says Ellis. "Sometimes young love can last a lifetime."

I'm taken aback. I wait for Ellis to undercut it with some smart-arse comment, but he doesn't.

"Yeah. Yeah, exactly," I say eventually, tucking my hand back into its pocket. What the hell has gotten into him?

Ellis stares at me again for another drawn-out moment. Only, it's not in a gawking way, like I get from Paris and his goons. It's something else that I can't quite describe.

"Stop it," I say. "Stop looking at me like that."

"You are amazing," he says, clearly lying.

"I know, right?"

"You hide behind sarcasm," he says gently.

I open my mouth for a comeback and find I've got zilch.

"Apparently I do it too," he continues, smiling. "I also chew my lip when I am worried."

"What is this, a therapy session?" I'm thrown by the sudden oversharing.

Ellis doesn't answer—he just starts back up with the too-deep staring. As I'm choosing between insults, he snaps himself out of it and goes to check his watch. Except the watch isn't on his wrist anymore—I guess he lost it when we were running.

"I have to go," he says abruptly. "I have to go upstairs. To see if the man in the gas mask is coming."

He leaves the room. I stare out the window at the fading sunlight and wonder what the hell just happened. Then I hear a small sound behind me.

Ellis didn't leave—he's standing in the doorway. "I know that it feels like everything is moving terribly fast right now," he says, "but just trust your heart. It will be all right."

And those words? They're exactly the kind that I've longed to hear so badly. That I've wished so hard a boy would say to me in real life, as opposed to just on the page. Because yes, everything with Romeo was so fast, so rash. To the point where I've sometimes wondered if my heart could even be trusted. Now here's some near-total stranger, allaying my secret fears? And telling me, no less, it will all be okay? What is this, some kind of cosmic joke?

"Will you quit pretending you like me?" I say, feeling weirdly exposed.

I hear the first chime of the broken clock tower. I've been hearing it in the distance my whole entire life, but this is the first time I've heard it so close.

"Who's pretending?" Ellis says.

....

12

Ellis

2056

"Jules?" I yell, glancing around the abandoned department store. No answer. Jules is definitely not here. Somehow, she did not jump with us. Shite. *Shite, shite, shite.*

"She is the blasted *mother*," I say to the others, confessing everything. "The man with the mismatched eyes, who saved me from drowning? The one who built Frogs and created the Deadenders? Jules Capulet is *his* mother."

"So if she dies, the man with the mismatched eyes is never born," says Iggy, like it is a well-known fact. "Frogs is never built. The Deadenders are never formed. Which means we're all dead, centuries in the past. And there's no hope of saving the future."

"That is more or less where I was heading . . ." I trail off, confused.

"Frogs told us after you left," says Beth. "*Many* times."

"Frogs, what is going on?" I direct my question to what remains of him.

SANTANA

"You won't get much out of him," says Iggy, gently cradling Beth's handbag, which contains the mess of circuitry. "He made us hack out his mainframe." Iggy is a little choked up. I will confess that I am too—recent betrayals aside, Frogs was a friend.

"We do not know how, but the man in the gas mask tracked us down on the bus," explains Henry. "Frogs told us to bring you and Jules to 2056, then he sacrificed himself to save us."

"The man in the gas mask," I say. "Who is he?"

"Not sure," says Beth. "Somehow he's been piggybacking off our jumps. Frogs made us promise to destroy his mainframe as soon as we got here so we couldn't be followed."

Except we cannot do that, because Jules failed to jump with us.

"Hold on." The logistics sink in. "There was no time for all of that."

"You've been gone three months, Ellis."

"*Three months?!*" For me, it has been but hours since I left to wake Romeo.

I add, "Look, there is something else going on with this mission." I think about the note in the crypt and me knowing how to make Cat-9. "Things Frogs kept from us."

"Yes, we came to suspect as much," says Henry.

"Frogs *lied*," I say more bluntly.

"He would've had a good reason," says Iggy defensively, hugging the mass of circuitry tighter.

And what possible reason could that be?

"Either way, the mission's real," says Beth. "And important."

"What makes you so certain?" I say.

"Because Frogs *died* for it."

COCKER!

Beth winces. "Sorry, *mostly* died."

"So, what are our next steps?" asks Henry.

"We have to go back for Jules," says Beth firmly.

"No can do," says Iggy. "Frogs doesn't have the juice to program another jump. We *can't* go back for her."

"So *what*, then?" I throw my hands up in frustration.

"We use pods," says Beth suddenly. "We steal them."

"Pods are the most in-demand item on the planet right now," Iggy reminds us. "Pretty much everyone still left here is desperate to jump. How are we going to get our hands on any?"

"I don't know," I say, "though Beth is right." I look around at my friends, the Deadenders. This is what we have been training for. This is what we cheated death for. "Somehow, we must save Jules. *And* wake Romeo. They have to be together. Everything—*the whole future*—depends on the two of them being together."

....

13

Jules

2083

Standing in the cruddy Chinese restaurant, Ellis takes my hands in his. *Both* of them. Nobody touches my dead hand—it's like this unwritten rule. I'm about to object in spectacular fashion, when he bends down and *plants a goddamn kiss.* Seriously—a kiss on the hand, like some outdated gentleman. But a boy acting all hero-of-romance-y is exactly the kind of thing that I put in my story. It feels like I'm being mocked. Like *my story* is being mocked.

I yank my hand back. Then I add an emphatic, "You're a fool."

"And *you* are smart and brave and beautiful and strong," says Ellis, so earnest that it's obvious he's teasing. "But I really do have to go upstairs now. Quickly see if the man in the gas mask is coming."

I simply stand there, hating myself for not having some cracking comeback.

"Check your book. Page forty-nine," says Ellis, right before he disappears around the corner.

My book—he must mean my story. But why would he tell me to check that?

I get the notebook out of my backpack and flick through the pages as the broken clock tower slowly warbles through its chimes. Always thirteen, dragged out way too slow, always at random hours.

On page 49, there's a note written straight on top of my play. I stare at the individual letters . . . because they're mine. It's the quirky handwriting that I developed after what happened. After my left hand went dead and, for the first time in my life, I had to hold a pencil with my right.

The note says: *Wake Romeo before first nightfall.*

It's impossible, of course, since I never wrote the note. *Can't* write it, in fact—at least, not so neatly. And yet there it is, impossibility be damned.

I wait for everything to hit and knock me sideways. Because that's what happens, right? In stressful situations, I deal poorly. I panic. I act decidedly *rash*. I should be a mess right now. Crying and hysterical at the very least, given my track record. I don't know why I'm not. Maybe you only get one colossal lose-your-shit per lifetime. Maybe after that, it's all a bit whatever.

Or maybe some crucial part of me is just numb and unfeeling, like my arm.

The can't-shock-me-twice gives way to a smidgen of panic. I can taste it, rising like bile. But I can't go there, not again, especially not now. I have to *stay strong* and *dig deep*, à la Mum's nauseating pep talks.

When these feelings hit, I normally go for a pencil. I write away the muck with a verse about love. I'm clutching my story to my chest, so it's technically an option . . . but rhyming couplets here? Now?

Instead, I start pinching my arm by way of distraction. I can't feel the pain, though the act of it feels like control. A few more dragged-out chimes and Ellis comes back downstairs again.

"I don't understand," is all I can manage. Understatement of the centuries.

"Time to buck up, soldier," he says gently. Then he takes the cuff-thing from the table and hands it to me. "It is pre-programmed. All you have to do is click it around your wrist and you will travel back in time. *Trust me.*"

A few minutes ago, I would have thought that he'd lost the plot or was messing with me. But that note in my book, written by me, but *not yet*?

"Ellis, what's going on?" I ask.

"Best not spoil the ending." He picks up my backpack and zips it up for me. "Though perhaps time really is more like a circle—no end and no beginning." He guides the backpack strap over my arm.

Whatever the hell *that* means.

The broken clock tower makes its thirteenth chime, which is always the last one. Ellis's eyes travel left; he's seen something behind me. He grabs me and pushes me out of the way.

I don't hear the gunshot. Like so many things in life, it's silent. But I see the impact and the damage; blood seeps out of Ellis's chest. He sways for a fraction of a moment, staring at me, like time really is standing still. Then he falls to the floor and doesn't move again.

I scream.

It's like a sick kind of déjà vu, throwing me back to an earlier time and place. The World War II uniform, the gas mask—the shooter is dressed the same as Romeo was the night of that party. And there's a boy dead at my feet, just like before. It's a horrible mash-up of beginning and end; a gruesome abridgement.

I can't bring myself to keep looking at the man with the gun, so I stare at his boots instead. Brown, with a splash of Ellis's blood on them. His breathing is loud through the gas mask. In my peripheral vision I see him raising the weapon. *I'm next.*

And I can't help but think . . . isn't a dramatic end what I thought I wanted? Isn't that what I chose, last time around?

This time I choose the other option. Hugging my story tight to my chest, I use my chin to click the cuff-thing around my wrist.

And just like that, I disappear.

....

14

Ellis

2056

We are standing in the ransacked department store, fresh out of ideas, when Jules suddenly appears. She is clutching her notebook to her chest, looking decidedly shocked.

Beth does not hesitate—she grabs her purse from Iggy's arms, tips its contents onto the floor, and stomps on the circuitry until it breaks into tiny pieces.

"Did he follow us?" she asks while grinding Frogs beneath the heel of her saddle shoe. "The man in the gas mask, is he there?"

I peer out the window at the street below. There is a strange mix of abandonment punctuated by chaos, which is typical of the post-Fall years. I see a few lonely humans roaming the debris, and I believe I spy a wolf, if I am not mistaken. But no one who looks like they are straight out of World War II.

"I think not," I say, turning back to the others. Jules is staring at me, shaking her head like she cannot believe it.

"What?" I say, when she does not stop staring.

"But you . . . you . . ." her voice trails off.

"But I *what*?" I snap. Frogs might have lied, but he still practically raised me. And now he is dead. I know that is not exactly Jules's fault; however, I am rather inclined to blame *someone*.

"Nothing," she says. And then, focusing on the others, "Do *you* know who that was? The man in the gas mask?"

Beth opens her mouth to speak, so I cut her off with a curt, "Confidential." Who knows what she will say? We need to preserve the timeline as much as possible.

"Look, you should probably know that . . ." Jules's voice peters out. She is staring out the window in disbelief. "This . . . this is the past. You really *are* Deadenders."

"Confidential, huh?" Beth crosses her arms and raises an eyebrow at me.

"How do you know that word?" I demand of Jules, alarmed.

"*You* told me."

"I most certainly did *not* tell you!"

"You told me just then," says Jules. "*Before*. In the Chinese restaurant."

"I have never even *been* to a Chinese restaurant."

"Yes, you have," says Jules, confused. "We were there just then. *Just now*."

"Well, it was not me. I was right here the entire time."

"It wasn't you *yet*," clarifies Iggy. "If she saw you there, but you haven't gone there, then it means you haven't gone there *yet*. You must go there in the future."

Oh. Right. *Obviously.*

"The important part is that everyone is here now," says Henry, ever the diplomat. "My name is Henry, by the way. That's Iggy and Beth."

Jules nods at each of them in turn.

"Charmed, et cetera," says Beth, moving things along. "So, what now?"

Beth is clearly talking to Iggy, Henry, and me—the Dead-enders. Jules nonetheless answers with a tentative, "I think . . . I think I need to wake Romeo before first nightfall."

"Before first nightfall?" I am increasingly annoyed. "You are keen to wake your precious beau. Understood. But *today* is clearly out of the question!"

Jules hesitates a moment, then holds out her notebook. "Page forty-nine."

I open the notebook to the particular page. Written in thick red pen is: *Wake Romeo before first nightfall.*

"It's my handwriting, except I never wrote it," explains Jules.

"Shit," says Beth.

My sentiments exactly.

"Do you think it means first nightfall here or first nightfall back where Romeo is?" says Henry, peering over my shoulder.

"*When,* not where," corrects Iggy. "Could be either. Assume both?"

"Wait, you believe me about the note?" says Jules. "Just like that? No giving me hell about being crazy?"

"I was pulled from the brink of death in 1812 to become a secret time traveler," says Henry gently.

"Ditto, darling," says Beth. "Except from 1950."

"1979," says Iggy.

I remain silent.

"So how do we wake Romeo?" says Beth, coming to the point.

"We?" says Jules. "Does that mean you'll help me? That you'll all help me wake Romeo?"

"Waking Romeo is *our mission*," I say stiffly, rebutting any suggestion that Deadenders perhaps have naught better to do than matchmaking. "It is why I was sent to your Settlement in the first place."

"Oh." Jules lets that sink in. Then she asks, "Why? Why was your mission to wake Romeo?"

The others turn to me—this is the obvious moment to admit what is really at stake. To tell Jules that she and Romeo are destined to have a son. That their son will be the man with the mismatched eyes. That he will one day build Frogs and create the Deadenders. That without their son, there is no hope of saving the future. That everything—absolutely everything, including our lives—depends on waking Romeo.

"No inkling," I say instead. "Probably nothing of importance."

Beth gives me a look. I ignore it.

"Category drugs—they are our answer," I add, to change the subject. "If we can lay our hands on some Categories, then I can make Cat-9 and wake him."

"Not to be all negative here, but Romeo won't be born for about a decade, and we've rather lost our ride," says Henry sadly, gesturing at what is left of Frogs.

His words barely reach me, for I am staring out the window again. Before, I only looked down, to street level. Looking up, there is a gold skyscraper. From this room—from the *specific spot* that Frogs jumped us to—you really cannot miss it.

"What year did you say this was?" I ask, focused on the building adjacent to the skyscraper.

"2056," says Iggy. "Why?"

"Remember the mission that Frogs sent me on right before I left to wake Romeo? Just as I was about to create the Cat-9, Frogs stopped me. He said he had made a mistake. That the whole building was going to collapse regardless, so there was actually no point. He jumped me back to the wasteland, leaving the drugs behind."

Beth frowns. "Frogs doesn't *make* mistakes."

"Indeed," I agree. Then, pointing out the window: "That was the building."

"Well, it clearly hasn't collapsed yet," says Henry. "The drugs—maybe they're still in there?"

Precisely.

"Wait, 2056? Frogs sent me here before too," says Beth. "That mission last year, where I had to write a note in the dust on a piano. The piano was in a music room. There were five pods stashed there."

"Do you remember the address where the pods were?" asks Henry eagerly.

Beth nods. "It was 11 Elsinore Road."

"Wait. *I* live on Elsinore," says Jules. "Number 11 is the empty block directly across from my house."

That cannot be a coincidence.

"What the hell is going on?" says Jules, looking overwhelmed.

I ignore her again. "Frogs sent us on missions to this exact time and place so that we would know where to find what we need," I say to Henry, Iggy, and Beth. "What we need to wake Romeo."

"Frogs knew that this was going to happen," says Iggy as it sinks in. "That exactly *this* was going to happen. *Frogs knew . . .*"

Our eyes fall to what is left of him, smashed on the floor.

"But *how?*" says Beth.

"Why did he not tell us? Or change things?" says Henry.

"Why didn't he save himself?" says Iggy.

Yes. All bloody good questions.

"I guess these are useless now," says Henry, taking the cuff off his wrist and dropping it onto the pile of crushed circuitry like flowers onto a casket. Iggy and Beth somberly follow suit. When my turn arrives, I add the cuff from my wrist and the cuff from my pocket as well, so that Frogs's remains are together in one place.

"Perhaps someone should say a few words," says Henry gravely.

"Nonsense, we're on the clock," reminds Beth. "First night-fall, remember?"

Except Beth is more sentimental than she lets on. When she tipped out her purse, it was not just the remnants of Frogs that fell to the floor. Among the circuitry, there is my copy of Emily's book, Iggy's prized Sid Vicious artifact, and the small case that contains the ashes of Henry's father. Beth grabbed something from the bus for each of us before they fled.

It is all we have left now.

"Perhaps—" says Henry, but he is interrupted by a loud gasp.

"It's him," says Jules, who has been across the room, looking out the window. "The man in the gas mask."

"You're sure?" says Beth urgently.

"Yes."

"Did he see you?" I ask.

"No."

The window smashes; we are being shot at again.

"Maybe."

Shite.

Beth focuses on me. "We'll split up. Henry, Iggy, and I will draw his attention while you sneak Jules out the back. Go straight to the pods. We'll get the drugs and meet you there before nightfall."

"No. Absolutely not," I protest. There is no possibility that I am sneaking off, leaving my friends in danger. I shall not do it.

"We have to keep her safe, Ellis," says Iggy. "Outrunning a gunman and entering a building that we know for a fact collapses at some point is arguably *not* the most prudent option."

"All right, then one of *you* take Jules to—"

"Proven track record, darling," says Beth. "We've been evading this chap for three months now, haven't we, boys?"

"But—"

"But *nothing*," says Beth, quickly fishing my book and the other personal items out from among the circuitry, then stuffing them back into her purse.

I reluctantly hand her the crumpled piece of paper from my pocket—the one with the details of my Cat-9 mission, including the exact coordinates.

"Last desk on the left," I say. "Be careful. Someone was there, in the laboratory. Someone was coming."

"One set of footsteps or three?" asks Beth.

Yes, of course—perhaps it was Henry, Iggy, and Beth that

I heard running toward me. Or maybe it was the man in the gas mask. Maybe he followed them. Maybe he caught up with them. Maybe my friends—

"I cannot be sure," I say, terminating that line of thought.

Beth nods with no hint of fear or hesitation.

"Do you need this?" asks Jules as Beth is about to shut her purse. "To find Elsinore Road? It's a map." She is holding out an *A–Z of London,* apparently grabbed from her backpack.

"Lovely," says Beth. And, to me: "Ten minutes, then out the rear exit, okay?"

Beth does not wait for my answer. She simply announces, "This way, chaps," and leaves with Henry and Iggy in tow.

....

15

Jules

2056

Romeo died . . . then it turned out he wasn't dead. Now the exact same deal with Ellis. What is this, a developing *theme*? The other Deadenders have gone, and I find myself staring. I mean, from my perspective it's only been minutes since—

"Why did you fail to jump with the rest of us?" says Ellis, clearly suspicious.

"The wrist thing was busted," I say. I don't mention why. "You fixed it."

"*I* fixed it?"

"You said . . . the causal loop was broken?" I try.

"What else? What else happened from your perspective?"

"We ran and hid in this crusty Chinese restaurant. You went upstairs to see if the man in the gas mask was coming. You told me to check page forty-nine of my book."

"And?"

You kissed my hand like it meant something. You died.

"Nothing else," I say.

"Well, try not to cause any more drama," says Ellis, rather unkindly. And yes, I know that time's all out of joint . . . but heroics and romance one minute, then this the next?

"I'm *not* causing drama."

"Yes, *clearly*," says Ellis as he carefully scoops all the pieces of metal and circuitry off the floor.

Only, given how the whole Romeo fiasco got blamed squarely on the silly, dramatic teenage girl, that girl being me? It's kind of a sore point. "You know, a boy once told me I'm smart and brave and . . . strong," I say, quoting him, though he doesn't know it.

Ellis laughs. "Did it work?"

"Did *what* work?"

"Well, you cannot believe Romeo said all of that just to be *nice*, surely?" he says, peering out the window, probably double-checking that the man in the gas mask isn't still down there.

I'm blushing. And fuming. *Both.* Clearly there are two versions of Ellis, and the one who died to save my life was pure fantasy.

Then something occurs to me.

"Why did Henry say that you had to keep me safe?"

Ellis pauses, and then offers, "Perhaps you struck him as incompetent."

But as he throws all the pieces of metal out the window, scattering them, I notice it: *Ellis is chewing his lip.*

"You chew your lip when you're worried," I say automatically.

The insight catches him totally off guard, and for an instant I see it. The same thing I saw in the Chinese restaurant. A kind of . . . I don't know. Difference? *Something*.

"No. I chew it when I am *annoyed*, sweetheart," says Ellis, the mask back in place.

"You hide behind sarcasm," I say, on a roll now.

Ellis clearly has no idea how to respond to that, to the changed behavior from me. He stares for a long moment, then deadpans, "I deeply appreciate your observations. Catch the sarcasm in that?"

"Yes," I say. "Kind of proves my point though, right?"

Ellis glares at me and announces, "Time to go," without checking his watch, which is back in place again. Then he adds a gruff, "Try not to slow us down." Only, when we get to the stairwell, he holds the door open for me to walk through—he's being a gentleman again. I don't think he's even aware that he's doing it.

The stairs take us down to the ground floor of what was once a department store. It's your typical post-Fall mess—broken glass, rat poo, graffiti, mold—although there are also plenty of items for purchase remaining.

"I can't believe all this stuff is still here," I say, looking around. I always had the impression that, beyond our Wall, there was nothing useful left.

"You cannot fit much in a pod. Travelers had to be selective," says Ellis, all curt.

Weird to remember that he's not really a Traveler.

"Why do you call yourselves Deadenders?" I ask as we walk through a graveyard of plastic pine trees in some long-forgotten lead-up to Christmas. At the Settlement, we adore Christmas—all the traditions are king.

"Because it sounds so cheery," says Ellis, again with the sarcasm. He's being deliberately short with me. And yes, my knee-jerk reaction is to bite back with something cutting. But I force myself to focus on his words from before instead: *Trust your heart.*

And the thing is, my heart just isn't quite buying his hardened routine anymore. Not right off the back of him trading his life to save mine.

"I know, right?" I say, pretending that he meant it as a joke. "Makes me think of storybook unicorns and fluffy kittens. I mean, if rainbows . . ."

My eyes drift left, and what I see stops me in my tracks. Over near a make-up counter there's a pod, melded with wheels and plastic. I guess a shopping cart or something must have rolled into the exact wrong spot.

Of course, this isn't new to me. Pods reappearing somewhere that's no longer empty, merging with whatever's there? It's been part of the landscape my whole life. A constant backdrop, like the painted-on scene in a one-act play. Except in *my* time, on *my* side of the Wall, the carnage is a thing of the past—sun-bleached bones, rust, nothing to offend the senses. This is of the "now"—fresh and disgustingly present.

At a guess, I'd say that it's only a few weeks old—a month at most. I see rotten-flesh lips molded into metal. I see teeth and eyes alongside buttons and dials. Long blond hair flows in places, like a grotesque game of dress-up. A decomposing hand juts out the side, almost like it's waving. The hand is small—*a child*.

Shit, I can *smell* her.

When I arrived in the crypt that terrible night, I thought Romeo was dead. He *looked* dead. There was a faint pulse, apparently, but *I* sure as hell couldn't find it. So, to my mind: dead. And here's the thing—I couldn't imagine anything more awful. Romeo not breathing? Most. Tragic. Thing. Ever.

But I was wrong. There's apparently room for *much* worse.

Glancing away, I stare at my feet instead. I thought I knew what a tragedy was. I thought I understood its structure—the arcs, the loss, the moral to the story. Except there's no moral here—no poetic meaning, no lessons learned. This is real—*real* tragedy. It has stench and gore and a terrifying mess about it.

I quickly lean forward and puke my guts up. Once my stomach's empty, I keep going, dry retching, trying to purge what's not there. *Tragedy sounds like feuding parents. Tragedy feels like Romeo.*

Tragedy tastes like bile.

I wipe some of the vomit off my hair. Then I keep staring at the puddle of sick on the floor so I don't have to look up again.

"Are you finished?" asks Ellis once the dry heaves have stopped. His tone is gruff, but he's moved to block my view of the Picassoed girl. It means stepping in puke, although he doesn't seem to care. *Romeo* would care. Romeo would find it all very disgusting. He wore nice shoes—loafers. Maybe the last pair of loafers left in all of creation. They were lovely. He took proper care of them.

"Here," says Ellis, taking a bar from his pocket and giving me half. "Try not to spew it up, mind, for I have no other food, and these parts appear scavenged clean of all things edible."

I take a big bite, and soft sweet oats override the sharp taste of bile. It helps. As I chew, Ellis leads us away from the pod. He chats as we walk, which isn't like him. It's a distraction, I realize—something to fill the air other than the smell of her. A small act of kindness. But hell, isn't it always the small things that give us away?

I step outside; the street is eerie in its emptiness. Things aren't quite falling apart yet, like they are back home. That comes later. *Oh boy,* does it come. But here? Everywhere's a little bit wrecked, sure, though it's mostly just abandoned. Like everyone simply up and left . . . which of course they did. The only clue as to the how and why of it are terrible clumps of silver and gore. I count five—no, six—melded pods from where I'm standing.

And zero people.

We're not really completely alone out here—not everyone jumped. At least, not yet. I can hear noises off in the distance. Evidence of life, of—

"Which way?" says Ellis, pulling me out of my thoughts.

"Not sure," I say. The truth is, I've no idea whatsoever. I've never been beyond the Wall—not once in my whole life, before today.

"Do you at least know the general direction?"

I shake my head. Ellis sighs, clearly annoyed at me.

"Did it even occur to you to—" His voice cuts off. "Hold on. You did not know how to get home, yet you gave Beth your map regardless?"

I shrug. It seemed like the right thing to do.

Ellis stares at me for a moment, then mutters a reluctant, "That was good of you."

It's the first time he's given me a compliment, besides in the Chinese restaurant. From his perspective, the first time, full stop. I guess he must be conscious of that too, because there's an awkward pause. Then he clears his throat and says, "Close your eyes."

"What?"

"Trust me."

It's what he said before, in the Chinese restaurant. *Before he died for me.*

I close my eyes.

"Imagine yourself back home," says Ellis. His voice is soft and calm, a total contrast to an alarm that's just started screeching somewhere nearby. "Imagine yourself to be somewhere elevated."

So of course, I picture me on my balcony.

"What do you see?" says Ellis.

I see Romeo beneath my bedroom window. He's a mash-up of the real and the storybook version. Full period costume . . . but drunk and puking on the shrubbery.

"Shrubbery," I say, without elaboration.

"Look up," says Ellis. "What else do you see?"

"Nothing, it's dark."

"Make it lighter."

In my mind the darkness transforms into clear blue skies, like some cheesy metaphor. And then I do what Ellis said—I look up, away from the boy. I look *outward*. I see hints of a whole world out there, beyond my bedroom, beyond the Wall.

"Describe it to me," says Ellis. "Describe what you see."

"Mine eyes doth see the folds and flows of fleeting futures," I say, accidentally slipping into the old-fashioned language that I use when I'm writing my story. When I realize what I've done, I'm mortified.

I open my eyes.

Sure enough, Ellis is staring. Then he catches himself. "We need landmarks. Recognizable ones."

"I can see the tip of a black triangular-type tower to my left, and about this far away I can see a dome-shaped one," I say, holding my fingers apart to indicate the distance between them.

"I know those buildings," says Ellis, orienting himself. "I can probably get us there with that." He leads us down a side road, and I notice a ransacked shop called Tescos—it reminds me of the Supermarket. *Our* supermarket—Dad's and Tybalt's and mine. But, of course, these past few years, I'm the only one who still goes there. I cruise the aisles alone like some midnight shopper and research my story. "Cereals & Bread" for facts about Verona; "Biscuits" for books about fourteenth-century clothes.

Even when I was little, the Supermarket was always empty. When Dad took Tybalt and me for "crisps," we never saw another human soul, shopping for answers. I guess no one wanted to read about the past, they merely wanted to live in it. Except now I'm wondering . . . why? Why go to all the trouble of putting books in a supermarket, only for no one to read them?

Turning a corner, Ellis sees something and deliberately hangs back a little. I don't call him on it—instead I spy on him in the reflection of a shop window. I see him pass his half of the muesli bar to a bundle of rags. No, not rags—it's an old man, sitting so still that I hadn't even noticed him.

But Ellis did.

The old man starts eating hungrily. Ellis gave his last bit of food to a total stranger, I realize. Romeo never once did a noble deed without wanting praise. Yet Ellis tried to *hide* it?

I was wrong before. There aren't two versions of Ellis, like some dramatic disconnect—*Jules versus Juliet.* The boy I met in the Chinese restaurant? The one who told me to trust my heart . . . and who said that I was smart and brave and beautiful and strong . . . and who died for me? *He's* the real one. Ellis can pretend all he wants, but I see him now. And once you've truly seen a person . . . well, unlike with time, there really *is* no going back.

....

16

Ellis

2056

"So, you broke his heart," I say bluntly as we walk past a decrepit Tube stop. The stairs leading down are covered in bird shite and bat droppings, and the mouth of it spews out flies.

"What?"

"Romeo. He tried to end his life. You said he was heartbroken . . ." I trail off.

Jules stares up at a murder of crows that have started to circle. After a moment, she says, "Our parents hated each other. Romeo and me being together . . . it was forbidden."

Yes, I understand forbidden all too well. *A dark-skinned brat, a gypsy imp of Satan*—that is what Mr. Brontë called me when he read Emily's journal. When he discovered that his daughter loved a boy who was not white. It was October of 1831, in the kitchen of their home. Mr. Brontë waved the journal around in a terrible rage. Emily stood her ground, refusing to apologize. She calmly stated that whatever souls are made of, hers and mine were the same. Mr. Brontë was furious. He grabbed me by the scruff of the collar, took the skillet hanging above the fire, and smashed it into my forehead . . .

"Who you love is nobody else's business," I say now. It must come out with a bit too much heat, because Jules is staring at me again. Staring like she's trying to force out some truth, using nothing but silence.

"You're a *romantic*," she says at last, like I am some manner of riddle that she is pleased with herself for cracking.

"I am not like your beau," I say. "I care naught about love."

Ironic since, as far as nineteenth-century literature is concerned, I am quite the shining example.

Jules raises an eyebrow.

"You do not even know me," I snap, irritated.

"I know you better than you think," she says. "From my perspective, we've spent more time together."

The Chinese restaurant. I wonder what exactly happened in that additional chapter between us.

"Did I cover myself in glory?" I ask, testing the waters.

Jules remains quiet.

Right. Something definitely happened. Of course, from my perspective, I have done naught. But then I think of that rainy afternoon on the cliff with Emily. The kiss that I should have taken, yet failed to. And I remember that sometimes it is the things that you do *not* do that haunt you forever.

"I shall make a note to redeem myself in style," I say as we round a corner . . .

. . . and come into clear view of the Road.

I have encountered the Road a few times in my travels—the denseness is the first thing that hits you. The way the pods and bodies melded together so *efficiently* as they competed for the same space in the same time. It reminds me of the wasteland, except on a much smaller scale. These are the rotten seeds of our stillborn future.

Judging by its current size, I would guess that the Road must have collected a few thousand souls so far and counting. There are no survivors. The only life that it holds are feral: rats and mongrel descendants of abandoned pets. They gnaw at the wreckage, sniffing out fragments of flesh. Yet even *they* end up part of it eventually—absorbed when a new pod arrives. Wrong place, wrong time. The crows do better, circling above, sticking to easy pickings.

"What *is* that thing?" asks Jules in barely a whisper. She looks like she might vomit again, although she does not turn away. Instead she cranes her neck, taking in the terrible whole of it.

"Yellow Brick Road," I say. "That is the nickname for this particular stretch of highway."

"Like in *The Wizard of Oz*. But why's it so much worse than everywhere else?"

"Because they were *told* to jump here," I explain. "When it all got out of hand, the government closed off the highway and told everyone that they had to jump here, or else there would be chaos. They had a system. They had schedules," I add, as though that is what mattered. As though that should have fixed everything, human nature included.

I have seen the so-called ordered system firsthand. Thousands of rectangular bays marked out in yellow paint so that, from above, they look like bricks. Numbers for every bay, notice-boards with schedules and arrival times and endless warnings to KEEP CLEAR. A hurried attempt at order from what was left of the government. An easy system from the few well-meaning officials who were not already long gone for the glorious future.

"Anyone who followed the rules . . . is dead?" says Jules as the truth of that sinks in.

"Or *will* be dead, as soon as they get here," I say. "Though this was not some accident. Beneath the mess of pods and bod-ies, there are couches and chairs and TV sets. Debris that was deliberately dragged onto the old highway to ensure it became a deathtrap."

"But why?" Jules is suitably horrified.

"I do not know for sure," I say, which is true. "Though I sus-pect that some of the people left behind . . . well, perhaps they decided there was little point preserving a future if it was not going to benefit them personally." It would not be the first time.

"*That one might read the book of fate, and see the revolution of the times make mountains level, and the continent, weary of solid firmness, melt itself into the sea,*" says Jules quietly. "Shakespeare wrote that. I wonder what words he'd have used if he knew how the story ended. That humanity was destroyed not *in* time, but by it. Contagion to this world . . . at the hands of a god-damn *clock.*"

"The cancer was there long before pods were invented," I say, facing away from the Road and walking us around.

"What do you mean?" says Jules, following.

"Even before time travel, people failed to invest in the now," I say bitterly. "When they saw an issue, they refused to change. Instead, they passed the problem on to the next generation."

I have seen polar ice caps melt, species go extinct, and global temperatures soar. I have seen skies, lands, and oceans grow sicker and sicker. Time and time again, whole nations turned their backs. I guess sometimes the things that you do *not* do haunt you forever . . . and sometimes people do naught, with no care in the world.

"Action versus inaction," says Jules, her brow furrowed, like the idea of it has struck a chord. "None were noble enough to take arms against a sea of troubles."

With words like that, she reminds me of Emily—of the poetry that pooled in the soul of her. The comparison is unwelcome.

"More like a sea of *pollution*," I say, deliberately gruff. And then, "Pick up the pace, we have much distance to cover."

"Of course," says Jules, with no hint of sarcasm.

After three blocks at a brisk trot, we pass an old dumpster where stagnant water has collected. Inside, there is the corpse of a long-haired boy floating face-up, surrounded by blooms of mold. Jules observes him, saying nothing. And as we walk, I, in turn, observe Jules. Occasionally, she pauses to read some of the graffiti that's been scrawled on once-grandiose façades, but she otherwise keeps moving. There is a stoic quality about her that I missed upon first meeting.

Then I catch myself. Juliet Capulet's character traits are *not* my concern. Instead, I focus on practicalities—like navigating through London, at speed, without getting us killed.

* * *

"Bollocks," I say—the first word I have spoken in over an hour. It is in response to the collapsed shop front blocking our path.

Among the camping store debris, I see a flashlight. I grab it and click it on and off—solar-powered, so it works. That could be handy if the pods are stashed somewhere dark. Or if we miss the "nightfall" deadline, and . . . actually, best not to think about the consequences of *that*.

"I'll walk around and meet back up with you," says Jules.

I nod, distracted. "First, put this in the backpack." I hand the flashlight to Jules. She is too slow to grab it with her functional hand, and it smashes on the ground.

"Get a good look?" she says, because I am gaping. "Got some clever comment about the grossness of imperfection?"

"Perfection is overrated," I say gently.

"Yeah. *Sure.*" She stares at a piece of rubble by her foot, avoiding my gaze.

"Jules, I have no doubt your arm can be a major hassle for you, but for me, it is rather refreshing," I say, and mean it. "I have never been enamored with everyone looking the same," I add. I do not make a fuss of it—just a statement of fact.

Jules glances up and stares at me—properly stares, like I have uttered something mildly shocking. Eventually she shakes her head and says, "Wow. You really *are* a good guy."

"Hardly." I glance away. "I have been called a blackguard, a devil, a brute, a thief, and a—"

"—fiend," Jules finishes for me. I remember too late that I have already described myself to her in those words. *Precisely* those words.

"That's quite the shit list to know by heart," she says quietly. "Someone sure did a number on you, didn't they?"

Part of me wants to lash out for cutting so close to the bone. Somehow, I cannot. Our dynamic has changed. And apparently, all it took was Jules seeing some good in me. But of course, that is exactly what it took the first time too.

With Emily.

"I am *not* a good guy," I say again, thinking of the fictional "me" in Emily's book—the overtly masculine brute with all gentler traits erased. Worrying, as always, how he measures up to the truth.

At that, Jules looks me right in the eyes and says, "I don't believe you."

17

Jules
2056

We walk in silence again, block after block, with no words whatsoever. Then, out of the blue, Ellis asks, "Does it hurt?" And in my mind, I'm screaming, *Yes, of course it hurts. It's goddamn agony. These past two years . . .*

Then I realize he means my arm.

"It's dead," I say. "Can't feel pain, can't feel anything."

Would it were, that the same could be said of my heart.

"Dead?" says Ellis. "That is a very negative word to describe a part of yourself."

"All the happy sunshine words were taken."

"In a utopia like this, it is no wonder," quips Ellis, not missing a beat.

I can't help smiling.

As we continue in silence again, I keep coming back to this

one radical thought. In the Chinese restaurant, Ellis seemed to genuinely like me. He said I was smart and brave and beautiful and strong. He somehow saw *all of that* in me. Under normal circumstances, I wouldn't believe it. *Couldn't* believe it. In fiction, sure, but not in real life.

And because I couldn't believe something like that, I've always acted accordingly. Hardened accordingly. A self-fulfilling prophecy of the heart. Only, that tiny moment of time in the Chinese restaurant? It's taken the guesswork right out of everything. Ellis *can* like me, because he *did* like me. And so, the go-to insecurity—and the defensiveness because of it—somehow just isn't there.

In some version of the future, Ellis likes me.

And here in the now, that changes everything.

"What?" he says, because I'm staring.

"Nothing," I say. But my mind keeps wandering back to him kissing my hand. Nobody's really touched me in years, so I guess it makes sense that I'd think about it. That I'd imagine . . .

No, *not* appropriate.

I force myself to think about my husband kissing me instead. *Our* first kiss. It wasn't at a masquerade ball, like I put in my story. It was a party at an abandoned history museum. There was a lot of drinking. I remember Paris dirty-dancing with a Neanderthal figure, and his girlfriend swanning about in a priceless Egyptian headpiece, complete with cow horns. I remember Laurence pissing on the fake campfire in one of the dioramas, pretending to extinguish the papier-mâché flames. I remember feeling completely overwhelmed. I remember Romeo lifting off the World War II gas mask to reveal those oh-so-dreamy eyes. I remember him smiling right at me . . .

The gas mask. The uniform. *The same.*

I shove it from my thoughts.

We pass a melded pod which has been overtaken with vegetation. Ellis stops and picks a stem of it, like you might pluck a rose. He holds it out to me, one hand behind his back, all formal. It's like some weedy twist on the boy-gives-girl-a-flower moment. So, of course, I'm instantly awkward. Ellis grins, and then—in total contrast to the old-fashioned vibe—he chomps the top of the plant off!

I stare, agog, while he chews. We were taught to never eat wild plants—that some will poison you, just like I put in my story.

"Care to try?" says Ellis. I shake my head. Smiling, he crushes a leaf between his thumb and finger, then holds it under my nose.

The smell—*it's incredible.*

"Basil," explains Ellis.

No, it can't be. I've been eating basil my whole life. It's a key player in the industrial-sized vat of McGill's Mixed Herbs that we've been slowly working our way through for a solid decade. It doesn't smell like *this*.

Ellis hands me the crushed leaf and, with one last hesitation, I tentatively put it in my mouth. The flavor—it's fresh and alive, like nothing I've ever tasted. And I can't help thinking, *Why didn't we do this before? Why did it never even occur to me that—*

Then I realize, it *did* occur to me. We'd been down at the Supermarket. Dad had just read Tybalt and me *Jack and the Beanstalk*. When we got home, I asked if we could plant our own vegetables. Mum got all weird about it. She told me to be grateful for what we had. She almost seemed cross at me for asking . . .

"We should keep moving," I say abruptly to hide the unsettling feeling that's growing in me. The feeling that I've been missing something, maybe for a while now.

Another few steps and Ellis grabs me by the shoulder, stopping us both in our tracks. The gesture has a definite "danger" vibe, but Ellis seems . . . awed? Without a word he points to a nearby tree by the side of the road. There's a horse beneath it—*a real, live horse.*

"*My kingdom for a horse,*" I whisper, quoting *Richard III.*

Ellis smiles wide. "Sounds like a fair trade to me."

"Shakespeare wrote that, not me," I admit.

"Mere details." Ellis brushes it off. Then he adds, "*My Lord,* she is a beaut!"

The grass around the tree is mostly dry and patchy, but the horse has found itself a clump that's thick and lush—rich green among a sea of faded yellows.

"Funny how some things thrive and some things die," I say, staring at the grass but thinking closer to home. "Just fate or luck, I guess."

"Look up," says Ellis, not taking his eyes off the horse.

There's a plastic bucket tied to one of the tree's branches—I hadn't noticed it before. Some kind of makeshift nozzle is attached with duct tape.

"Bucket shower," Ellis answers my unasked question. "The grass is green because that is where the water falls." Clearly distracted, he adds, "A man might fish with a worm that fed on a man, then eat the fish that fed on the worm. Circle of life. Everything is connected."

Ellis checks his watch, briefly wages some kind of internal battle, then announces, "Three minutes—we can spare three minutes. *There is time.*" With obvious pleasure, he starts approaching the horse. I stay on the road, not wanting to scare her.

The horse is nervous at first, you can tell. But Ellis is a natural—so patient, so careful. He doesn't rush in. He moves slowly, whispering calm reassurance. She still isn't sure, so he holds out his hand. He's allowing her to get comfortable with him, I realize. Showing her through his actions that he's not a threat—that she's safe, and that he can be trusted.

Ellis is displaying skills that I've never seen before. Never even *imagined* before. And yes, I'm a little bit impressed.

The horse eventually drops her guard enough to let Ellis get close, to let him touch her. But he still doesn't rush it. He begins with long, gentle strokes down the length of her nose. When she's ready, he pulls her into him by the mane—gentle yet firm—and presses his forehead against hers.

And the image of that connection? It's what I was fumbling for in my story, with all that "*It is the east, and Juliet is the sun*" stuff. It never occurred to me to think more broadly. To imagine a much bigger picture than just human hearts.

The horse's ears suddenly prick up, and she bolts without warning.

Ellis and I both watch her go—something alive and vital against a crumbling backdrop. It's funny; my whole life I've grown up knowing that I might be one of the last surviving people on the planet. But I never really thought *beyond* people, about the world as a whole. Our Settlement, with its wire fence Wall? I'm suddenly struck by the idea of animals in a pen . . . except *we're* the animals. And we put ourselves there; we *made* ourselves separate.

As the horse disappears into the distance, I wonder if she's cantering or galloping—I've read both words, but never seen either in real life. I start to think about that—what it means. What it says about me and the place I call home. Maybe the idea that "everything is connected" isn't just about "past–present–future" or "cause and effect." Maybe it's about *more* than that. I look up at the bucket shower, then down at the patch of green grass, surrounded by dead yellow. It's thriving precisely because . . . the thought trails off as I spy movement.

"A bird." I stare in wonder at the tiny creature that's drinking from the bucket. It's the same breed as the one that's half-painted onto the backdrop of the old theater.

"A *sparrow*," says Ellis, distracted.

Huh. I know *Othello* and *A Midsummer Night's Dream* practically by heart. I've studied Elizabethan language like a fiend, and—given the end-of-days predicament—I might be the world's leading expert on the symbolic meaning of hallucinations in *Macbeth*. And yes, I've read about all kinds of flora and fauna down at the Supermarket. I've seen birds in general too—the Wall couldn't keep them out.

But I never thought to wonder about *that* bird. I saw it as nothing more than a painting on a stage. I thought about the metaphor of it, sure. Yet I never stopped to consider the reality. The fact that it's a painting *of* something, of a beautiful living creature, perhaps no less important than me . . . and it has a name.

"A sparrow," I say to myself, enjoying the sound of it. Maybe people *aren't* the paragon of animals. Maybe the world . . .

I clock that Ellis isn't merely distracted—he's on high alert.

"What?" I spin around, trying to see what the threat is.

"That horse was scared," says Ellis quietly. "She heard something."

We both stand perfectly still, perfectly silent.

"I don't hear anything," I say at last.

"Horses hear better than humans," whispers Ellis.

We wait some more.

Now I *do* hear something. Something that was maybe there before, just quietly. But it's getting louder now, more difficult to ignore.

"Do you hear that?" I say.

Ellis listens for a moment, then, "Quick, off the road."

"What is it?" I ask, alarmed, as the noise gets closer.

"You shall see," he says. Only, Ellis doesn't seem worried anymore. He's . . . smiling?

....

18

Ellis

2056

Jules stares with an obvious sense of wonder as the car speeds past us. I am from the 1800s; I never saw a car until I became a Deadender. Jules would not have seen a *working* one either. I was born too early; she was born too late. Despite us both being the right age to hold a license, neither of us can . . .

Then I remember the ridiculous plastic chair in the wasteland.

"I probably know how to drive a car," I say, as the idea takes hold.

"You *probably* know?"

"Theoretically, I know. I have simply not done it before."

Jules looks at me, an eyebrow raised.

"Frogs . . . I mean, the computer. He insisted that I learn to drive for some future mission." Though perhaps there was no future mission. Perhaps it was always for this, for now. "I practiced on a . . . proxy arrangement, yet I have not driven a car. Never even been inside one, actually."

There is a pause, then Jules says, somewhat tongue-in-cheek, "Well, there's nothing quite like your first time."

There are abandoned cars aplenty—people just left them behind when they departed for their better, brighter futures. But what we need is a *recently* abandoned car. One where the tires are not flat, and it is basically in working order. After a few minutes of searching, Jules calls from the other side of the road: "Here, this one."

It is a tiny little squirt of a thing, canary yellow.

"This one has three good tires," I say, referring to the luxury red sports car that I am inspecting. That I am really *rather keen* on driving.

"This one has four," says Jules.

"But—"

"*Four,*" repeats Jules, inviting no argument. With one last longing glance at my chance of driving a vintage Ferrari, I head for the yellow hatchback.

The keys are not in the ignition, though that does not matter. My fingers move of their own accord, overriding the car's internal computing system. It is a very specific skill that I picked up a few months ago for an unrelated mission. Coincidence? More and more, this all seems like part of the weave. Like Frogs knew exactly what was coming and did naught to stop it. *Or to warn us.*

"This is what is known as a seatbelt." I demonstrate how it clicks into place. Jules struggles with hers—it is clearly a challenge one-handed.

I reach over to assist, but she pulls away. "I can do it myself."

"As you wish." I withdraw.

Silence for a moment, then Jules adds, "I don't need your sympathy."

"I did not offer sympathy," I say, matter-of-fact. "I offered help."

"No, you didn't," says Jules. "You just assumed that I needed help, without even asking."

I flush with shame, for she is right. Having the use of only one arm must present constant challenges. There are probably tasks that Jules can manage herself, and those that she cannot. Though that is for her to determine; I had no right to decide for her.

"Please accept my apology," I say. "I acted without thinking."

"Happens to the best of us," says Jules, concentrating on the seatbelt.

Three more tries and the buckle finally clicks in.

"Here goes naught," I say, turning on the engine, shifting into gear . . . and drive. *It is exhilarating.* Emily taught me to ride horses, and galloping through the paddocks at a breakneck pace gave me a feeling akin to what I am experiencing now. There is an absolute thrill in tearing down the road. My hands are clenched tight on the wheel as I focus on the speed, on the *rush* of it.

I risk a quick glance at Jules. She is staring back at me, deeply unimpressed.

"We could *walk* faster," she says.

Indeed, a stray dog off to our left is more or less overtaking us. I check the speedometer—two kilometers an hour.

"This is the speed at which I am comfortable," I say, defensive. But I put my foot on the pedal until we are driving at least twice as fast. Five, maybe even six kilometers an hour. More than a sensible pace, given the circumstances. Arguably *excessive*, even.

"You keep an eye out for any signs of danger." I steer us around an abandoned garbage truck and head west.

"But everything's whizzing by so *fast*," she deadpans.

"Humor me," I say. And with that, Jules winds down the window and stares out at the world. Or rather, what remains of it. Every block, we see a few lost souls looting or roaming the streets, yet the city is largely empty. The pods were just too tempting, the future just too bright compared to the lackluster "now." Almost nobody stayed, nobody rebuilt. This era ended up basically abandoned. By the close of the decade there were not enough people left to keep even the most basic infrastructure ticking over. So I guess, one way or another, most of the people that we are seeing here now will simply . . . disappear.

"Have you seen the future?" says Jules, still staring out the window. "I mean, further forward than when *I* live?"

"Yes."

"What's it like?"

I think about the wasteland, where the bus is parked. The huge mounds of melded-together pods, like gruesome metal mountains, set against . . . nothingness. Everything that ever was, reduced to rubble and dust. The ultimate graveyard at the deathly close of time.

"I would not be inclined to build my holiday home there," I say.

"You should build your holiday home within walking distance," says Jules, obviously making another reference to my driving.

"I am traveling at a speed roughly equal to that of a horse and buggy," I retort. "And I will have you know that such a pace suited *many* eras just fine."

"*When* exactly are you from?" she asks as I carefully steer us around a downed helicopter.

"Oh, long before your time, me lassie." I ham it up. "I am practically ancient," I add, which is truer than not. Henry was born in 1798, so he beats me by twenty years. Other than him, I am technically the oldest living person by a colossal margin.

"And you're from London?"

"The moors," I say, automatically. "I was born in London, yet the moors were my home. 'Twas a harsh land of scrub and marshes, yet—"

"Hey, Ellis?" Jules cuts me off. "I think we have a problem." She is looking behind us, concerned. I check the rearview mirror and see a white car in the distance, gaining on us. It is a convertible. I can see quite clearly that the driver is wearing a gas mask.

Shite.

"Fear not," I say instead. "Since becoming a Deadender, I have watched a plenitude of classic cinematic masterpieces. This is what is known as a car chase."

"Well it's going to be a short-lived one if you don't drive faster!"

"This is my first time behind the wheel!" I protest as the white car closes in on us.

"Which button makes it go faster?" asks Jules, fiddling with the air conditioning, engaging the hazard lights. Another button and music starts blasting. The music is loud and distracting, though I don't dare take my hands off the wheel to switch it off.

"Stop it! Stop pressing things!" I yell to be heard over the song. "There is a *foot pedal* for speed!"

Jules looks down at my foot, which is resting gently on the accelerator. Then she unbuckles her seatbelt.

"What are you doing?" I shout, as she climbs onto me.

"What do you think?" says Jules. Then I suppose she realizes that she is effectively lying on top of me—her legs between my legs, her face buried into my chest—because she adds a hasty, "Don't answer that."

From a position that is rather akin to a lover's embrace, Jules stomps her foot on top of mine, pressing the accelerator all the way down.

"Stop it, you shall get us both killed!" I bellow as we pick up speed in an instant.

"Trust me!" she says.

"We are going to die!" I scream as we approach an impossible corner.

The tiny yellow car careens on two wheels, yet I somehow—miraculously—keep it steady.

"My reflexes are impressively good!" I yell as the car comes back down onto all four wheels. Up ahead there is a broken table, dumped on the road. I use it as a ramp to launch us skyward so we clear a mound of dead appliances.

"I appear to be able to drive with quite reasonable skill!" I shout as we sail through the air, skid, spin, and turn back the way we were going.

"Good news," mumbles Jules, who is now stuck facedown against my chest, unable to see a thing.

I check the rearview mirror. The white car is still there, though we are gaining distance from it.

"Your computer toad delivered," says Jules into my chest.

Correct. Frogs has been giving me reflex training for years, which is why I was able to keep the car steady on two wheels. And using the table as a ramp? I learned that trick for the Barcelona mission, except it was a skateboard, not a car.

"I am quite possibly the best driver *on the entire planet* right now!" I say.

I may have spoken too soon. Ahead of us there is a fallen power pole blocking the street. I slam on the brakes, and the car goes into a sideways slide. I stare in awe at my hands—the way they handle the wheel with dexterous skill, just like Frogs had me practice, hour after hour, month after month, on that plastic chair in the wasteland.

The car comes to a final stop.

"*So* impressed with myself right now," I say quietly, shaking my head, equal parts relief and disbelief.

I hit a button on the dashboard, finally turning the music off. Adrenaline is already pumping hard through my system . . . and then Jules doubles it by pulling herself up. She is effectively sitting on my lap now. This is by far the most proximate I have ever been with a woman. I freeze, suddenly acutely aware of the physical situation. The time period that I am from . . . having a young woman sit on one's lap was *not* the proper thing. My heart is pounding—I tell myself it is purely as a result of the car chase. An obvious lie.

"How did you know that I would be able to drive so well?" I ask.

"I didn't," she says. "Took a chance."

Took a chance with our lives without even flinching. Perhaps she is not entirely unlike Emily after all.

Jules's gaze travels up, over my shoulder.

"Quick, get out," she says. "The white car—it's coming."

....

19

Jules
2056

"If he finds us, are you going to bust out some lethal moves?" I whisper. We're hiding in the dressing room of an abandoned clothes shop. It's been twenty minutes, and still no sign of the man in the gas mask.

"If he finds us, I am afraid that *dying* seems more likely," says Ellis.

"What, no heartfelt words of affection first?" I think of what happened in the Chinese restaurant.

"Anything particular in mind?" whispers Ellis.

"Oh, I don't know. Thought you might *at least* like to tell me I'm beautiful or something," I say, kind of as a joke. But also, beneath that, kind of serious.

"This is the middle of the twenty-first century, when gender equality was briefly the fashion," says Ellis. "As such, should it not be *you* telling *me* that I am beautiful?"

The door opens. We both shut up.

I can hear footsteps moving around the shop. I stare at the shabby carpet. The changing room curtain doesn't go all the way to the floor—in the gap, I see the rough khaki fabric of World War II army pants. Beneath them . . . sneakers?

The man in the gas mask—he's less than a meter away. I'm expecting to be discovered, for it to end in death. *Like what happened with Romeo and me, our forbidden romance.* But this time, I'm spared the tragedy. Unlike me two years ago, the man in the gas mask just walks away. A moment later, there's the sound of the door again. He's gone.

We wait, frozen, which I guess is ironic. Because hasn't that been my life before today? Frozen in time, waiting for Romeo to wake? A life officially on hold?

I glance at Ellis; he's biting his lip again. It reminds me of a line from my play—this thing that I wrote about *two blushing pilgrims.* I was describing Romeo's lips. Thinking about it now, I wonder why I chose such delicate, bashful words. If I had to describe *Ellis's* lips, I'd—

No, never mind.

Looking away, I stare at my reflection in the changing room mirror. What with the greasy hair and the too-big hoodie, I'm a real *vision of loveliness.* But there's a mirror behind me too: infinite versions of me, getting smaller and smaller.

"He is surely gone, though we should give it another minute," whispers Ellis at last.

I'm very conscious of how close we are; our bodies are

basically pressed together. My hand has come out of its pocket, and it's touching Ellis's hand—

I flinch, pulling my body back. It seems like I've just recoiled from him, though it wasn't really that. It was a knee-jerk reaction to him touching my dead arm.

"So, you think you're beautiful, huh?" I whisper, to hide the awkwardness.

"I was *not* proclaiming myself to be beautiful," retorts Ellis.

But he *is* beautiful. Handsome, and he must know it.

"Yeah, I'm sure life's been real tough for you," I say, teasing him. "Tall, muscled physique, chiseled cheekbones. So, tell me, in which era exactly did *that* go out of style?"

Ellis looks struck. I see pain in his eyes, as opposed to vanity. I wait for him to shut down, like I usually do. Like he has before.

"*All* of them," he says, quietly. "Every single era of humankind—past, present, future. Every time, the color of my skin has been an issue. *Hate* has been an issue."

I understand what it's like to be hated because of your appearance. Paris and his goons? The teasing over my arm is never-ending. But it's not the same at all. I wasn't hated just for existing. The truth is, I *can't* understand what Ellis has gone through. I'll never really relate, and I have no right to compare.

"People are historically shit," I say in lieu of sympathy.

"The absolute shittiest. Not a decent one among the lot of them," deadpans Ellis. Though on his lips, there's the ghost of a smile.

We give it another minute before leaving the changing room. I go to tuck my arm back into its pocket, and I see what's missing. *I lost it,* I think to myself. Even in my own head it comes out sounding like some cheesy metaphor: *lost my youth, my innocence, my mind.* Except I'm talking practicalities. My wedding ring—it's not there. I touch the spot where it should be. There's no poignant strip of white—no tan line, no mark left behind. The ring's just gone without a trace. Of course, I didn't feel it leave me. *I felt nothing.*

I remember the wedding that I gave to myself, like a gift, in my story: quaint little church, flowers and candles, longing gazes, heartfelt vows, full period costume. Then the image morphs into what really happened: church smelling of piss, pews piled tall, graffiti everywhere. Romeo high as a kite, tongue-in-cheek as he slid the ring onto my finger . . .

I tell myself that the ring doesn't matter, except that's a huge lie. The band of gold *does* matter, though not because of its connection to my husband. Romeo never gave me a ring—he forgot, so we used one of mine. It belonged to my mother. She gave it to me back when I was little and we were close. Before she became nothing more to me than a source of dramatic tension.

"What is it?" asks Ellis. I'm still staring at the place where the ring should be.

I'm about to tell him, then I remember what he said in the Chinese restaurant when he saw my wedding ring. *Sometimes young love can last a lifetime.* I kind of don't want to overwrite the memory of that with something different from him now. Something less. So I say, "Nothing. It's nothing. I just lost a piece of jewelry, is all."

"Shall I buy you something sparkly, by way of replacement?" Ellis gestures expansively at rack upon rack of women's clothes that have us surrounded. There's a lot in the way of sequined miniskirts and barely-there tops in tiny sizes.

"Gee, *would* you?" I say.

"No, I actually *would not*," says Ellis, heading for the exit. And yes, I'm a bit sad about the ring, but I'm still smiling. Because the man in the gas mask? He was wearing gray sneakers just now. Back in the Chinese restaurant he was wearing brown boots, splattered with Ellis's blood. Things can change. The *future* can change. *Ellis doesn't have to die.*

And it turns out, I care more about that than a band of gold.

. . . .

20

Ellis

2056

As we make our way out of the city, we see all manner of depravities, all manner of horrors. Jules observes them without a word and keeps on walking. We have been silent for so long that I get a proper start when she suddenly says, "Stop!"

"What? What is it?" I spin around frantically, expecting the man in the gas mask.

Jules smiles. "Listen."

Somewhere in the distance, I hear a chime.

"It's the clock tower," she says. "We must be close."

We run toward the sound, and it leads us to a large stone clock tower.

"Time's fell hand defac'd no more," she says cryptically. And then, "In my day, the tower was faulty. Like time was broken, but the poor clock just"—she pauses, turns to face me—"didn't know it yet."

The way Jules is staring at me now, her expression— something about this clock tower seems to have upset her.

"Tip-top condition *now*, though," I say. "Tickety-boo. Tickety-*tockety*-boo?"

Jules does not smile at my attempted humor—she is simply quiet for a long moment. Eventually, she shakes off whatever had her worried and says, "You're right. Of course you're right. Things aren't set in stone."

"Except for clock towers," I say, patting its smooth surface as I would a filly.

This time I am rewarded with an eye roll, and then we head off.

We walk through the suburbs. It is effectively a ghost town— abandoned bicycles and cars, squalid piles of garbage, black swimming pools, vacant lots where houses have burned down. Though the gardens—albeit overgrown—are thriving.

"Rich soil," I say, absently scooping up a handful of dirt as we walk. "Would make for good farming—living off the land, instead of off the past."

Jules is staring again.

"What?"

"Nothing. It's just, back home, it never—it almost never occurred to me that that was even an option," she says. "That we might . . . I don't know. Plant the seeds. Create our own future."

"You are not alone in that," I say, placing the dirt in her hand. "I have visited most eras, and rest assured, it is a recurring theme."

"It must be incredible," she says, inspecting the dirt. "Traveling through different centuries, visiting the last syllable of recorded time."

"A house, a vegetable patch, a dog, maybe a horse—" I break off, choosing not to voice the rest of my private wish list: *A family of my own and a love that I can count on.*

"I would rather have that than all the time in the world," I finish instead.

And suddenly I am remembering a moment from my past, with Emily. The two of us, just kids, out on the moors, dreaming of finding the right place to build a house—a life—together. Yet it was naught but a fantasy.

"What's wrong?" says Jules, perceiving the change in me.

"It is unimportant."

"Don't do that," she says. "I hate it when people do that."

"Do what?"

"Pretend that everything's nothing."

"Just . . . sometimes my past catches up with me," I say, going for clichéd but secretly literal.

"*Time heals all wounds,*" says Jules, letting the dirt drop from her fingers. "You know, I read that once. Although lately I've been thinking it's backward. Time—"

"—*creates* all wounds," I finish for her. I have had that exact thought myself. It feels like a moment of connection between us. When I first met her, I thought she was like Romeo—that they were peas in a pod. Well, not *that* kind of pod. Now I am starting to think it is a case of opposites attract. She is the wild one, and he is the conformist.

I must still seem torn, because Jules gives me a playful little punch on the arm and says, "Time to buck up, soldier."

I do a double take, because that is exactly what Frogs always said. He would utter it whenever I had been sitting on the steps of the bus for too long, staring out into the wasteland. When I was mooning over Emily. When it all became too much.

"You okay?" says Jules, because now *I* am staring.

"Yes, fine." I shrug it off. Frogs was never "alive" as such, yet in his death, I do miss him.

We keep walking until we reach a stretch of dirt that appears no different from any other, and Jules comes to a stop.

"This is where the Wall was," she says, gazing at her feet, like they are teetering at the edge of an invisible barrier.

"Need me to cut you an imaginary hole, or can you manage?" I say. Except Jules is suddenly in no mood for jokes.

"*The weakest goes to the wall,*" she says quietly. "I wrote that about something else, but perhaps I always intended a secret double meaning."

I do not understand.

"The Wall," she says. "I lied before. Until today, I'd never gone beyond it. Not once in my whole entire life."

She had never gone beyond the Wall? Never ventured beyond the borders of such a tiny little world? In that case, she is coping remarkably. When I was yanked out of *my* known universe to become a Deadender, I sure as shite did not handle the change so well.

"When I was growing up, they said that the Wall was to keep the Travelers out," continues Jules. "But there *weren't* any Travelers on the other side. There were none left . . ."

Correct. By the 2070s, almost everyone had already jumped ahead. They were collecting at the end of time in the wasteland. Or on the Road.

"The thing is, I *knew*," says Jules, still staring at the empty space in front of her. "I knew that the Wall was pointless, but I stayed behind it anyway."

Looking at her now, something in me softens. Fear is what kept Jules behind a false barrier, clinging to the illusion of safety. It is the same thing that kept me from letting myself go, with Emily. I understand completely.

"It is never too late to change," I say quietly, wondering for the first time if that is perhaps true. Then I have an idea. "Wait."

I find a stick and draw a line in the dirt, level with Jules's boots, marking the spot for her to step over.

"Is that the start line or the finish line?" says Jules.

"Both."

"Deep," she says with a laugh.

"Cardinal rule of time travel," I say. "There is no beginning or end."

Jules looks at me as if the words carry meaning. Then she says, "Guess we'd better focus on the middle, then." And with that, she crosses the threshold into "home" again. I pause for a moment, smiling to myself as I watch her march on ahead without turning back.

And then I follow.

ACT III

. . . .

21

Jules

2056

These past two years, I've so often wished that I could wind the clock back and restore myself. Somehow return to the younger, less crumbling me. Turns out *home* got that particular do-over. Staring at Number 10 now, it's the house that I grew up in, but without the decay eating away its dignity. It's been renewed, like magic . . . except that the magic was *time*.

This is the past, so my relatives must be living here. I suppose I should stay away, though the temptation's too great. I sneak up the path and peer in the window. Inside it's shut up, dusty. Abandoned, like so many other houses that we've passed.

It makes no sense.

"People should be living here," I say. "The Capulets have been living at Number 10 since forever. They were one of the founding families of the Settlement."

I don't wait for Ellis—I head around the side to where the crypt is. It still says CAPULET, but the rosebushes haven't even been planted yet. I stare at the crypt, long before my secret will be hidden in it. And then, just like back home, I look away.

Walking quickly to the front of the house, I turn my attention to Number 11, across the road. In my time it's a vacant lot—overgrown grass, empty except for the two old pods. Not *merged* pods, like so many you see. *Sabotaged.* The mechanisms ripped out, so they don't work anymore. Tybalt and I made pretend rocket ships out of them when we were kids.

Right now, Number 11 is a mansion. Not like ours—not Victorian with latticing and balconies. It's what they called "modern," back in the day—clean lines, blond wood, glass.

"The pods must be in there," says Ellis, glancing at his watch.

I take one last look at Number 10, the house that I grew up in. There's an old saying: "You can never go home again." It's about time—you can't go home because things will have moved forward. Apparently, it's also true in the other direction.

We walk across the road to Number 11.

It's locked.

"We need a long, thin piece of metal," says Ellis, hunting around in vain.

"Like this?" I point to the cuff-thing that's still around my wrist. I didn't take mine off when everyone else did, back at the department store. I felt self-conscious about my arm, so I kept it tucked away in my pocket.

"Perfect," says Ellis, taking the cuff off my wrist and crushing it beneath his heel. "The most sophisticated technology in existence, repurposed to jimmy a lock," he mutters to himself as he fishes through the debris. "I think Frogs would have approved of that, actually."

Ellis finds what he needs and pokes it into the lock, jiggling.

"Deadender training?" I ask.

"Misspent youth."

The door clicks open.

Before entering the house, Ellis carefully scoops up all the little pieces of metal from the doorstep. "Our technology does not exist in the past," he says, finally opting to explain. "You cannot be too careful." He throws all the tiny pieces into the garden, scattering them.

Inside the house, there's a grand spiral staircase right as you walk in the door. Beyond that, there are low-set modular chairs and pale timber floors. Everything's wood and white and clean except for a layer of dust. It's practically empty, although not ransacked-empty. *Minimalist* empty—tasteful and sparse.

We go from room to room, searching for the pods. Beth said they were in the music room. This place is huge—that could be anywhere. I catch sight of a painting hanging on the far wall: a girl standing in front of a small village, her face half-hidden by flowers.

That image. I move closer, staring intently.

"What is it?" Ellis follows me over.

"The girl holding the flowers ..." I say, staring at the painting.

"Not flowers, *herbs*. There's rosemary, that's for remembrance," says Ellis, pointing. "But Jules, why have we paused here?"

"The painting. Something about it seems familiar, but I can't place what." I shake my head. Then I notice the dust—there's a section of floor that has no dust, stopping at the painting. Shoeprints going nowhere? And the frame. Most of the frame is dull, except one small corner is shiny. Like it's been touched often. I press on it. Sure enough, a panel clicks back, then out. A hidden door.

"I thought that, in your time, this was an empty block," says Ellis.

"It was," I say. "I mean, it *is*."

"Then how did you know *that* was there?"

"I didn't. It was the painting—that's what caught my eye. I feel like I've seen it before, but not quite."

Shrugging it off, I pull the secret door open and step inside ... *to a room full of books*. It's a library, hidden behind the walls. Whereas everything in the rest of the house is minimalist, in here is a hoarder's paradise, filled to the brim with pilfered artifacts. Weird items—mousetraps, a suit of armor, two wooden clowns, a big red flag with a white cross on it, a painting of a castle, a poster boasting PURPLE RAIN, a giant tapestry. I feel my imagination starting to click over, getting inspired. This place, with all its quirky stuff, would make the seeds for such a wonderful story. I examine it, drinking everything in. The ceilings are high, and all the way around the edge of the room there's a mezzanine level, draped with blankets and quilts.

I step further inside, craning my neck, marveling at the wonder of it. The treasures, the *books*. I've always loved books, histories in particular. Stories about the past and those who ruled countries, before time ruled all. I'm about to head to the nearest shelf and scan the titles when Ellis grabs me by the shoulder and subtly nods to my left.

Two monitors—jarring against all the historical items. One shows the front door that we just came through. The other shows a back door. *Surveillance.*

Ellis starts quietly ushering me toward the secret painting entrance.

Then a voice says, "Is my castle *under siege?*"

A boy with golden hair steps out from behind the tapestry. He's about our age—late teens. But he's holding a sword and is wearing a flashy crown that might actually be real.

"The sword is merely for theatrics," says Ellis quietly. "The others have guns."

I look around the library—I don't see anyone else. My eyes rest on the mezzanine level—the blankets over the banisters. They weren't for decoration, or to give the place a cozy aesthetic. They were for hiding. One by one, the others stand. I count twenty of them, all teenagers. Ellis was right. Unlike the would-be king, they all have guns.

"Thieves!" says an impish girl from the mezzanine level.

"So clean, so well fed?" says the king, strolling the floor as if he's sizing up prey. "They're *Travelers.* Here recently, too."

"Where are your pods?" demands someone else from above us.

"Pray, do tell," says the king. He's grandiose, like a bad actor, except it's all some strange performance. He seems *off,* somehow. He sways, not quite steady on his feet. Sheathing the sword, he fishes a little glass vial from his pocket and puts a drop of blue liquid in each eye. Drugs.

"To see or not to see. That is . . ." He seems to lose his train of thought. His pupils are like saucers; he's clearly high. Maybe he thinks he really *is* a king.

I watch as he pours wine into a ceramic mug, squirting in some of the blue eye-drop mixture. I can't place his voice, though he somehow looks familiar.

Then one of the others says to him, "What do we do with them, Montague?"

The name sinks in my gut like a stone. The wild king? It's *Claude Montague*. Romeo's father, as a teenager. But that's not possible. He wasn't a teenager now, in *this* time.

"My words . . . fly up?" he asks in lieu of an answer. He's staring in awe at a stained-glass panel in the roof. It's of Mary Magdalene—the same classic image that Mum always loved.

I take a closer look at the others, who've now all made their way down from the mezzanine level. And it's like my vision shifts, finally letting me realize what I'm actually looking at. Or rather, *who* I'm actually looking at. The impish one is Trudy, Romeo's mother. The Reynaldos, the Osrics. Rosencrantz and Guildenstern—they're not dead. It's all the founding families, back when they were teens.

My gaze stops on the two young women standing at the bottom of a narrow staircase. One is about my age, the other a bit older. Pale skin, dark hair, the matching dark eyes—unmistakably sisters.

"I know you." I stare at Aunt Miranda . . . and at Mum.

Montague glares at them, an accusation.

"She's lying," says Mum, totally steady.

"You're Omelia Capulet and Miranda Capulet," I say in disbelief.

"Omelia *Manningham* and Miranda *Manningham*," corrects Aunt Miranda, clearly confused.

What is this, some twisted joke? Ellis nudges me—a warning—but I ignore him.

"No, not *Manningham*." I'm getting flustered. I glance from Montague back to Mum and Aunt Miranda again. "It's the Montagues and *the Capulets*. There's a feud. You hate each other."

"Why would we *hate* each other?" Montague drapes his arm over Aunt Miranda's shoulder in a proprietorial way, rubbing a hand over her belly.

I register the bump. Aunt Miranda is pregnant, clearly with Montague's baby. Tybalt . . . Tybalt was a *Montague*?

I take another look at the king and his disciples. It's not right. Nothing's right.

"No, no, no," I say, half to myself. I turn to Miranda and Mum, desperate for them to believe me. "You were both born in the big white house across the road—Number 10. Your family has been there for generations. When everyone else jumped, they stayed put. The Settlement, the Wall, the stash at Laertes Health Club . . . they built a community. A community of *Settlers*."

"She's clearly not sane," says Mum.

"Agreed," says Ellis, probably trying to defuse the situation. "Ignore her."

I don't want to be ignored. I try to think of specific details about Mum. Things to prove that I actually do know her. But I can't manage any. I guess I never really thought about her as her own person, outside of just being "Mum."

Instead, I spin to Miranda and, pointing at her belly, I say, "It's a boy. He's born in 2063. You name him Tybalt."

Miranda starts to say something, but Montague shuts her up by raising the mug to her lips. "It's a boy! A toast to our unborn son!" he says, abruptly jovial.

Montague doesn't seem to notice that Miranda has clamped her mouth shut, refusing to drink the drugged wine. Or that, because he keeps pouring, the wine is spilling down her chin and onto her clothes. Or that she has tears in her eyes, clearly humiliated. Maybe scared, even.

He definitely hasn't clocked the fury in my mum. That she's balling her fists, readying for a fight, regardless of consequences. And it's the weirdest thing—after so long resenting my mother, I suddenly feel *protective* toward her.

"No, you call your son Romeo!" I blurt out, to move Montague's attention back to me. "After your brother, who died."

His demeanor changes instantly. The sword is long—one swoosh and two steps is all it takes for him to have it pressed against my throat.

"Did you just threaten my brother?" Montague says quietly.

Shit. Romeo, the uncle, *my* Romeo's namesake. He's not dead yet. Or not dead here, in this upside-down place. Sure enough, a young boy—maybe only twelve years old—calmly steps forward and says, "I don't *like* being threatened."

He has the same hazel eyes as my father-in-law. His voice is angelic, except he instantly gives me the creeps.

"Lower your sword," says Ellis.

The other members of the motley gang are slowly closing in around us.

"Lower your sword," repeats Ellis, undeterred.

"Gut her," says a girl with a shaved head, also clearly on drugs.

Back home she was Mrs. Cisco, the headmistress—Rosaline's mum.

"Now, let's not be hasty," says the blond-haired boy that Trudy's linking arms with. He seems to be her boyfriend, though that's not right either. In my time—my world—Trudy was with Claude Montague, Romeo's father.

"We need their pods, remember?" continues the blond boy, calm and coaxing. I'd say he's one of the few—besides Mum and Aunt Miranda—who's sober. "Even with all our stashes, we're still six pods short. If you kill them, they can't tell us where they've hidden theirs."

I should be focusing on the blond boy's words, since it's maybe a life-or-death moment. I'm not; I'm focused on his voice. It takes me a moment to recognize it, but that's no surprise. I mean, it's been two years since I've heard him say anything except "Hell is."

He's decades younger, and the scratchy beard is gone altogether.

But the blond boy is my dad.

....

22

Ellis

2056

"Kill her and your fate will be likewise," I say ever-so-calmly. It has the desired effect—all eyes are on me now.

"Revenge?" says Montague, wide-eyed and nodding. "Yes, yes, I like it. That's good, that's interesting . . ."

The chap is so high he is officially off the planet.

"Let's *force* them to tell us where their pods are," says the little brother with a disturbing smile. "Let *me* do it. Can I?" His eyes are wrong—not drugs, something worse. I have dropped in on history enough to know that there are some who simply enjoy the dark side of things. I would bet good coin that he is one of them.

"Everyone stay calm," says the blond boy, obviously trying to de-escalate.

Montague lowers his sword and steps backward, but the little brother grabs it and lunges.

Jules steps in front, putting her body between me and the weapon.

There is no sound.

For a moment I assume that the brother must have missed, then I register his confusion. Jules's arm is bleeding impressively, though she acts as if it hurts not at all. Which is the truth, I realize. It was her numb arm that she put between me and the sword.

Brave *and* smart.

Of course, the little brother does not know such stuff. From his perspective, Jules is hard as nails, entirely unflinching. She stares him down, not making so much as a whimper. He seems disappointed.

Montague, clearly rattled, grabs the sword back from his brother. He is high and flustered—not a winning combination. He starts blinking furiously, then he focuses on the tiny splotch of blood that has dripped from the sword to the floor.

"Look, it's in the shape of an animal," he says, suddenly fixated. "A weasel? I heard about weasels. They lived in deserts, with humps—went for months without water." He tilts his head to observe the blood from a new angle. "Now it looks like one of those giant creatures that lived in the ocean. What were they called again?"

This chap is a *very* long way from logical thought. I take advantage of the confusion and pull my T-shirt off, wrapping it tightly around Jules's arm and holding it there. She might not be able to feel the pain, but she is still losing blood.

She did this for *me*.

"Should I get that stitched up?" asks the blond boy, the peacemaker.

Montague nods, still mesmerized by the red on the floor. Until the brother says to him, "You're getting *soft*," loud enough for the others to hear. "What's wrong, afraid to take action?"

The loss of face shakes Montague out of his daze.

"Wait," he says, reacting. "Lock them in with the sleepers."

"No, you can't put them in there!" says the younger of the two dark-haired girls—one of the sisters whom Jules believes she knows.

"Claude, *please* don't," begs the pregnant one, more gently.

"Take them away!" he says, overcompensating with volume. He turns to us and adds, "To the sleepers with you both, until you tell us where your gods are! No, wait, that's wrong. Where your *pods* are." And then, to a skinny kid, "You—you go with them."

"Just tell them where your pods are," the blond boy—the diplomat—urges Jules and me again.

We remain silent. Because, of course, there are no pods. In fact, it is appearing increasingly likely that we are actually here to thieve *theirs*. Thank you for that, Frogs. Thank you for naught.

The blond-haired boy and the skinny kid shepherd us upstairs, their guns at our backs. As we walk, I whisper to Jules, "You put yourself between me and harm's way."

"Learned from the best," she says with a complicated expression. I feel an irrational pang of jealousy—she clearly means Romeo.

"Perhaps—"

"No talking," the blond cuts in.

For some reason, Jules gives a humorless little snort and mutters, "What, not even two words?"

At the end of the hallway, there is a large double door with a bike lock threaded through the handles.

"The backpack. Confiscate it," says the blond as he enters the combination.

But Jules is wearing the backpack and I am holding her arm like a vise. The skinny kid cannot remove it because I refuse to relinquish my grip.

"Let go of her arm," he says, struggling.

"No," I say, and mean it. Jules has lost a lot of blood. Gun or no gun, I am *extremely* disinclined to budge. The kid hesitates, clearly not sure whether to pursue the issue. In the end, he unzips the backpack and peers inside. He grabs the bolt cutters as though they constitute a prize.

"Anything else?" the blond asks.

"Just a book," the skinny kid says.

"Leave it," says the blond with a shrug. "No harm in carrying a *book* around."

Jules snorts again, like the comment is somehow funny, then catches herself.

Must be the blood loss.

With that, we are shoved inside, the door locked behind us. Glancing around, I see this is the master bedroom—huge yet sparse. A fireplace, a walk-in wardrobe, an ensuite . . . and right in the middle, a bed. The bed is not empty. Two bodies lie atop the covers, naught but bones. They've been here too long for there to be much of a lingering smell, though the sight is far from pretty.

When pods became rife and the world went to shite, not everyone jumped. Some found *other* means of escaping the "now."

I cast my eyes around the room, assessing our options. The floor-to-ceiling glass panel is double-glazed—there shall be no breaking that. I try the door behind us with my free hand—definitely locked.

"I can make us a fire," I offer, "since I for one am freezing." Jules has lost a lot of blood; a fire will help.

Her gaze falls to the huge panel of glass. Outside, the sun sinks ever lower in the sky.

"The others shall come for us," I say, with a confidence that I do not entirely feel. "We shall be out of here before nightfall."

"*Rescue, fair lord, or else the day is lost,*" says Jules, clearly quoting something.

"Let us assume the *first* option," I say, resisting the urge to check my watch again. We are running out of time . . . but time is out of my control. I cannot get Jules beyond these four walls—not yet, at any rate. I *can* get her warm, though, and hopefully distract her.

I let go of her arm for a moment to take stock of the fireplace. There is still wood in the hearth, matches on the mantel. It does not take me long to strike a fire. Practical matters—such has always been my forte.

"What do you think they were like?" says Jules. I turn and see that she is holding up a framed photograph. It is of a handsome young couple together with a toddler and newborn baby, the epitome of wholesome. My eyes inadvertently flick to the bones on the bed—the couple as they are now.

"Total degenerates. Into very strange things," I deadpan.

"Yes, you're right. The way they're staring adoringly into each other's eyes? Perverts, for sure."

"No one puts their *real* selves on display for everyone to see," I say, nurturing the flame.

"No, I guess not." Jules puts down the photo.

We have to wake Romeo before first nightfall. Except there is no way out, the sun will soon set, and—on top of all that—Jules is hurt.

This mission is a disaster.

....

23

Jules
2056

I'm staring at the skeletons on the bed, at their untimely embrace. Two lovers, together in death, just like I once thought I wanted. Huh. Doesn't look quite as romantic as I'd imagined. In my head it was all, *to die, to sleep—to sleep, perchance to . . .* I dunno, *something*.

"It is not too bad," says Ellis, carefully taking the backpack off me and letting it drop to the floor. He means my arm. "Come, we shall get you fixed up good as new."

Funny, one of the early responders said something like that two years ago: that she'd "put me back together, good as new." I don't know if she was referring to the knife wound or all my other flavors of broken. Maybe neither. I was bleeding a lot—it was probably just one of those empty things people say.

"Those two girls downstairs. How did you know all those

things about them? And why did you believe their name to be Capulet?" says Ellis, leading me into the ensuite, his hands clamped over my arm again.

"They're my mum and my aunt," I explain. "The boy who brought us here? The blond one? He's my dad. They're my *family*."

"Shite," says Ellis.

Yeah, exactly.

"What the hell is going on?" I say instead.

And I guess old habits die hard, because I'm half expecting the Romeo Effect. For the handsome boy to deliver some pretty line so that sweet Juliet doesn't worry. A gentle, lying smile, perhaps? But Ellis doesn't smile. He looks me right in the eyes and says, "Damned if *I* know."

Inside the ensuite it's your typical bathroom scene, just with everything covered in dust. Water would be good, but the taps won't work—plumbing didn't last after pods were invented. People who worked with toilets and crap—so to speak—well, they tended to *not* stick around.

Ellis riffles through drawers, hunting in vain for a bandage.

I hesitate a moment, then say, "Use the hoodie."

There's a pair of rusty scissors in the third drawer down. Ellis cuts the sweatshirt off me, then rips it into strips.

"Are you really a doctor?" I ask, trying to distract myself from how exposed I feel with just a T-shirt on. I've been wondering for a while now.

"Afraid not. Dealt with my fair share of flesh wounds, though," he says. "Recruiting Deadenders tends to be . . . messy."

As Ellis bandages my arm, I watch him in the mirror. I should probably look away—avert my eyes all demure, since he's still half naked. But I don't. I stare at his muscles, his form.

And *because* I'm staring, I see them—scars, rucking his back. Scars as bad as mine.

"What happened?" I ask.

"*Hate* happened."

I hesitate. Then I move my T-shirt down just a fraction, revealing the tip of the thick purple scar. "*Love* happened."

"That looks naught like love to me," says Ellis, dead serious.

I don't meet his eyes, yet I hear it. Worry. Anger, almost.

"Got a bit carried away," I say, trying to make light.

He doesn't say it, or make me say it. But the word is there, unspoken.

I turn my head away and Ellis takes my chin, forcing me to look at him. It's a courtesy I denied everyone—including Mum—after what happened. I hid myself behind defiance and anger and blame. And Dad? Well, he was too lost in "Hell" to focus on me anyway. But now there's nowhere else to look, so I see it staring back at me. The magnitude. The *holy shit* of attempted suicide.

All these years, I've worn my scar like a puckered badge of honor, pinned straight to the flesh. Because I've had to. Because I refused to apologize. *Because of my secret.* I've wished the scar gone many times, but always because of how it looks. Now I'm wishing it gone because of how it got there. I'm wishing *that* wasn't a thing that would mark me forever.

"Why would you do that to yourself?" says Ellis, barely a whisper.

I shrug, regretting I ever said anything.

"She couldn't bear the whips and scorns of time, so she . . ."

I don't finish the sentence.

Ellis gently touches the top of my scar, then moves his fingers south a little. It pushes the fabric of my T-shirt down too. Nothing indecent—just enough for him to see that the scar goes further. Straight to my heart.

I've imagined a boy setting eyes on this scar. Imagined it many times, usually for torture. But what I'm seeing now, in Ellis? There's no revulsion. None of the disgust that I thought was a given, like night follows day. He's looking at me with something different altogether. Something softer.

"Why?" he asks again.

"It was love," I say automatically.

Ellis steps away, running his hands through his hair.

"You wish to be reunited with a boy who would let you do that to yourself?" he says, getting worked up.

"Starting was such sweet sorrow I mean *parting*. I mean—"

"That is not what love is," says Ellis, surprisingly forceful. "Love is the opposite of that. It is about *protecting* this." He puts his hand firmly over my scar, over my heart.

I'm waiting for Ellis to chastise me or otherwise dig me in deeper. But he doesn't have any of the usual reactions that always push me away. He does the opposite—*he pulls me in*. He rests his chin on my head and his arms move carefully around me. Where his skin touches mine, it's infinite lightness. It's the ghost of a hug—being held without any pressure.

Mum tried for hugs after what happened, but I refused her. I kept my distance. There was this no-go zone around me, like outside the crypt. A Wall; a barrier. Except Ellis doesn't know the rules around my heart. He just waltzes right on in.

"It . . . it was a grand gesture of love," I stammer. Again, that's not quite right—it was never so simple.

Ellis doesn't say a word, though I hear him sigh, and his arms around me tighten. "It was . . ."

Instead of finishing the sentence, I squeeze my eyes closed and go for the usual comfort—I imagine a scene from my play. Romeo and me, both dead in the crypt, full period costume. There's zero blood; it's totally poetic. I've just delivered my final line—*O, happy dagger! This is thy sheath; there rust, and let me die*—like it's some epic love story.

Then I let myself remember what really happened that night in the crypt. The mess and the pain and the blood and the absolute panic. That there was nothing serene or beautiful about it. It was the total *opposite* of poetic. Because sure, a lot of my story was fiction . . . but the knife in my hand was real.

"Jules. Jules, talk to me. Are you all right?"

I open my eyes. Ellis is leaning away, holding me by the shoulders. He's worried.

"Give me a minute."

He says nothing. He doesn't leave, either.

"I'm fine. Just give me a minute."

He keeps staring at me, all noble concern. But I can't cope with kindness right now. *Mean*, I could handle—*kind* will definitely break me.

"Please!" I snap, raising my voice, even though I shouldn't.

Ellis looks struck—he takes a step back so we're no longer touching.

"Of course," he says with this odd formality, quickly pulling his T-shirt back on. It's black. The blood doesn't show, but the stains are still there, whether or not you can see them.

He shuts the door behind himself. After a moment I turn

to my tired reflection, seeing myself head-on for the first time in years. Juliet Capulet. *Jules.*

My eyes are hot, verging on tears. I've cried plenty since what happened. I've shed rivers of tears over my husband, though they were mostly the civilized kind, like Rosaline musters. Romeo got my pretty tears. But the ugly ones, the ones that make me keen and shake and let out strange noises? They belong in the dark, to my secret, and they can't come out now.

Something has to come out now, though—I can't keep it *all* down. So in the reflection with me, I imagine Romeo. Only this time I see him as he really was. A world away from the fourteenth-century honor and frills of my story.

"*Did my heart love till now? Forswear it, sight, for I ne'er saw true beauty . . .* ," he whispers in my ear as he kisses my neck, as his hands run the length of my body. But, of course, that's not *quite* the line he delivered that night in my bedroom. His language was mostly grunts and moans. The precious few words that he used were . . . less poetic.

"Juliet Capulet tried to kill herself over a boy that she barely even knew," I say to my reflection. That's what I put in my story. I reduced all my sharp, messy threads into a neat little arc, then dressed it up as romantic. But it wasn't really about one single thing. There's no simple cause and effect, except in fiction. The truth is, *a lot* of things led me to that moment. And yes, what happened with Romeo played a part.

But it was never the *whole* story.

Looking away from my reflection, I stare at the scissors. I haven't held a pair of scissors in years. They all "mysteriously" vanished right after what happened. For my safety, probably.

But I'm not feeling fragile right now. I'm feeling bold for the first time in . . . well, quite literally ages.

I zero in on some locks and start cutting. I don't actually care about my hair—haven't for years. I didn't do that dramatic thing of hacking it all off when Romeo didn't wake up. It just became a bit of a nonevent. I trim it when it gets too long, I wash it when it gets too greasy—that's about the extent of my efforts.

When I'm finished, I glance at myself in the mirror. The haircut isn't great; I haven't missed my calling or anything. Yet this suits me. My face has been hidden behind a grubby fringe for so long, it's almost a shock to see myself clearly. I've changed. I've grown up. The puppy fat around my face is gone so that all you notice is dark eyes and cheekbones. I don't look pretty, exactly—not like the girl in my story with the doe-eyed smiles. But this is better.

This is me.

24

Ellis

2056

When Jules opens the bathroom door, I can do naught but stare.

"Continuity might be an issue," I manage eventually, clearing my throat.

And then I find myself doing the opposite of staring—I am looking anywhere but at her.

"What?" she says. "Is it really that bad?"

"In my day, women were not permitted short hair." Then I mumble, "Bloody shame if you ask me."

Jules smiles. The haircut—she can tell that I like it.

"Care to join me?" I say, pretending we have a choice in the matter. I double-checked while she was in the bathroom—there is no way out of this room.

"Sounds grand," says Jules. Though as she leaves the bathroom, she holds onto the doorframe for a moment. The gesture is subtle, but I notice. She is dizzy.

I glance at her injured arm—fresh blood is seeping through the makeshift bandage.

"Indeed, most grand," I say, trying to hide my concern.

Jules comes out into the bedroom proper and wanders closer to the bookshelf.

"Do you read?" she says, scanning the titles.

I cannot help but smile at that. "I do," I say, remembering Frogs and his interminable lessons. The endless tutorials, giving me a superb grasp of language that I initially used for naught but swearing more richly. Frogs, the machine that lied.

"I read every day," I add.

"What kind of books?"

"Anything and everything." Then, quieter: "But I always circle back to one book in particular. A . . . work of fiction." Somewhat ironic, since I am uniquely positioned to know that is not *entirely* true.

"You must really love that one book," says Jules.

"I despise it," I say, trying to keep my voice light. It is no use—my airy tone does not quite sit, and the comment hangs there.

"Fixating on a book that you despise is a tad messed up, Ellis," continues Jules. "Any specific reason?"

There are plenty of lies I could give. Instead, I say, "It was written by a girl I once knew. I left her behind."

Jules knows that I am not a Traveler. She knows that by "left her behind" I do not mean that I jumped.

"You loved her," says Jules.

And the truth of it cuts—I *did* love her. Though I was scared that I could never quite trust it. So I could never quite *voice* it.

"Yes," I finally say, years too late. "We were young, but I loved her very much."

"Young love," says Jules, with an edge to her voice. "Was it a whirlwind of rash, sleep-deprived choices, and fumbling sex?"

I smile at just how wrong she is.

"We never even kissed," I say softly.

"You loved her and you never even *kissed* her?"

"I have never kissed anyone."

"Wait, *never*? Not even, like, *on the hand* or something?"

I shake my head. "Are you going to mock me for being old-fashioned?"

"No."

Jules is staring at me now, like she is trying to work me out. Yet I cannot bring myself to tell her the truth—that I was only thirteen. That my first life ended in 1831. How, after that awful scene in the kitchen with her father, Emily and I ran away. How, when we got to the coast, there was that moment. The moment when she leaned in to kiss me, but I stepped back. And I would have changed my mind. I would have been braver and kissed her like I wanted to. Only, it was raining on the cliff that afternoon, and when I stepped back . . .

"I left," I say instead. "Years later, she wrote a book. She only ever wrote one. In it, she . . . sort of imagined how our lives would have turned out if I had stayed."

"She wrote the better version," says Jules, as if she understands. "She wrote the version of her life that she wanted."

"Not quite." I sound more than slightly bitter. "Not even

close, actually. There is passion and love, yet also such rawness and cruelty."

"And it's about you?" she says, doubtful.

"I am in every word of it. I am in the people and the places and even in the weather. It is full of little jokes and references that only I would understand," I add, without humor. "She even used my Christian name for her character, and my surname as the pseudonym that she published the book under—it is *all* in reference to me. Everything comes back to me. She was—"

I break off, unsure how to finish. I have never spoken of Emily to anyone. Frogs knew. In the first year when I pined for her so keenly, Frogs matter-of-factly announced that she had written a book. Afterward, he found me a copy and taught me to read it. Though we never *discussed* her.

"I think it was more than just a story," says Jules when I fail to continue. "I think it was something she wrote to deal with the loss."

"Perhaps." I am unconvinced.

"No, I *really* think it was just her way of coping."

"Duly noted," I say, though Jules has no way of truly knowing. Nobody does, which is the torture.

Jules keeps staring at me, like she is weighing something. Then she mutters, "Screw it," picking her backpack up off the floor and opening it.

"*The Love Story of Juliet & Romeo.*" She holds up her notebook with a self-mocking flourish. "A tragic tale of two young lovers, which bears almost no resemblance to the actual truth. I didn't go with a raw and painful version, like your girl. Instead, I went in the opposite direction. I made it all about noble swordfights and declarations of undying love. It sounds kind of ridiculous, but in a way, it helped. Before I started writing, I used to fixate on the what-ifs. What if we'd taken it slow? What if he'd gotten my note?"

Jules waits for me to respond. I remain silent.

"What I'm saying is . . . I don't actually believe that what I wrote is true." Jules sounds surprised as she speaks, as though she has just worked that part out for herself. "I don't think that the version of Romeo in these pages is the *real* boy or that it's what his character is *actually* like, deep down. The story is simply . . . an alternative version of events to help me move past the real ones. Maybe it was the same for her. Maybe your girl wrote that story, not because it was true, but because it *wasn't*."

I have no reply to that.

"May I read it?" I nod at the notebook.

"No, it's silly," says Jules, without missing a beat. "I wrote it in the style of Shakespeare, so the language is tricky. Besides—it's not finished. I'm having trouble with the ending."

"Please?" I say, holding out my hand. "I once inspired a rather lengthy novel—surely that counts as credentials."

"I don't think so, mister."

"View it as cathartic, then," I persist.

"That's your argument?" she says, mocking my attempt at being earnest. "That it'll be cathartic? Wow, you really know how to convince a girl, Ellis."

"All right. Curiosity," I try. "I want to see how this Romeo character measures up as a romantic ideal."

"Now that's more like it," she says with a chuckle. After one final hesitation, she hands it over.

I turn to the first page, which is covered in messy scrawl. "*Two households, both alike in dignity* . . ." I read aloud.

"Nothing but dignity to see here, my friend. Nothing but dignity," says Jules, gesturing vaguely at the bloody arm and the general mess of us.

I flip a few pages and read, "*O Romeo, Romeo, wherefore art thou Romeo?*" Then, looking up at Jules, "What, you misplaced him?"

"*Why*, not *where*. 'Wherefore art thou Romeo?' It means *why* are you Romeo?"

"Yes, *obviously*."

I keep reading aloud, stumbling over words here and there, hamming up the parts that are clearly begging for it. Jules interrupts from time to time to mock herself, or to razz my silly voices, yet she does not pull the book away or otherwise try to stop me.

As we read, Jules fills me in on the story—how it is a tale about the Montagues and the Capulets, set back in the 1300s. Two powerful families; some ancient feud that is never quite explained. Their children—Romeo Montague and Juliet Capulet—fall in love, but their love is forbidden. There is a misunderstanding, a sleeping potion, a lost note. Romeo takes his own life because he thinks that Juliet is dead. When Juliet wakes and sees his lifeless body, she takes her own life too.

I wonder how close that is to what actually happened.

And then I think of her words from before: "*What if he'd gotten my note?*" And I cannot help but speculate . . . what are the chances that the note in question was *not* the one that Frogs sent me to retrieve from her family crypt all those years ago? The one with the two entwined hearts on the front, which smelled of perfume? The odds are not good, I would wager.

"Life can be complicated," I say quietly. "I am sorry you were in a place where the light could not find you."

Jules says nothing, so I wait.

In her own time, she turns back to me.

"Darkened with the smog of pain, polluting. O wretched grief, a poison to thy soil."

"Did you compose that just now, in your head?"

Jules shrugs, indicating yes. I am more than slightly awed.

"The stuff in there is a lot more polished," she adds quickly, nodding at her story.

"Then I ought to continue."

Except as I keep reading, it all starts becoming too much—too raw. Jules has captured the pain of young love and loss in a way that is far too close for comfort. It is as though she is speaking my truths with a clarity that I could never approach. I find it overwhelming.

I flick straight past Act V like a coward—all the way to the crossed-out section. And that is where I *truly* see Jules in the writing. In the way she keeps trying, with revision after revision, to conceive of her own happy ending. The way that, no matter how the action plays, it simply will not come together for her.

Yet hiding from heartbreak cannot relieve the pain of it. I learned that lesson many years ago. And so I eventually turn back to Act V—to the part where the lovers die, like Emily thinks I did. To the final act that is written.

"*Oh, here will I set up my everlasting rest, and shake the yoke of inauspicious stars from this world-wearied flesh,*" I read aloud quietly. "*Eyes, look your last. Arms, take your last embrace. And lips, O you the doors of breath, seal with a righteous kiss a dateless bargain to engrossing death."*

I had not meant to deliver the lines with such feeling. I had meant to jest and make light, as before. Yet I could not. Her words, the heart she puts on the page, the heart she puts in the world, even when she is defensive—*especially* when she is defensive. The fearlessness with which she speaks her truths about love and pain. I cannot keep hiding how her words *reach* me. The weight of them; their beauty. I cannot pretend I do not feel it.

I stare at the page to avoid looking up at Jules. I knew she was unique. Frogs told me she was important in relation to the timeline. Damn that. Forget how she is important in relation to others, or the world, or as a mother.

She is important *unto herself.*

....

25

Jules

2056

My heart's pounding. The way Ellis delivered my words is exactly how I imagined them being said. Only difference is, I'd imagined them being said by Romeo. In my mind, the talk of a righteous kiss was in my husband's melodic voice. After hearing Ellis, I'm picturing something . . . well, *deeper*.

Ellis finally glances up, and the way that he stares is like he's looking right into my dark, complicated little recesses. But it doesn't feel like he's trying to fix them or change them or make them light—just that he sees them. Sees *me*. And the expression in his eyes isn't lust, like I thought was the one-trick pony of teenage boys. It's something altogether different.

"You have an extraordinary mind," he says.

"*Weird*, you mean," I say, playing it right down.

Ellis holds my gaze for a long, drawn-out moment. Finally,

he says, "Whoever told you that the most powerful version of yourself was *less* attractive?"

I don't answer, but my mind whispers: *everyone*. Keep yourself small—that was always unspoken. Being smarter than the boy isn't attractive. *Demure* is attractive. Pretty, sweet, feminine, doting, vapid, naïve. *Juliet* is attractive.

This feels like tricky ground, so my defenses kick in.

"Got a thing for strong women, do you?" I say, raising an eyebrow.

But Ellis refuses to let me make a joke of it. Instead, he looks right at me and says, "Should I have a thing for weak women?"

And hearing that sentiment from a boy, knowing he means it, is way more of a turn-on than pretty words of love. Heathcliff, the moors, the past—the novel that Ellis inspired must have been *Wuthering Heights*. I read it down at the Supermarket one time.

The girl who loved him was Emily Brontë.

And yes, I can definitely see it. Staring at Ellis now, I can understand how a bookish girl might have fallen hard for him. Might have written words of passion and . . . and I'm suddenly very conscious of how close we're sitting. Of how I can hear his breath, practically *feel* the heat of him. How leaning in is all it would take. There isn't a universe between us anymore, there's merely space. *And it's tiny*.

Ellis pulls away.

"The others shall come. They shall get here in time. It will all work out," he says, a little flustered. He adds, "You will be with Romeo."

In *Wuthering Heights*, the lovers don't end up together—

they were star-crossed, just like the kids in my story. Heart after heart, beat after beat, never a happy ending.

"If you say so, Heathcliff Ellis," I say quietly.

He looks shocked by that, properly struck.

"How do you know my name? I have not told *anyone* my Christian name."

"Well, in the Chinese restaurant, you told *me*," I say. Though I guess everything will be different now, so that moment will never happen. Ellis won't die.

And he won't kiss my hand either, like the start of some old-fashioned courtship.

I'm feeling a wee smidgen of regret about that last part, which is *not* model behavior. Hell, I met Ellis *this morning*. I've known him less than twenty-four hours, which is the kind of intense rush that happened last time. I mean, is this an emerging pattern of behavior for me? A developing theme?

Fortunately, I'm spared the trouble of diving too deep on that because there's a commotion in the hallway. Footsteps coming toward us. We get to our feet, but Ellis doesn't stand in front of me. Instead we stand side by side, shoulder to shoulder. And it occurs to me . . . is this it? Do our minutes hasten to their end, like in that sonnet?

I turn to Ellis.

He turns to me. He opens his mouth to say something—

The door opens: it's Henry, Iggy, and Beth.

"I never doubted it," says Ellis, rushing toward his friends. He thinks we're saved—that they're here to rescue us.

He's wrong.

Henry, Iggy, and Beth enter the room, sure enough.

But it's at gunpoint.

"*Love* the new hairdo, darling," says Beth when she sees me, as though the threat of imminent death rates zero mention.

"Are you okay?" says Henry, clocking my bandaged arm.

"Quiet!" says the skinny kid, who I think is a young Mr. Marcellus. Rick Marcellus? *Yorick?* Not sure. I didn't know him well. Or like him any.

"Check her purse," says Dad.

Marcellus grabs Beth's purse and starts poking through it. Beth doesn't try to stop him. She just smiles sweetly and says, "Two romance novels, hairspray, and some *feminine hygiene products,* darling."

You can almost see Marcellus's brain slowly ticking over, deducing that the discreet little box that he's currently holding must contain the "feminine hygiene products." He quickly drops the box back into the purse and hands it to Beth like it's contagious. Yep, that which I see before me is *definitely* Marcellus.

After a bit more fussing, Marcellus and Dad leave, locking the door behind them. Once they're gone, Henry turns to Beth and says, "Did you just pretend that my father's ashes were feminine hygiene products?"

"Yes," says Beth, unapologetic.

Henry slowly shakes his head. "Brilliant."

I decide that I rather *like* these Deadenders.

"Got the drugs," says Beth, reaching under her skirt and somehow producing a small silver case. I guess I must look slightly agog, because she smirks at me and says, "It was between my knees, you dirty-minded scamp."

Only she doesn't say it meanly, or with any offense taken.

She doesn't try to cut me down or embarrass me in front of the boys, like most of the other girls that I know would. She says it with a cheeky grin, like we're coconspirators.

Yes, I definitely like them.

Then I clock Iggy's expression—unmistakably grim.

"We might have the drugs," he says, "but I don't think *time* is on our side."

We all follow his gaze to the huge glass panel. The sun is low and spewing out all those impossible colors. It's starting to set. Ergo . . .

We failed.

"I am so sorry," says Ellis quietly. For a moment I wonder why he's looking at me in particular when he says it. And then—a beat too late—I realize.

We cannot wake Romeo.

A flush comes to my cheeks that my husband wasn't my first thought.

Shit. If this were my story, that would be a *terrible* first reaction. We're talking near-zero levels of world-ending-because-I-love-the-boy-so-much poetry.

I need a moment alone to process. Except the closest thing I've got is the other side of the massive bedroom. So that's where I go. I stare out the floor-to-ceiling glass panel. In the distance, a building collapses. Somewhere else, there's smoke from a fire. It's a city in chaos. No, not just a city. There's a *whole world* out there, going to ruin. But the world at large? That's not my focus. That's *never* been my focus. Instead, I stare at Number 10—the house where I grew up. The place where it basically all happened, on the Romeo score. It represents my history, my universe, my everything.

I try to channel all the heartbreak and disappointment that should be overwhelming me right about now. I try to feel the can't-live-without-him panic that hit when I thought that Romeo was lost to me the *first* time. Except I just . . . can't. And so I do what I always do when the doubts set in: I rely on the made-up version.

I stare at the all-too-familiar balcony across the road and imagine a scene from my story. Romeo all earnest, in old-fashioned clothes, with his "*Soft, what light through yonder window breaks*" lines. And in my mind Juliet's there too, lapping it right up. But the glass panel is reflecting the image of the *real* me over the imagined one. The me of now.

Who I've become. The messy girl who's *actually* there.

With a slight shift of focus, I can see the Deadenders too, here in the reflection with me. And I find myself wondering . . . is this my new life? Given that we failed, maybe this is where I stay. Maybe this is the "fresh start" that Mum was always going on about. A place that's a world away from my past. A time when all my mistakes haven't even happened yet. A life where the boy might be Ellis instead of Romeo. A *new* love story.

And I have to confess . . . I'm not entirely heartbroken.

26

Ellis
2056

"Um, small question," whispers Henry, glancing at Jules, who is across the room, watching London falling. "Her son created the Deadenders. If we failed—if Romeo is never woken and their son is never born—then we never became Deadenders. We technically died *rather a lot* in the past. So what happens to *us* after nightfall?"

Nobody knows, so nobody answers.

"Well, if we're facing our own imminent demise," says Iggy, "I'm leaving my mark." With that, he goes to Beth's purse and retrieves his precious artifact. Not hairspray, like she pretended: spray paint. We all listen to the *click-click-click* as he shakes it. The can is Iggy's prized possession, once touched by his idol Sid Vicious, back in the late 1970s. Iggy has never used it—not a drop. The fact that he is expending it now has a certain finality.

Iggy scrawls, "*Ignatius Jones, born 1966*" straight onto the wall, then solemnly hands the spray can to Beth.

She writes, "*Elizabeth Fujiyama, born 1936.*"

"What happens to these names if we cease to exist come nightfall?" says Henry as Beth hands him the can.

"Does it matter?" asks Iggy.

Henry does not reply. He simply writes, "*Henry Hawkins, born 1798.*"

They do not know my Christian name. I hesitate, then I add, "*Heathcliff Ellis, born 1818.*"

"Heathcliff?" says Iggy, scrutinizing me. "Like in *Wuthering Heights*?"

"You were named after the character in that book you keep reading?" says Iggy, confused.

"1818, darling," says Beth, sharp as ever. "Other way around, apparently."

They all gawk at me for a moment as that sinks in. Then, one by one, they follow my gaze to the wall. Those names, together, were the Deadenders. Four miscreant teens who briefly tried to save the world. Four—

No, not four. *Five*. With another shake of the spray can, I add one final name.

Frogs.

"I think we did a rather decent job of leaving our mark," says Beth.

"I especially appreciate the composition," says Iggy, pretending the messy scrawl is an artwork. By "composition" he clearly means us. *All of us, together.*

"They look like tears," says Henry, watching the drops of

paint that are falling from our names like tears down a cheek. I glance across—sure enough, Henry is crying.

I am done with the conceit, so I simply pull all three of them into a rough embrace. We stay like that for a long moment, saying our silent good-byes. Then my eyes drift to Jules. Beth notices.

"Chaps, a word with you in my office?" she says, linking arms with Henry and Iggy, shepherding them into the ensuite to give Jules and me privacy.

I walk across to Jules and stand by her side. She does not turn to me—she just keeps looking straight ahead, through the glass. Out of nowhere she says, "Do you know much Shakespeare?"

"A little," I admit. Emily devoured his plays—sometimes she would read me passages or explain the plots as we wiled away the hours.

"Well, he wrote this one play called *Macbeth*," says Jules. "In it, there are these witches who predict the future. But really, they're based on the Fates from Greek mythology—three sisters who control destiny. One spins the thread of life, another measures out how much each person gets, and the third one cuts it when it's time to die. Only, with all this time-travel stuff, I sometimes wonder if all the threads are in a massive tangle."

"Entwined destinies?" I say, raising an eyebrow. It was a theme in Jules's story. Emily's too, in point of fact.

"More like *messy* destinies," she says with a snort. "Or maybe just messy people and messy lives."

I am beginning to suspect that there is no other kind.

"You pinch your arm when you are nervous," I say instead. "Are you not nervous now?"

Jules seems surprised when she looks at her arm.

"I guess not," she says. "Everything depended on waking Romeo. That's pretty much been my whole mantra for two years. But maybe waking Romeo *isn't* everything."

She is entirely wrong. Only, I am suddenly not thinking about Romeo, because Jules is staring right at me. Right *into* me.

"Who even *are* you?" she whispers.

Who am I? The brute Emily painted me as? A ghost in time? A dead end?

I might not know who I am, but contemplating the messy, complicated girl in front of me, I suddenly know what I want. Come nightfall, chances are I will have drowned, hundreds of years in the past. I have naught to lose, and that makes me daring. I take Jules's numb hand in mine and tenderly rub my thumb against the warm skin. A caress, even though she cannot feel it.

Jules blinks at her hand in my own, like the act of it—the sight of it—is shocking. "How can you do that?" she whispers. "How can you make my heart beat fast just by touching the dead part of me?"

"No part of you is dead. Different does not mean *less*."

My words must penetrate, for she is suddenly all vulnerability. There is fear in her eyes of a very familiar kind. Fear of letting the walls down; fear of trusting.

Her movements are slow and careful as she tentatively places a hand atop mine. Now she is holding my hand in a way where she can physically feel it, skin against skin. Though it is more than just that. She is also holding *her own* hand—the numb one.

She locks her eyes on mine. Gently, she reaches up and runs a finger along the scar that marks my forehead. The wound that had been fresh when I fell off the cliff.

"Also hate?" she asks.

I nod, my heart pounding.

Next, she traces the line of a thick white scar near my wrist. "This too?" Her finger rests tenderly on the old wound. I nod again.

Suddenly, her brow furrows. She grabs my hand and stares at it.

"The paint," she says eventually. "*Green paint.* It was there in the Chinese restaurant. What does it mean?"

I look down: some of the fingers on my right hand have Iggy's paint on it. The magnitude sinks in.

"It means we did not fail."

"What?" says Jules.

"We can wake Romeo. We *will* wake Romeo . . ."

I remove my hand from hers—we cannot indulge in this moment. Not anymore.

"You will be with Romeo."

I let myself feel the kick to the guts of that, but only briefly.

"Everyone, back in here," I shout to the others. As soon as the bathroom door opens, I say, "Quick, pass me the drugs."

"Why?"

"Because we did not fail!"

I take the case with the drugs from Iggy, flick a switch, and a 3-D hologram of various molecular structures appears. The device is terrifically complicated, but Frogs made damned sure that I knew how to use it.

"Category drugs have a tiny effective life," says Beth, clearly worried. "If you activate them now, they'll be useless in an hour."

"It matters not, all shall be dandy," I assure her.

When I finish adjusting the molecular composition, I press a button and the syringe fills with goo.

"Now it does not have to be me," I say. "*Any* of us can wake Romeo."

"Do I point out the obvious impediment?" says Henry.

"Which one?" says Iggy. "By my count, there are several."

"So what now?" says Jules.

"Now something happens," I say.

They all look at me as though I am talking gibberish.

"Something happens because it *did* happen," I attempt to explain. "The green paint—it was on my hand when Jules saw me in the future, at the Chinese restaurant."

Still blank stares.

"*The die is cast?*" I say, trying another angle. That phrase is one that Frogs used often. It means that the moves have already happened.

"Huh?" says Jules, still not following, though understanding dawns on Henry, Iggy, and Beth. Because it all fits. Frogs was training us for *years* to understand this moment.

"The note that Frogs got me to write in the dust on the piano," says Beth. "That was it. *The die is cast.* That's what I wrote. I never made the connection."

"It's already happened," says Iggy as it registers. "The future is already past."

"The mission that Frogs sent me on," continues Beth, talking fast. "The one where I saw the pods? They're in the music room downstairs. Five pods. *One for each of us.* We just have to get to them."

"Any bright ideas?" asks Henry.

Only silence.

Beth glances out the window at the setting sun. "It has to be now."

Still naught.

Then Iggy walks to the door and starts banging.

"You have a plan?" says Henry.

"Nope," says Iggy. "But we're running out of daylight. Whatever's going to happen, this kind of has to be the moment, right?"

The door opens and the two guards from before appear, both with guns.

"What?" says the skinny one. Iggy does not answer—he just looks to the rest of us as if to say, *your turn.*

More silence.

And then Jules says to the blond guard, her father, "We're ready to take you to our pods." She grabs her backpack for emphasis.

Time to improvise, apparently.

As we are being led from the room at gunpoint, Beth kicks the can of spray paint. It appears to be an act of clumsiness, but Beth does not *do* clumsy.

It is no accident that the can lands right by the edge of the fire.

....

27

Jules

2056

Dad and Marcellus lead us down the stairs at gunpoint. When we reach the secret library, I count twelve kids. Some are harder to recognize because I knew them when they were decades older—the ravages of time, et cetera. But yep, I pretty much know all the faces.

"They've agreed to take us to their pods," announces Dad.

"Excellent," says Montague. "There'll be enough for us all soon. We can finally get out of this hellhole. On to a brighter future."

The drugs are clearly still in his system; he looks a smidge off the rails.

"So?" he says. "Pray tell, *where* are they?"

I hadn't exactly thought this far ahead.

"The map," says Henry at last. He reaches for Beth's purse

and is quickly met with a dozen guns, all drawn and pointed right at him. They think he's going for a weapon.

"The map," he says again, hands in the air. "It's in her purse."

Montague motions for someone to take the purse from Beth. Once it's in his possession, he pulls out the *A–Z of London*. Then he glares at Dad and Marcellus.

"They have a *map*? You didn't appropriate a *map*? You didn't think that might have, oh, I don't know, *been worth taking*?!"

"She said it was a romance novel," says Marcellus weakly.

Montague shakes his head at Marcellus, then tosses the *A–Z* to Henry and says, "Where?"

Henry flicks through the pages, blustering. He doesn't have a plan; none of us do. While he's stalling, Aunt Miranda sidles up next to me.

"The baby," she whispers, one hand resting on her belly. "I never told *anyone* that I wanted to call him Tybalt. How did you know?"

I'm about to tell her the truth, then I think better of it. So instead I whisper, "You have to help us."

Aunt Miranda is the kindest person I ever met, by a landslide. Yet this time, she hesitates. She looks at Montague, clearly a bit scared, and shakes her head.

"Show him where your pods are, and he'll probably let you go."

"I can't," I say.

"You *have* to," she whispers. "He can be all right, but not when he's like this. When he's been using. Just give him the pods. *Please*."

"Aunt Miranda, there *are* no pods."

I didn't mean to say the "aunt" part—pure force of habit. I

can't take it back now, though. She stares at me—my dark eyes, so exactly like her own. The silence stretches on and on while Henry bluffs about a secret location, referencing made-up street names.

And then I see it in her face. For some reason—my whole life—when it came to the crunch, Aunt Miranda always believed me. And she does it again right now.

"Go. Hurry. Get out of here," she says at last, passing me her gun. I stare at it, heavy in my hand. I've never touched a gun before. I don't know how to shoot one. Besides, I'm naturally left-handed. I'm still getting used to holding a pencil with my right, let alone a weapon.

Beth subtly takes the gun from my hand and holds it behind her back, hidden in the folds of her full skirt.

"Come on, come on," she mutters, clearly waiting for something.

Then it happens. Just as Henry's running out of invented street names, there's a loud explosion. Almost everyone ducks, me included.

"What the hell was that?" shouts Montague.

"Aerosols and open flames don't mix," says Beth, calm as anything. Then she adds, "Weapons on the ground please, darlings."

Beth has the gun inches from Montague's head. Her frock and hairstyle are kind of at odds with the seriousness of the moment, though only a fool would underestimate her expression.

"Get behind me," Beth says to us—the Deadenders, plus me. We all huddle behind her.

"Whose gun is that?" says Montague's younger brother

in the sweet voice of an angel. But again, something's just *off* about him. "Who gave them a gun?"

Aunt Miranda trembles, a little bit teary, giving herself away.

"You?" yells Montague, thunderous.

Unnoticed, Mum tucks her own gun into the back of Aunt Miranda's waistband and steps forward.

"It was me," she says. "*I* gave the girl my gun."

Montague shoots Mum a look like he might *actually* kill her.

Mum is totally unflinching. How is this the same woman who cared about nothing except schmoozing and me "growing up" a fraction?

"That was very naughty of you, Omelia," says Montague through gritted teeth. He's high and clearly unstable. In this state, he *really might* shoot my mother.

And then it happens—Dad steps in front of Mum, putting himself between her and harm's way. He doesn't say a word. He simply stands there like a shield. Then he glances back at Mum ... and the look that he gives her? Love. Unmistakably. I peek at Trudy, his girlfriend. Yep, a clear face of betrayal. Woman scorned if ever I saw one.

"Uh-oh," says Montague's brother. There's something very wrong with the fact that he's smiling.

"Romeo, go upstairs. Check on what that noise was," instructs Montague.

"I don't want to. I want to watch. I want to—"

"Check on the noise!" yells Montague. The kid reluctantly troops upstairs, and Montague turns his attention back to Dad.

"Lucian," says Montague with frightening calm. "What are you *doing*?"

"I'm protecting Omelia," says Dad, channeling valor like nobody's business.

"Like *hell* you are," says Mum, moving in front so that she's protecting *him* now.

Dad whispers an indignant, "Omelia—" He never gets to finish because there's a loud bang and a smash. Beth just shot out the stained-glass panel in the roof. What was once a beautiful Mary Magdalene is now in pieces, nothing left but a brief rain of glass and sharp edges.

"Weapons on the ground *now*, please," says Beth, her gun trained squarely on Montague again. Then she adds, "I'm a *superb* shot, darling," with a smile, cool as ice.

There's a beat, then Montague finally says, "Do it."

The other kids lower their weapons obediently.

"Kick them over," says Beth ever-so-sweetly. "And my purse, please."

There are too many guns to carry, so we load them—and the purse—into a pram that's among the pilfered artifacts. A pram for Tybalt, perhaps? Except that he's not meant to be born for over half a decade . . .

"If memory serves, the music room's down that hallway," whispers Beth once we're done. "Get the pods ready. I'll hold them off."

The four of us turn to head for the music room. But then Montague gives Mum and Dad a murderous glare and says, "We'll settle *this* score later."

Ellis hears it and stops short. He pauses a moment, clearly torn. Then he mutters a heartfelt, "Shite."

"What?" says Beth urgently, out the side of her mouth. "What is it?"

"Those two are her parents," whispers Ellis. "*Jules's* parents."

An awkward moment as we all stand huddled together behind Beth.

"We cannot just leave them," says Henry eventually. "If they die here, then Jules is never born ..."

"But there are only five pods," Iggy reminds us.

If we take my parents, then two of us won't have a way to leave. Two of us will be stuck here ...

"The die is cast," says Beth in a somber tone. And then, in a louder voice to my parents: "You and you. You're coming with us."

Dad starts, but Mum doesn't move. "No. I won't go anywhere without my sister."

"You *have* to," says Beth. "Now move."

"No," says Mum, not budging. So stubborn. Ironic that stubbornness is what Mum so often accused *me* of.

Beth glances back at the other Deadenders and says, "Well, chaps?"

If we take Aunt Miranda too, then *three* of us will be stuck here. Might even *die* here ...

Braver than me, they all nod their consent.

"You too, then," says Beth to Aunt Miranda. "Now *hurry*."

Mum, Dad, and Aunt Miranda silently join us, defecting.

Montague fumes at Aunt Miranda. Then his rage suddenly switches to calm. "Miranda, my sweet, *you're confused*," he says with wide-eyed sincerity. "This isn't what you want."

Miranda hesitates.

"These antics of yours, they're madness," he says in the tone of a lover's whisper. But him telling her what she wants? Him telling her that she's confused? The talk of madness? On instinct, I reach out and take Aunt Miranda's hand. I give it three little squeezes, kind of like I used to do with Romeo in the hospital. Aunt Miranda squeezes back, firm and decisive. Then she hurries toward the music room with the rest of us.

Beth stays put, her gun on Montague, buying us time.

The music room is quirky by anyone's standards. For starters, it's round. Then there's the fact that it's wallpapered floor-to-ceiling with a landscape scene. On the section directly in front of me, I recognize Kronborg Castle—Dad showed me pictures of it during one of our Supermarket excursions. But it's the *middle* of the room that has my attention. Because yes, in among the cello, the recorders, and the harp, there they are.

Five of them, all metal and sleek—the shape of a tear fallen sideways.

Five pods, ready and waiting.

"Nobody steals from me," yells Montague, back to rage again. It's unclear whether he means the pods or Aunt Miranda.

"What year did you say the baby was born?" Ellis asks me.

"2063." Tybalt was two years older than me.

"Climb in," he says to Mum, Dad, and Aunt Miranda. "Set your dials for 2063."

"I know where you're going, my little lambkin," shouts Montague from the hallway. "I'll find you eventually. You can *count* on it."

Shit, that's right. *I told him.* I told him which year Tybalt was born. I even told him that they lived in Number 10, across the road.

"Change the year," I say urgently.

"No," says Ellis.

"But—"

"No, you *cannot* change it," says Ellis, firm as anything. Then he adds, "Trust me."

Trust me? It shuts me up.

Mum, Dad, and Aunt Miranda climb into pods—one each. In my time, they were Settlers. In *this* time, they're Travelers. Some things are different . . . but maybe some things are the same?

I go to the pod that Aunt Miranda's in. Just before she closes the hatch, I whisper, "Tell Tybalt to never go to the old theater."

Aunt Miranda looks at me for a long moment, then nods.

One by one, the three pods—carrying my mother, my father, and my aunt—all disappear for the future.

28

Ellis

2056

"Can I get a hand?" calls Beth just as the third pod vanishes. Amid the chaos of the fire, she has slowly backed herself into the music room. Her gun is still trained on Montague, though, which is the only thing keeping the others at bay.

Beth shuts the door, and together, we push the upright piano against it. On the bright side, the only way in here is now thoroughly barricaded by a rather heavy piece called "Steinway." On the downside, there is no longer a gun on Montague, creating a deterrent. Clearly, at least one gang member had a second weapon, because they start firing almost immediately. We do not have much time.

There are two pods remaining and five of us. That means Jules, plus one other person.

"One of you take it," I say to the others, inviting no argument.

Henry shakes his head. "It has to be Jules and you. You know that it does. *The die is cast.*"

"No, I will not leave you here!" I say as a bullet slices through the door and hits the piano keys, making a *twang*. "Not like this."

"Bigger picture, remember?" says Iggy as a section of wood above his head is struck by another bullet.

Out in the hallway someone screams, "Fire! Upstairs is on fire!"

I say it again: "No."

They are my friends—I cannot just *abandon* them. Moreover, I *will* not.

"Jules saw you in the Chinese restaurant, Ellis. So it *has* to be you," says Beth quietly as she hands me the small case of Category drugs, together with my copy of *Wuthering Heights*.

Yet I still hesitate.

The kids outside are now trying to break through the door.

"But it doesn't have to play out *the same*," says Jules.

"It's already happened," says Iggy.

"Things can be different." Jules suddenly sounds desperate. "Things can *change*. The gray sneakers—"

Another hard thump against the door. Beth fires a warning shot into the ceiling.

Jules adds, "In the Chinese restaurant, the man in the gas mask turned up."

"He must have found a pod," suggests Henry.

"Makes sense," says Iggy, putting his back against the piano, lending his weight to the barricade. "He doesn't have the 'nightfall' deadline. He could have taken *months* getting his hands on a pod, and still jumped forward to that exact moment."

"No, you don't understand," says Jules. Then, to me: "He shot you. *You died.*"

There is a beat; nobody says a word.

A huge crash sounds outside the room. Someone yells, "The roof's collapsed!"

Montague screams, "Romeo? Where's Romeo?"

"But now we'll do things differently," continues Jules, talking fast. "The broken clock tower was chiming. Right after the last chime—*the thirteenth chime*—you got shot. You took a bullet to save my life. So this time you'll just duck or something, okay?"

I glance at the others—they look as stricken as I feel. Henry opens his mouth to speak, but I shake my head.

"Duck after the last chime. Understood," I say, forcing a smile as I tuck the Category drugs and *Wuthering Heights* into my pockets.

"Yes, yes, exactly," Jules babbles. "You'll duck, or—or whatever. *Something.* You'll do something different and everything will change. Everything will be fine."

While Jules is distracted talking, I remove my watch and slip it onto the wrist of her numb hand—she will need it more than I. Jules does not notice; cannot feel it. And then I take one last look at my friends. Beth is grinding her teeth, tough as always. But Henry and Iggy both have tears in their eyes.

"Everything will be fine," I say, echoing Jules. The irony is, my friends and I know that—at least for me—it will not be. "Resilience," I add quickly, before they can speak. "I have decided that the collective noun for Deadenders should be resilience. A *resilience* of Deadenders."

They will understand my meaning, the message.

"No," says Beth. "Family. A *family* of Deadenders."

"Yes, family," agrees Iggy.

"Family." Henry nods, in tears.

My gaze falls to the piano that their backs are all up against. The note that Beth wrote in the dust used to say, "The die is cast." Most of the letters have been smudged by us. Now the only legible word is "die."

How perfectly appropriate.

....

29

Jules

2056

Ellis stares at his friends for the longest time, and I know why. He's worried that they're going to die. The door won't hold out much longer. On top of that, the house appears to be burning to the ground. It's a fairly hopeless last stand, if ever I saw one.

"A little send-off music?" says Iggy, reaching up from where he's sitting on the floor. Without looking at his hands, back against the piano, he starts playing. I know the song—it's the super-easy one that Tybalt and I used to play together, side by side on the piano stool: "Heart and Soul."

"Romeo is dead!" yells Montague, somewhere on the other side of the door. "You murdered my brother!" He furiously bangs against the door, rocking the piano.

Ellis turns to me and says, "Into the pod."

I hesitate. I feel like I should say something to the other

Deadenders, even though I hardly know them. But then there's another loud bang and the door pushes open a little. Beth fires a second warning shot and Ellis says it again, more urgently this time: "*Into the pod.*"

I run to the nearest one, head down to avoid the bullets, throw my backpack inside, and climb in after it.

"How does this thing work?" I shout above the sounds of the gunfire and the music.

"Spin the dials. Set the date, then the time. Input 5:11 p.m.— that's ten minutes before Iggy, Henry, and Beth first appeared near the overgrown playground," yells Ellis.

"5:11 p.m.," I repeat.

Iggy gets to the part of the song where you need another person to complete it. It's meant to be a duet, so his last note just kind of hangs there, lonely. You need two people, *two hands*.

But then Henry starts singing the missing part—a deep baritone set against the destruction and chaos. It never occurred to me that there might be a different way to make the music. That the love song might have *words*.

I set the dials on the pod. It's over two decades after the year that Mum, Dad, and Aunt Miranda just jumped to. They will have been there more than *twenty years* by the time we arrive.

I try to pull the hatch shut, only I can't because I can't get the buckle done up one-handed. Ellis sees that I'm struggling and leaves his own pod to come to me. When he arrives at my side, he stops short, like there's an invisible barrier.

There's too much danger and chaos. "Please help me with this?" I ask.

Ellis nods and quickly fixes the strap. I watch him. And

suddenly, preparing to go back to the time and place where he died? I'm nervous. I realize: *I care.*

"Duck, okay?" I say, even though I've said it already. "Right after the last chime of the broken clock tower. The thirteenth chime. Got it?"

"Got it."

When I'm buckled in and ready to go, Ellis touches my hair. It's this gentle caress that's a whole world away from stiff words of love or rhyming couplets, a universe beyond all fictional verse. Then, despite the obvious need for haste, Ellis leans in. I close my eyes, thinking he might kiss me. *On the lips,* this time.

But no, Ellis's lips don't find mine. Instead, they land softly on my forehead. He lingers there, so close that I can hear his breath, *feel* it on me. And then the kiss is over. When I open my eyes, Ellis is giving me this intense look. The kind of deep-as-the-heart stuff that I put on the page in abundance.

Then he says, "Pods are rough. Try not to spew," totally undercutting the moment. I laugh, despite everything. Can't help it.

Ellis pulls the hatch shut, then runs back to his own pod amid the gunfire. I look over at the others. I can still see Iggy playing the piano, Henry singing, Beth shooting. I see Montague's sword pierce the door that's already in tatters . . . but there's no sound. The pod has turned the whole scene to silence.

A moment later I hear Ellis's voice, tinny through the pod-to-pod communications: "Press the red button."

I press it, presumably starting the launch sequence. No backing out now—in just a few moments I'll be hurtling through time.

I'm amazed at how easy it is. To be or not to be a Traveler— that was the question my whole entire life. It was this massive deal. Turns out, all that really separated the two was the touch of a button.

"Jules, I cannot explain right now, but know this—the whole future depends on you waking Romeo," says Ellis through the speaker, all earnest again.

And yes, I used to think the same thing—that everything depended on waking Romeo.

"Romeo's just a piece of my past," I say, and finally mean it. "A pretty piece of—"

"There is a bigger picture," Ellis cuts me off. "You *have* to wake Romeo."

"*We* have to wake Romeo." A chunk of piano goes flying across the room. "We'll do it together."

"Go directly to the hospital," continues Ellis.

"What are you talking about? We'll *both*—"

"Go directly to the hospital," he says again, more forcefully. Then he adds, softer: "I am sorry."

"Why?" I'm confused. "Sorry for what?"

Ellis says nothing.

On instinct, I look down at the dials and notice straightaway: he changed the time of my jump. He made it *later*. When he kissed my forehead—when my eyes were closed—he changed the dials. Only by fifteen minutes, though timing is everything. I try to change it back, to turn back the clock—

But it's too late. I disappear.

ACT IV

....

30

Ellis

2083

My pod arrives in the empty block opposite Jules's home. It takes a second for the pod's hatch to release. As soon as it does, I leave the Category drugs on the grass for Jules to find when she arrives here, fifteen minutes from now. And then I run.

Years of Deadender training means that I am good at remembering directions. I do not find it hard to retrace our steps back to the fence with the envelopes stuffed through it. The hole in the wire—the one that I cut—is already there. I quickly make my way through, then traverse the rubbish. Up ahead I can see Jules and me from before, walking away. This is mere moments after we crossed the so-called Wall for the first time.

I loop around, making sure I do not cross paths with the earlier versions of us. The new route takes me past the clock tower. Sure enough, it is broken—one hand stuck forever in one place. Only, now that I am back to this time, I see that the culprit was not a melded pod or vandals, like one comes to expect. I would say it was simply the tyranny of old age.

I cut back toward the main street, where the ice-cream shop is. Then I hide and wait.

A few beats later they come into view—Jules and me, from earlier. And perhaps I should be staring at myself, having an existential moment. I am not; I am staring at Jules. Her hair is longer again, and she is still wearing that oversized sweatshirt with a hood. So much has happened since, yet not for her—she has not lived this chapter yet. She looks so different, and it is not just the hair or the clothes. Seeing them both one after the other like that—Jules from later versus Jules from now—it is clear how much she has changed. *Will* change.

I wish I had more time with her. And because of that, a reckless part of me wants to unravel everything. To warn them about the man with the gas mask, to alter the past.

But the die is cast.

So I watch events play out again like a scene from a book— the same, to the letter. *Henry, Iggy, and Beth running into view with the spare cuffs . . . the man in the gas mask appearing . . . him shooting at us . . . everyone running for cover.* Just like before, Jules splits from the others. Henry, Iggy, Beth, and the earlier version of me are over by the pharmacy. Jules is behind the ice-cream shop, less than a meter from where the current me is hiding.

Jules smashes the cuff against the wall, trying to get it off.

I wait. My friends and the earlier version of me all vanish— jumped back in time to the ransacked department store.

Now is the moment. I step forward, out of hiding.

"You have broken it already," I say, grabbing Jules by the

wrist before she can smash it any further. I am wearing the exact same clothes—she does not know that I am from her future. That for me, time has passed. That I have gone and come back; that everything has changed.

Jules is about to say something, so I gesture for her to be quiet. Then I take her by the arm, and we run. Jules said that we hid in a Chinese restaurant. It is several blocks before I find it.

"In here," I say, entering the building.

"Who were those Travelers?" demands Jules. "And why did they put this thing on me?"

"They are not Travelers. Neither am I. We are Deadenders," I explain, somewhat stiffly. "The cuffs are how we travel backward and forward in time."

It feels strange revealing our secrets, but Jules said that I told her about the Deadenders here in this restaurant. Besides, from *my* perspective, she has the truth already.

"You know, I'm kind of not in the mood for bullshit when I'm *being shot at*," she says, heavy on the sarcasm. "Can we be serious, please?"

"Trust me," I say. Though from the look on her face, that is currently a bridge too far.

I take the damaged cuff off her wrist and start carefully fixing it. "I am reconnecting the causal loop, all right? The *causal loop* was broken. That is why you failed to jump with the rest of us."

"Sure. The *causal loop* is why I didn't jump in time without a pod." Jules clearly does not believe me.

I put the repaired cuff on the table next to her. "All you have to do is click it around your wrist and you will travel back in time."

"You can never go back," she says.

And in a way, that is true: I can never go back to before, when Jules knew me. I will die with her thinking that I am practically a stranger. It is like we have already lost our connection, and I want it back, even if only for a moment. I will be dead soon. I cannot tell her anything that matters, though I need to say something—one true thing.

"Heathcliff," I say quietly. "My Christian name is Heathcliff. Ellis is my last name."

Jules shrugs and says, "Hey, what's in a name?"

She is blasé, dismissive. Except I know better.

I smile at her. Just like before, I am freed by the fact that I will be dead soon. I can finally speak my heart.

"Jules, I need you to know—"

I stop short. Her left hand has come out of her pocket. "You are . . . you are *married*?" I stare in shock at the ring on her finger.

"So?" she says, warily.

"I just . . . the ring. I did not notice it before."

"My hand's been in my pocket the whole time, genius."

From my perspective, it has not. From my perspective, I have seen her left hand. I have *held* her left hand. And there sure as shite was no *wedding ring* on it.

"Yes, of course," I say, confused. "I just did not realize you were already married." The piece of jewelry that Jules said she lost—it was her wedding ring. She has belonged to another this entire time.

"Look, whatever you've got to say about us being too young, I've heard it all before," she says defensively.

"I was not going to say you are too young," I reply softly. "Sometimes young love can last a lifetime."

Jules seems surprised—like she was expecting to have to fight me on that.

"Yeah. Yeah, exactly," she finally mutters. I must be staring again because she adds, "Stop it. Stop looking at me like that."

"You are amazing," I say, because it is true.

"I know, right?"

I cannot resist. "You hide behind sarcasm." Jules appears caught out by the insight, just like I was when she said those words to me, back at the department store.

"Apparently I do it too. I also chew my lip when I am worried." I smile at the memory of how she called me out on *that* as well.

"What is this, a therapy session?" Clearly Jules is not amused.

The broken clock tower will start chiming soon—I am running out of time. I glance at my watch, but of course it is not there. I gave it to Jules in the music room.

I remember that Jules said that I went upstairs, so that is what has to happen.

"I have to go. I have to go upstairs," I say, avoiding her eye. Then I add, "To see if the man in the gas mask is coming." It is the first excuse that comes to mind. Then without turning back, I walk away.

Upstairs, I head for the front room. It is a bedroom—a child once lived here. There are lots of dusty models of the solar system from back when kids dreamed of traveling in space instead of just in time.

I pace the room, full of pent-up emotion. *I have to do this.* Romeo and Juliet are crucial. Their son is the only chance of saving the future. Without him, Frogs will never be built. Without Frogs, it is over—the human race will hurtle forward to its ultimate demise. And there will never be a way to go back and undo the mistakes made.

I stare at my reflection in the mirror: *Heathcliff Ellis.*

The first death that I was slated for ruined Emily's life— even a cursory read of her book made that much apparent. But if my *actual* death can deliver Jules her happiness? If by dying I can make sure that Jules gets a life and love?

Well, perhaps that redeems me.

....

31

Jules

2083

The music room's gone. The *whole house* is gone. The fire at Number 11—it must have burned everything to the ground decades ago.

While I wait for the pod's hatch to release, I check my surroundings. Sure enough, this is the empty block across from the house that I grew up in. Turning to my right, I see two rusty old pods covered in bird shit, nestled in overgrown grass. They're the ones Tybalt and I transformed into pretend rocket ships when we were little. I can still see the remnants of the flag that we made. It's the same. But why? Given that so much else has changed, why is *that* the same? And why are there only two old pods? If Mum, Dad, and Aunt Miranda arrived here twenty years ago, shouldn't there be *three*?

A few tense seconds later, the hatch finally releases. I quickly grab my backpack and climb out. To my left, there's Ellis's pod—shiny, new, and . . . empty. I put my hand on the metal—still warm. Looking down, I see the little case of Category drugs is sitting on the grass. He clearly left it there for me.

Ellis told me to go straight to the hospital. That I *had* to wake Romeo. That everything depended on me waking Romeo. That there was a bigger picture at play. True to form, I choose the other option. The *boy* option. I shove the drugs into my backpack and run toward the decrepit Chinese restaurant—toward Ellis.

It only takes me a few minutes to reach the Wall, with all its forlorn letters. A pointless barrier that I never went beyond until this new chapter. I don't pause to contemplate the divide this time. I just step through the hole that we cut and keep running.

I hear it—the first chime of the broken clock tower. *It's started.* I keep running, becoming more and more panicked. Problem is, I don't know where I'm going. I've only been past the Wall once in my life.

The broken clock keeps on with its dragged-out chimes, marking the passage of time. *Time*—the very thing that I'm running out of. Tears are streaming down my face, but since when have tears helped anything? I keep searching, desperate, becoming more and more frantic.

Finally, there it is—the cruddy Chinese restaurant. But I'm too late. I hear the last chime; the death knell . . .

I don't hear a gunshot. It was silent the last time too. I *do* hear the scream. *My* scream. The sound of my own pain, from before. I feel it again right now, right here, with so much more force. *A man can die but once* . . . yet I lived it double.

Ellis is dead again. And here I am, alone all over. It's a tragedy, like in my play.

I crumple. I collapse to my knees and stare at the restaurant. I can't quite let myself believe it; my poor old heart just won't paint it real. I want to fall back on my usual comfort when the truth's too sharp. *Fiction.*

Except I can't hide my pain in made-up worlds. Not *this* time. Not again.

Not anymore.

It's then I notice Ellis's watch. It's on my left arm—he must have put it there when I wasn't paying attention. I look up at the setting sun. *Time is running out.*

Maybe *this* is "first nightfall"?

The Deadenders seemed to think that waking Romeo was the most important thing in the world. It was Ellis's final message to me. So maybe there are other forces at work; matters bigger than just me and my heartbreak. Maybe I have until the sun sets on *this* day to wake Romeo before it all goes to shit.

Maybe I really *am* all those things that Ellis saw in me. Maybe I'm *brave*, maybe I'm *strong*. Maybe if I can believe that about myself, I'll goddamn *make* it true.

And just like that, something changes in me—like a thread finally pulling together. A thread that's tougher than I thought.

So *this* time, I don't stay down. I don't indulge the inaction. I don't quit because the boy is dead.

I get up off my knees, I wipe away the tears, and I run.

....

32

Ellis

????

Into the nothingness comes music. I must be dead. This must be heaven or hell. But then I hear the lyrics to "Disco 2000" and change my mind.

It takes me a few moments to reconnect with my body, to remember how it works. Then I open my eyes. I am in a bed, a room. My chest is completely bare. Am I naked? I lift the sheets, and relief—jeans still on. Though there is a square of white on my chest. A bandage? Yes, I was shot. It is all coming back to me now. *The man in the gas mask. The Chinese restaurant with Jules. Being shot . . .*

As I peel back the bandage, I see stitches in the shape of a cross over my heart. *Cross your heart and hope to die.* I am glad that I did not. *Why* not? And why am I without pain? I have never been shot before, but I assume it should hurt. Rather sure that is a given.

I survey the room. There is what appears to be medical equipment, but not like anything I have ever seen before. And I have traveled history enough that I should know. This equipment looks like it has been rebuilt entirely from scratch using spare parts, as opposed to being either new or scavenged.

Tentatively getting to my feet, I test if I am okay to stand. Yes, I seem to be. I walk to the antique chest of drawers that is against the far wall. On it, there is a neatly folded black T-shirt, identical to the one that I was wearing. I pick it up—underneath is my copy of *Wuthering Heights*.

After carefully pulling the T-shirt on, I head to the window—

What I see shakes me right out of my daze. I recognize where I am—this is Jules's Settlement. Except now it is completely different. I am observing a thriving community, bustling with people dressed in clothes from what seems to be every era. Some wear complete historical garb, like they have been plucked straight out of a particular time period and have decided to stay dressed that way. Some wear a mismatch. Some have hairstyles or facial hair that is at odds with "when" they are dressed from. It is like they have hand-picked the things that they liked best from throughout human history.

And the Settlement itself no longer has that too-empty, decaying feeling about it. From what I can see, the houses that were falling down have been cleared to make way for vegetable patches and orchards. New structures have been built, and graffiti has been scrubbed off those that remain. This is a community that takes pride. And it is not just filled with *people*, either. I see goats, ducks, chickens, dogs—you name it.

In among all the greenery, people, and animals, there is also technology. Not slick, modern technology. It is reclaimed metal and parts from across the ages, repurposed to make something new—the ultimate in upcycling. I stare at a horse and cart that rolls past. It is of historical design, but made with some kind of lightweight alloy—a true melding of concepts.

Then I notice the tree right outside my window. A sycamore, with a pod absorbed into its trunk. I recognize it. I take a closer look at the room that I am standing in. *I have been here before.* The furniture is different, and the curtains are of plain, hand-made cloth instead of balding velvet. I know precisely where I am, though. This is the room where Romeo was unconscious. Everything is the same, yet not quite.

Something has changed in the timeline.

I should probably leave Romeo's old hospital room. Try to get my bearings, not to mention some answers. But before I do, I find myself staring out the window again. The Settlement—it really is like a twist on what I saw before. I shake my head in disbelief as a woman with a state-of-the-art prosthetic leg milks a cow, right in my line of sight. I am about to open the window and call out to her when I sense someone behind me.

I turn . . . and it is Jules. Jules, but older. *In her forties.* Her hair is still short; she still looks largely the same, though she has aged more than twenty years. I just stare and stare.

"Time to buck up, soldier," she says.

There is a beat while I try to process what the blazes is going on.

"How long ago did you *first* say that to me?" I eventually manage.

"It's been a while."

. . . .

33

Jules

2083

When I make it to the hospital, I'm breathing almost as loud as the man in the gas mask was back at the Chinese restaurant. I decide against going in the front door. It's past visiting hours now, and there could be questions. I figure I'll climb in through the window instead.

I can tell which one is Romeo's room by the tree outside— the sycamore that got hit by that pod and simply kept on growing. I don't even pause to catch my breath—I just head straight for it. My arm makes climbing tricky, especially in terms of balance. And I have to use the gruesome pod/trunk/bone mess for handholds and footholds. It's doable, though. I'm almost level with the window when I hear a snap. Something comes loose and—

I'm holding a human skull in my hand, like the Magdalene

was in that stained-glass panel. I stare, face-to-face with death. A *woman* in death, judging by her jewelry—the lady of the sycamore. And I can't help but wonder: *Did someone kiss the lips that used to be right there?*

Nope. *Not* the time for poetry. I chuck the skull over my shoulder and gracelessly bumble my way in through the window.

I hear a voice. A *familiar* voice—I know it all too well from those cursed assemblies. *Rosaline.* She's sitting in my chair, chatting to Romeo like she's a regular. She stops talking when she sees me, clearly surprised by my unusual entrance. She doesn't let go of Romeo's hand, though. She's entwined her fingers with his, which seems obscenely intimate.

"What the hell are you doing here?" I shout-whisper.

Nobody ever visits Romeo—except me. Okay, maybe his parents sometimes. But I'm the only one who comes, day after day, regardless—or *because*—of everything. Why is Rosaline here? It's horrible timing that she showed up right when I was planning to wake him.

"Please, Jules, calm down," says Rosaline, all milk-of-human-kindness.

"What's going on?" I demand.

"I thought you knew," she says softly, "that I visit him after you leave."

I feel sick. "How long? How long have you been coming?"

She smiles sadly. "Always."

Rosaline has always come? I think back to all those cheesy tribute assemblies and the rivers of fake tears. Were they real after all? Was it *all* real? Does she genuinely love him?

"We were together for years before you entered the picture," Rosaline reminds me. "I care about him too."

My face must mirror how I feel because she stands up and says, "Don't worry, I'll go." She gently places Romeo's hand back on the bed and walks out of the room, shutting the door behind her.

I stagger to the chair. The chair that I sat in every single day for almost two years. The one that I've been warming up the whole time for Rosaline.

And here he is, right where I left him—Romeo, still sleeping. If this were a story, it would be a words-of-love or a rhyming couplet moment. But in real life? There's only silence. I suddenly realize that, despite my daily visits, I never *really* believed that Romeo would come back to me. I've never thought about the proper implications of what would happen if we ever had the chance to talk again, face-to-face.

But I can't back down now. The note in my book said, *Wake Romeo before first nightfall. I* wrote that note, and *that's* who I have to listen to. I have to be true to myself.

I get the Category drugs out of my backpack and their case, jab the syringe into Romeo's neck, and deliver the antidote. Fingers crossed it's sleep no more. A few minutes later there's a murmur; the rest is no longer silence. And there it is—my miracle.

Romeo is waking.

His leg twitches, and it's enough to send one of the monitors into a frenzy. It seems too impossible—it's all happening so fast.

Once upon a time, I was living for this storybook moment. I fantasized about what I'd be wearing when Romeo finally opened his eyes, the delicate words of love that would flutter between us. It was all *Good morning sweet prince* and *Flights of angels sing thee from thy rest.* In reality? I'm thinking practicalities. The nurses will be here soon, befuddled by the miracle awakening, with questions I can't answer. Time to go. I stuff the syringe and its case into my backpack so there's no evidence left behind.

Climbing out the window, I step into the sycamore tree. Through its branches, I can see the inconstant moon. It's both light and dark tonight, like the circle's been half painted over. I can't tell if it's waxing or waning—whether it's getting smaller, or closer to whole.

Looking down, there's that mangled mess again—pod mixed with Traveler. I stare at her lonely bones and wonder what good is interred with them, what good it did her . . . the woman who didn't like her "now" and decided *not* to try to change it.

She couldn't bear the whips and scorns of time, so she took the easy way out.

I overheard Mum say that right after I tried to kill myself. She was talking to Aunt Miranda, and she was furious. Yelling levels of cross, churned in with some sobbing. At the time I thought she was angry at me. That she *blamed* me.

I couldn't cope with that, so I shut her out. I built a wall between us.

But it was Aunt Miranda's response to Mum's comment that made no sense. I figured I must have heard wrong. Except now, with all this traveling backward and forward in time? With chapters out of order and stories being rewritten?

She said, "I can't believe it's happened *again*."

·········

34

Ellis
????

Rude or not, I keep staring at her—*Jules from the future*. She might be decades older, yet she is more hale and hearty than when I first met her. Lean, muscled. Her face has wrinkles and scars, with plenty of laughter lines too. She has led a proper life, a *real* life. Not like the girl in her book. Or the girl in Emily's book, for that matter. Her time was not cut short by some doomed romance—it has been full, you can tell. And based on the muscles and scars, she has not been idle. There is even a fresh smudge of blood on her T-shirt—not exactly the hallmark of a bookish lass.

Her numb arm is in a sling across her chest, not tucked away. Also, the T-shirt is cut low. Whereas once Jules was shy about the scar, now she wears clothes that pointedly reveal it.

"What year is this?" I ask.

"2107," she says. "This is twenty-four years after you were shot in the Chinese restaurant."

Glancing out the window again, I see people of all different cultures, all different creeds, working together. If this is indeed the future, it is like none that I have ever witnessed.

"How did I get here? How did I get from the restaurant to here? To *now*?"

"My son brought you."

My gaze falls to the numb arm, now supported by the sling. Sure enough, the wedding ring is back in place.

"I see you found it." I gesture at the band of gold.

"My *husband* found it for me."

"Wonderful," I lie. "You woke Romeo, clearly."

"Yes."

"You and he had a child? The man with the mismatched eyes?"

"Yes."

"So you got your love story, then."

"Absolutely."

Everything turned out perfectly. Because it was never just about "waking Romeo." It was about waking Romeo so that he and Jules could be together. Get married, have a son . . . a son who would create the Deadenders.

Everything—the whole future—depended on their love story.

"I am glad you got your . . . what was it that you called him? Your *pretty piece*?" I say, repeating her words from before, perhaps somewhat unkindly.

"*Pretty* . . . to imply *not manly*." Jules shakes her head. "Yes, I used to do that all the time, even in my head—describe 'feminine' traits in men as somehow a weakness. I didn't do it consciously. But even in my writing, the bias was there."

Is this a rebuke of herself *and* of Emily? *Wuthering Heights* is known for subverting gender stereotypes, yet also for portraying femininity . . . less favorably.

"Fascinating," I say in a tone that I hope will herald an end to the topic.

"It's funny," says Jules, pressing on. "I had this whole thing about girls comparing themselves to storybook ideals, but for the longest time I didn't even *think* about boys. How it might feel for *them* to be reduced to nothing except 'masculine.'"

In her novel, Emily rendered me as naught but that precisely. I have never understood why.

"Apologies, cannot relate," I say stiffly, turning to face the window again. I do not wish Jules to see my expression; this is not comfortable territory for me.

My gaze settles on a man in a wheelchair, which appears to be made of recycled cans. Looking more closely around the rejuvenated Settlement, I see rather *a lot* of differences, in point of fact.

I glance back at Jules's arm. The technology here is undoubtedly advanced, yet . . .

"Your arm. You could reverse the damage, but choose not to?"

Jules smiles. "My body's *already* whole," she says. "Besides, I am not enamored with everyone looking the same."

That is precisely what I said to Jules—from her perspective, many years ago. I am touched that, even after so much time, she still recalls it. I wonder if perhaps some tiny aspect of our time together left its mark. I wonder . . .

But no. She married someone else.

I clear my throat. "The man in the gas mask," I say, changing the subject. "The threat of him is no longer?"

"There never was a threat," says Jules. "It was all a performance."

"I do not understand."

"You will," says Jules. Then, "How's the wound?" And, when I fail to answer, "The gunshot wound?"

"Surprisingly fine, actually," I say. Touching my chest, I wonder what technology they used to heal me so well and so quickly.

"We're using next-generation meds, which makes recovery from injuries basically instantaneous. Also, we've pumped you full of some rather top-shelf painkillers. They're working?"

"Perfectly," I admit.

"Good, because we're about to dive into the past," she says. "Loose ends, et cetera."

"But only Deadenders can travel backward in time," I protest.

"I *am* a Deadender," says Jules. "I *created* the Deadenders."

....

35

Jules

2083

By the time I arrive home after waking Romeo, night is falling. I could sneak in the front door, but I don't want to risk waking Mum and Dad. And so I do something that I haven't done in years: I scale the latticework.

Two years ago, it was Romeo making this climb to my bedroom, with one thing on his mind. And now it's me, doing it alone. When I reach my balcony, I stop there a moment. Looking down, I remember the night that Romeo came to my window. Not the version that I put in my story, with the old-fashioned clothes and the too-pretty words. The *real* one. Romeo was down in the garden, mucking about with Paris and Laurence. He was laughing, about to throw a second stone. Only, being so drunk, he was going to throw it way too hard.

Paris caught his arm and slurred, "Softly! You'll break the window."

That was about the extent of the romance.

And me that night? I was sixteen years old, hair to my waist, wearing some frilly white nightie. *Love, love, love.*

I just couldn't see past it.

Now I stare at my reflection in the window—short hair, figure-hugging T-shirt, wedding ring gone. I focus on my arm—the left one. The one that I described as dead, even though it's a part of me. The one that I've treated like a hole in the otherwise whole. Pulling my T-shirt down, I take in the scar. *A wound caused the scar, the scar caused a wound*—around and around in circles, like a pain that had swallowed its own tail.

Behind my reflection, I see my bedroom. That's where I hid for almost a year after what happened. The tiny, domestic space was practically my whole world, just like the Juliet in my story.

Then I turn away from my bedroom, away from myself. And I do something that's badly overdue—I look outward into the starry, starry night. I can't see it, but somewhere between me and the empty city there's that other thing—*the Wall*. The flimsy divide that, when I was a kid, I thought was all that separated our island of "safe" from a tempest of Travelers. When I got older, I thought it was there to protect us from the awful truth of being alone.

Except being alone isn't the end of the world.

I *thought* it was. I believed I was half of a whole, despite how it made me smaller. Like so many things, I was mistaken. No, I *let* myself be mistaken. I never looked inward when I should have. I was the virgin, the martyr, the daughter, the lover, the wife.

I was Juliet.

And I was wrong—love isn't everything.

I decide that, if I ever write another play, it won't be a love story. It will be about action—taking action versus *not* taking action. Because standing on my balcony, looking out at the in-tatters world? It's becoming clear that we have to act. That we have to do it today, or tomorrow won't happen.

With that, my thoughts return to Shakespeare. His plays used to be performed at a theater called "the Globe." I figured it was just a cool name—I never really thought about the metaphor of it. The idea that all the drama was literally playing out on the world's stage. That each story, however small, was part of a bigger picture.

That everything's connected.

The Globe Theater was round, apparently. *A circle.* But Ellis was wrong about his "no beginning, no end" way of thinking. Because from where I'm standing?

Well, I can envisage an end just fine.

I finally go inside and light some candles, illuminating the childish bedroom that somehow suits me no more. I stare at the clock, inching by on the last of our batteries. It's almost nine p.m. Only three more hours and it will officially be tomorrow, making it two years exactly.

I run my finger over the hole in the plaster where I punched the wall after Tybalt died. I notice the spot on the carpet where I spilled the last of our cordial back when I was eight. Then something else occurs to me. I sneak to Mum's study, two doors down. Sure enough, hanging above the desk is one of her charcoal sketches. It's of a girl, half obscured by flowers. No, not flowers—*herbs.* Mum must have drawn it from memory after the original was destroyed by fire. Perhaps it's a portrait. Or perhaps it's nobody—just a nameless girl standing in front of a hamlet. Whatever the truth, that's why the painting at Number 11 was so familiar to me—a copy of it has been here in plain sight since before I was born. I must have seen it a million times, but like so many things, I never paid proper attention.

That iconic image, which Mum always loved—Mary Magdalene, holding a human skull. *It reminded her of the stained-glass panel.*

Kronborg Castle—when we stumbled across pictures of it down at the Supermarket, Dad didn't get all nostalgic for no reason. *It reminded him of the wallpaper in the music room.*

My parents lied. *All* of our parents lied. The founding families weren't Settlers. They were *never* Settlers. They were Travelers. Mum and Dad and Aunt Miranda *jumped* here from the music room that day. They weren't even really Capulets. They must have just taken the name because it was on the crypt, to sell the "been-here-for-generations" fiction. Or because *I told them* that they had. Everything played out the same.

Maybe time changes nothing.

Or maybe *time* was never the problem. Maybe the problem was always me. Me and my fluffy ideas about golden hearts and true love. Me and my needling hurt, beneath all the soft nonsense.

So maybe *I* can change, even if time—and everything else—doesn't.

Romeo is waking.

And after so much wasted plotting, I finally know *exactly* what needs to happen next.

....

36

Ellis

2107

"Beg pardon?" I say, stunned.

"I *created* the Deadenders," says Jules again.

I am completely confused.

"Put this on," says Jules, fishing a cuff from her pocket and handing it to me. The cuff is exactly like the ones that we had on the bus. I click it around my wrist, just like old times.

Then I notice that the cuff she wears around the wrist of her numb arm is different—it is wider.

"Manual version," says Jules, following my line of sight. "Lets me control the jumps myself."

"Frogs always controlled our jumps," I say, half to myself. "But I suppose, since Frogs was destroyed . . ."

"Frogs wasn't destroyed," says Jules, quite matter-of-fact.

That does not make sense either. The last thing I remember

is being in the Chinese restaurant. I wanted to kiss Jules, yet did not. I went back downstairs. I refrained from kissing her hand like I yearned to. Right after the thirteenth chime, I was shot.

The timeline—something must have changed.

"Grab that, we'll need it," says Jules, nodding at my copy of *Wuthering Heights,* which is still on the antique chest of drawers. I tuck the book into my back pocket, more for safekeeping than because she instructed me to.

Then the important part of the conversation sinks in: *They can send people back in time.*

"Henry, Iggy, and Beth," I say in a hurry. "If you have the technology, we have to go back for them. We have to—"

I never get to finish the sentence. Jules grabs the cuff around her wrist—

* * *

—and we are suddenly in an overgrown garden behind a wild rose-briar. The act of grabbing the cuff—that is what jumped us. Jules somehow controlled *both* our jumps.

"How . . . ," I start to say, but then a backpack lands on the grass not even a meter from where we are hiding. I look up and see Jules as a teenager, standing on the balcony above us. She is wearing her black hooded sweatshirt—the one that I ripped up to serve as a bandage. From my perspective, this is just after we first met. Before we went through the Wall. Before everything happened.

I watch as the teenage Jules grabs hold of the latticework,

preparing to climb down. Though I see fear and uncertainty in her face. She seems so different from the grown woman who is standing here beside me. Indeed, the teenager loses her nerve and goes back inside.

"She's going down the stairs and walking around," says the Jules by my side. "Quickly, grab the notebook. Page forty-nine."

I retrieve her notebook from the backpack and turn it to page 49. Jules takes a red pen from her pocket, pops the cap, and writes: *Wake Romeo before first nightfall.*

Five little words. But, of course, little words can change everything. I return the notebook to the backpack and zip it up again.

"I sure had a lot of work to do, back in this time and place," says Jules, looking around the Settlement. Though as she speaks, she rubs her numb arm. Not a pinch like before, but gentle—a caress, almost.

Checking her watch, Jules grabs the cuff around her wrist—

* * *

—Now we are in a hall that is humming with people. There is no lead-in whatsoever. Jules simply announces, "We call this the Control Room. Though technically, it's the old school chapel." She adds as an afterthought, "The same one where Rosaline used to give her Romeo tributes. For me, that was over twenty years ago. Since then, everything's changed."

I look around. There are still a few remnants of the past: plastic chairs stacked in a corner, a school coat of arms hanging on the wall. But there is also reclaimed equipment everywhere—the space is filled with highly sophisticated technology, all unasham-edly hodgepodge. And it is bustling. There are over a hundred people in here, monitoring equipment or moving with purpose—most of them children and teens.

"Who are all these people?" I stare at a young girl dressed in a tartan smock.

"Deadenders," replies Jules.

"Where I am from, *we* were the Deadenders," I say. "Beth and Henry and Iggy and me."

"Aye," says the girl in tartan with a thick Scottish accent—clearly eavesdropping. "All four of you on the bus, in the wasteland. But we are what happened next. We are what the Deadenders *became*."

"Beth, Henry, and Iggy," I say again urgently. "There was a gunfight in the music room. We have to—"

"They're fine. Or rather, they *will* be fine." Jules cuts me off. Instant relief.

"Come," adds Jules. "I need you to focus." With that, she leads me across the crowded room. As we walk, I stare agog at all the equipment and at the so-called Deadenders. They do not wear uniforms, like soldiers of time. They wear their own clothes, like *people* of time. A corseted girl with dyed black hair and black nail polish is shoulder-to-shoulder with a boy wear-ing naught but animal skins and feathers. People of all kinds, all variations . . . working side by side.

"We've been preparing for this day—this one critical se-quence of events—for years. And now it's almost over," says Jules, stopping at a huge golden sphere that is crisscrossed at a thousand points, like a giant ball of mechanical twine. Tiny windows exist in the gaps between the crisscrossed twine, every window displaying an image of the past.

"These are the moments that have to happen exactly right, or the Deadenders will cease to exist, along with the future," says Jules. "It took Frogs *years* to finesse this exact sequence of interconnected events. And we've been ticking them off, one by one, these past few hours."

Jules gives a nod, and an Indian girl dressed in an embroidered sari ceremoniously dims another window. The one showing the note on page 49, written in red pen. Another piece of the puzzle placed according to plan.

"When we started, the Web had thousands of tiny windows, all glowing bright, waiting to be actioned," explains Jules. "Now almost all of them are dimmed to signify completion."

I stare at the dark spaces that still have the afterglow of moments that I recognize. Moments like me tackling Jules to the ground by the fountain. Me in the crypt, remembering the lost note. Jules and me reading her story by the fireplace at Number 11. I linger on an image of me kissing Jules in the Chinese restaurant—my lips pressed tenderly against her hand.

"All the key moments that we sweated over getting right for years, now done and dusted," says Jules, nodding at the darkened Web. "But there are still a few windows burning bright, waiting to be dealt with."

I want to know about the kiss—why it is there, since that moment never happened. I never kissed Jules's hand in the Chinese restaurant. I thought about it, certainly. I *wanted* to. But she was already married, so I refrained. A missed kiss with Emily changed my life entirely. Was the missed kiss with Jules

significant also? Is that why the moment is somehow showing, even though it never actually happened? I am about to
ask when Jules calls out across the room, "You have the spare
cuffs?"

She is talking to a young woman dressed in a tunic and
cloak, who is holding an axe and round shield.

"Dæll," she says, without explanation.

"Remember, she has a gun," says Jules.

The woman—well over six foot—gives a dismissive snort,
clearly unconcerned.

"Well, can't say I didn't warn her," mutters Jules under her
breath as she places the red pen on a nearby table. "Book now,
please," she says to me without looking up.

With some reluctance, I hand her my copy of *Wuthering
Heights*. Jules opens it, turning to a blank page at the end. Beside it on the table, there is a crumpled piece of paper preserved
in plastic—clearly ripped from a book. Jules copies the note
word for word into the back of *Wuthering Heights*. Then she
slips the book into the dust jacket of a Holy Bible. The only
other thing left on the table is a white coat. It is just like the
ones that the nurses were wearing when Jules first took me to
the hospital to try to wake Romeo.

Jules hesitates for a moment, then she somberly dons the
coat and picks up *Wuthering Heights,* now disguised as a Bible.
She reaches for the cuff, but then stops. It is like she cannot
quite bring herself to do it. I notice a few Deadenders exchange
worried glances—something is wrong.

"We had a feeling you'd struggle with this one," says a voice
from behind us.

I turn—it is Jules's aunt and her father. The last time I saw them was in the music room when they were teenagers. Now they look to be in their sixties.

"Your mum wanted to be here too, but she's still not back from that last mission," continues Miranda. "We came for support."

Jules shakes her head; tears are welling in her eyes.

"I know there's a bigger picture," she says, barely a whisper. "I know that the future matters more than just hearts. I've *lived* that ethos. But hearts ..."

Jules trails off, staring first at her father, then at me. There is a deathly silence. While people are pretending not to watch, all focus is on Jules—I can feel it.

"Can't ... change ... *everything*," says her father.

"It's the only thread that works," adds Miranda with a quiet calm. "He knows that if there was any other way, you'd take it. But you can't, because it's already happened. Frogs ran the numbers a thousand times. Without this moment putting everything in motion, it all unravels."

"You ... *have* ... to," says Jules's father.

Jules looks up, out over the Control Room—all the faces, all the years of hard work. Yet she still does not move.

"I've been dreading this moment for most of my life," says Jules at last.

Miranda nods—clearly they have all been dreading it.

"Best get ... get it *over* with ... then ..." says her father. "*Hell* is ... waiting."

It seems to be some kind of private joke; in it, there is magic.

"Been waiting long to use that one?" Jules sniffs up the tears that were close.

"Dec ... cades," says her father with a soft smile.

Jules smiles back. She smiles in a way that is neither sweet nor agreeable. She is mess and pain and raw, bloody love all rolled into one. And in that look, I see it. I *know* it, right down to my soul. It is no mystery at all.

I am in love with her.

Romeo's the type to like his girls "girlie." He'll hate the haircut, among other things. And yet . . . there's almost *real* poetry in that. For years, I've quietly fretted about how I'd appear to my husband if he ever woke and saw me. All the little changes he might see and not like. Cutting my hair so that I look *completely* different? The haters will say it's just me being classically dramatic. That I hacked it off in some grand gesture. Except it doesn't feel that way. The hair feels . . . decisive. And so do I. For the first time in a long time, I know exactly what I need to do. And not just in fiction, in real life.

I remember the book that Ellis inspired—*Wuthering Heights*. It started with a ghost, if memory serves. And that's what I've been these past few years, isn't it? The ghost of Juliet. But I don't feel half gone anymore, like some washed-out wraith, or that sparrow in the old theater. I feel solid. *Strong.*

I shoulder the backpack—it's still got my notebook inside. I'd never *planned* on showing my story to Romeo, but I'm feeling kind of reckless. Like there's no telling what I might need in my arsenal today.

Taking the stairs quickly, I turn the corner and find Mum, Dad, and Aunt Miranda sitting at the breakfast table. They suddenly look so different—*so aged*—compared to the teenage versions that I was with in the music room.

"Well, what do you think?" I say, pretending to flick flowing locks that are no longer there. My hair's short, just like it was back at Number 11. I wait for them to recognize me.

"*Hell is, Hell is, Hell is,*" says Dad more urgently than usual. He's staring at the haircut, having clearly put two and two together. But with only a two-word repertoire, he can't really express it.

....

37

Jules

2083

ONE DAY AFTER WAKING ROMEO

The first thing I think when I wake in the morning is: *I need to see Romeo.*

I look at my crumpled uniform on the floor—the skirt with its scratchy wool. School will be buzzing today with news of the miracle awakening. There'll be some special assembly. They might even use the big hall. Not so long ago, I would have lapped up a day like today.

Times change, apparently.

I open my wardrobe. There are prettier things I could wear, more feminine options, but I choose jeans and a long-sleeved T-shirt that fits. I'm about to put on a hoodie—one of the baggy ones with the pouch up front. Then I decide no. I'm not hiding my arm or my shape—I'm not hiding *anything* today.

Once the clothes are on, I look in the mirror—*properly* look.

"Hush," says Aunt Miranda, touching his arm, trying to soothe him.

I spin to Mum, waiting for *her* holy-shit moment. It doesn't happen—she just gives a tired sigh. And the world-weary look in her eyes? I simply can't reconcile it with the spirited young woman who wouldn't back down, not even when her life was on the line. It's as if time has turned her into a completely different person.

"Sit down, Juliet," says Mum. The rare use of my unabbreviated name—it throws me, although I try not to show it.

"Someone from the hospital came around," she says, letting it hang there. "Romeo woke up last night. Trudy and Claude have taken him home."

They've taken him home already? They wouldn't have done that unless he was properly better. Cat-9 really must be as amazing as Ellis promised it would be.

"I'm going over there now, then," I declare, holding on tight to that rare decisive feeling.

"Juliet," says Mum, "the Montagues don't want you seeing him, and we agree."

"It's a bit late to tell me I can't see him. You know full well that I've been seeing him every day for two years."

"Trudy and I thought there'd be no harm while he was unconscious," says Mum, looking uncomfortable. "That maybe it would help you move on."

"What?" I'm totally rattled. The Capulets and the Montagues hate one another. And yet our mothers spoke, before? They *discussed* me? What else did they talk about?

"Did you know about this too?" I ask Aunt Miranda—an accusation. She keeps staring down at the table and nods.

"You're a bad influence on each other," says Mum. "The Montagues want Romeo to have a fresh start," she adds. "We think that's the best for both of you, given what happened."

She looks me in the eyes when she says it, and I know she's not talking about the "both almost wound up dead" part of the scandal. She's talking about the *other* thing. The *secret* thing. The thought of it has me suddenly off-balance, so I lash out with, "He's my *husband*"—and instantly regret it.

The fact that there was a "wedding" is still a sore point. It wasn't legal, of course. Hell, you don't even have to get it annulled when the reverend's a fake and the bride is barely sixteen. It was a public embarrassment for my parents, though, and evidence of just how out of touch with reality we star-crossed lovers really were.

I'm expecting Mum to fly off the handle at the husband thing, but she doesn't. She just gives me another tired, sad little smile.

"Juliet, you have to start growing up," she says, suddenly crying. "You *have* to put all of this behind you and take responsibility for your life. You're not a kid anymore. I keep desperately waiting for you to show me that you've changed, but year upon year you never do."

It's the tears that get me. I've heard this "take responsibility" spiel a thousand times, and it's always a tight-lipped sermon. Like she's preaching, *not* like she cares. Now, though? You'd think that lives literally depend on me growing up.

But maybe she thinks they do. Maybe she thinks that nothing's changed and I'm still prone to . . . problematic behavior.

"This can be a second chance for you too," she says once she's calmed down a bit and is almost back to her usual measured self.

"Now that you don't have this hanging over you, perhaps you can move on. It's a miracle, really. Two years to the day and somehow he wakes."

And suddenly I'm furious. Furious that Mum and Rosaline *both* got the date wrong. Furious that all of my kid years were wasted. Furious that they won't even let me see Romeo after all that I've given up in the name of him and our impulsive, epic romance. Furious about the lies. And about the biggest lie of all: goddamn *love*. Furious about *so many* things. All of it—all of that fury and emotion channels into the one small thing that feels like solid ground: time.

"It's two years *today*, not yesterday!" I yell, as though getting a date wrong is some kind of sacrilege. "Yesterday was the twenty-seventh. It happened on the twenty-eighth."

Mum just stares at me as though I've genuinely lost the plot.

And then, with infinite patience, Aunt Miranda says, "You tried to take your own life on the twenty-seventh. So two years ago *yesterday*."

Oh, no ... it *was* the twenty-seventh. Mum's right. Aunt Miranda is right. *Rosaline* was right. *Everyone was right, except me.* How could I have gotten that wrong? I've lived and breathed this stuff for years, so how is it even possible? How did I get the twenty-eighth stuck in my head? Surely—

And then I remember who died on the twenty-eighth, many months later, and I have to sit down. I hold onto the table, waiting for the world to stop spinning. When I look up, they're all staring at me—Mum, Miranda, *and* Dad. Dad, who hasn't been able to focus on anything in years, is watching me so intently you could almost believe that his brain isn't damaged.

Aunt Miranda asks, "Are you okay?" Her voice sounds

distant. I stare at my hand holding the table. The knuckles are white—I'm gripping it like I might fall down or drift away if I dare let go, even a little. What is it with me and holding on too tight?

Mum starts whispering, "Quiet," and then "*Quiet*" again, and then finally she screams, "Shut up!"

That snaps me out of it. Mum's not looking at me, though—she's looking at Dad. He's muttering to himself again. It's too low to make out the words, but I know what he's saying.

"Hell is *YOU!*" Mum yells back at him. "Hell is your husband leaving you to deal with the whole damn mess by yourself!"

My jaw drops. Somehow it never occurred to me that we *both* lost our husbands that night. That Mum and I shared the exact same torture of him being right there, but also *not* there.

"Hell is *you*," she says again, more quietly. Mum's tears from before were just a prelude—now she's *really* sobbing. I've never seen Mum cry before today, and now she looks like she might *never* stop.

I gaze at Mum and Dad, side by side at the kitchen table, but with a universe between them. From my perspective, it's been less than a day since they were young and in love. Since their feelings were fresh, unsullied by time. But, of course, all that endless love is just a racket. And my own parents are clearly the case in point.

I get up and leave.

I'm almost at the front door when Dad comes running, practically bowling me over. He shouts, "Hell is!" as though that unfinished phrase is a legitimate stand-in for all other language. And then he shoves his precious Bible at me.

I try to give the Bible back, only Dad won't have it. Maybe he thinks that with Romeo in the mix again, my damnable soul's in peril all over. I *really* don't want the book, but I also don't want the drama, so in the end I take it and shove it in my backpack.

"Hell is!" he shouts again.

And that's when it happens. Dad reaches out and touches my hair, my face. He holds my gaze and says, clear as day, "I love you."

What the . . . ? He could talk all along, he simply *chose* not to? All that time with me feeling like utter shit that maybe I'd somehow broken my own father, and he was just putting on a bloody good show?

"I love you?" says Mum from the kitchen doorway with a terrifying calm. She obviously overheard everything. "Nothing but two lousy words on repeat for years, and now three new ones? And they're *I love you?*"

Staring at Dad, I try to remember the last time he told me that he loved me. I try to sort out how I feel about it coming out now. And then it hits me. Dad wasn't making a declaration of fatherly affection—

"He finally finished his sentence," I say with a humorless laugh. "*Hell is I love you.* Well, Dad, that might just be perfect."

It doesn't get much more brutal than that. Because it's true, isn't it? Without the agony of love, the true depths of hell just aren't at your disposal. Love is what exposes you to the *really* exquisite torture . . . and for Dad, the torturer is me.

And suddenly, I can't take the guilt or the pain any longer.

"I'm going to talk to Romeo—there are things that need to be said." I let it hang there like a threat. "And none of you can stop me," I add for good measure, although it's a mistake. I sound like a petulant kid again, determined to get her own way, no matter what.

"You need to *grow up*," says Mum again, at the end of her tether. "It's *time* to grow up. I can't keep putting things off, waiting for you to be ready."

I'm in no mood for one of her pep talks, so I head for the door again. Mum moves to stop me from leaving, but Dad grabs her by the arm. I don't pause to analyze it—I take advantage of Mum's complete shock and storm right on out.

I go straight to the shed. I haven't ridden a bike in years. Not since the Romeo fiasco, when my arm—among other things— died. No, not *died*. I remember Ellis's words from before: *No part of you is dead. Different does not mean less.* More and more I'm realizing he's right. But it shouldn't have taken *someone else* telling me that for me to believe it.

I'm still grappling with the lock on the shed when a gentle voice from behind says, "Don't be angry with your mother. She hasn't made the connection."

As I turn to Aunt Miranda, understanding dawns. She remembers me from before, yet my mother doesn't. How can a mother not know her own child?

"I'm her *daughter*," I snap, letting the anger flow. "How can she not recognize me?"

"For us, it was half a lifetime ago, Juliet," says Aunt Miranda slowly. "We were young. It all happened so quickly, and we were under a lot of stress. Besides, sometimes people choose to remember things differently."

I think of me and my story. Ain't *that* the truth.

"But *you* knew," I say as it properly sinks in. "You *always* knew, my whole entire life. Because I told you." I'm practically vibrating with the shock, the realization.

"Yes."

And then I'm thinking about how it all played out. How everything happened because my cousin had died the week before. Tybalt was dead, so I went to that goddamn party. My heart was all bleeding and raw. I needed something to numb the pain, and there he was—Romeo. I used the attention of a boy as my drug and distraction.

Tybalt's death was the tragedy that sparked all disaster to follow. Without him dying, I would never have been at that party, would never have fallen for Romeo. My story would have been different. *Everyone's* story would have been different. So why the hell did Tybalt have to die?

"I *warned* you." I allow the emotions to take over. "Why did you let Tybalt go to the old theater when I warned you?"

"I didn't let him," says Aunt Miranda quietly. "We had a fight. It was the one place he was strictly forbidden to go, so he went there to spite me," she says softly, tears in her eyes. "Children sometimes *do* that with their mothers."

It was a self-fulfilling prophecy, like in *Macbeth*. Only this time, the architect of fate wasn't Shakespeare . . . it was me.

"It was my fault," I say eventually. "Everything was *my* fault."

"Oh darling, *of course* it wasn't your fault," says Aunt Miranda. "There are things in life that we can change . . . and things that we cannot."

"If I hadn't gone back in time, if I hadn't told you not to let him go there . . ."

My voice trails off as the magnitude of it sinks in.

"This whole place exists because of you," says Aunt Miranda, taking my right hand in both of hers. "What you said about the Settlement? That's what gave us the idea. When Montague and the others jumped here looking for us, we formed a glooming peace. We agreed that, together, we would start a Settlement—for real. Eventually, more Travelers who were passing through decided to stay. We had families. We built something from nothing. But *you* gave us the idea. Without you, without what you said back in the past, this place wouldn't exist. Everyone would have just kept going and going until there was no future left."

"My words killed my cousin," I say, not daring to look at her.

"Your words *changed the world*," she says, giving my hand three little squeezes, just like I squeezed her hand back at Number 11, all those years in the past.

Eventually I ask, "Why did you lie? Why did you all pretend that you'd been here for generations?"

"Because we wanted our kids to believe that it was possible. We figured that if you all believed that we'd done it, you'd truly believe that it could be done, and sustained."

Another self-fulfilling prophecy. Which of course just makes me think of Tybalt again.

"Your only son is dead," I say, willing myself not to cry. "How can you be okay?"

"Frailty, thy name is *not* woman," she says quietly. "Besides, he is with me always . . . *from this day to the ending of the world.*"

She's quoting *Henry V* now, trusting I'll get the reference. And of course, Aunt Miranda knows my secret, so her words are for me too. We stand there hand in hand, together in loss.

And then she adds, "*All that lives must die, passing through nature to eternity.* Our time together was short, though time isn't everything."

Love isn't, either.

"Why did you ever get involved with *Montague*?" I finally say, because I have to know. She's so—so *gentle*, like Dad. Mum I could maybe understand, but Aunt Miranda? The woman who introduced me to Shakespeare and who taught me the beauty of words?

She gives me a kind smile. "Our parents had . . . gone. Your mother and I were meant to go with them, except we didn't."

Their parents must have jumped; Aunt Miranda and Mum remained behind.

"We were hiding out in our mother's secret library, scared and alone, running out of food," she says. "Montague and his gang found us there. They stayed. At the time, it felt like he saved us."

Holy shit. Their parents didn't *jump*. They killed themselves. The house where we stumbled across the gang? Number 11? It wasn't some random squat. It was the house where Mum and Aunt Miranda grew up. The two skeletons in the bed, the sleepers? *They were my grandparents.* The adorable family photo that Ellis and I joked about—the baby in that photo must have been my mum.

Mum and Aunt Miranda—they had to deal with the grief of their parents' suicides back when they were teenagers. And then I almost put them through it a second time. Aunt Miranda's comment, right after what happened with Romeo—*I can't believe it's happened again.*

It wasn't about time travel. It was just history repeating.

Staring at Aunt Miranda now, I realize she was in pain

when she met Montague. Just like me, with Romeo. She let a boy "save" her; she let love be her solution. She fell into the exact same trap that I did.

Yeah, I get it now.

But then something else occurs to me. If our *parents* were the ones who started the Settlement, then . . .

"Why build the Wall?" I ask. "Why keep everything out, even the animals? Why not grow things or—or *plant* things? Why not at least *try*?"

There's a change in Miranda, like she's weighing whether or not to answer. She hesitates.

"Aunt Miranda?"

"We *did* try," she says at last, like a confession. "We tried to farm, and we failed. We tried to catch animals, and we failed. That first year, two starved. Anders was mauled by a dog, hoping to eat its meat—the infection killed him slowly. Jenny ate berries in desperation, which killed her fast—she was only twelve. A boy—I can't remember his name—cut his leg with an axe trying to clear some soil; we had no way to stop the bleeding. There was a murder over cereal . . . and a trial, of sorts. That first year, we didn't have enough of anything. It brought out the worst in us. We all did things that still haunt us."

I think of the Road. Humanity can be so ugly.

Instead, I say, "Why didn't you just *leave*?"

"Some did. We couldn't. Tybalt had been born. There was no pod for him."

I try to imagine our Settlement as a place of violence and desperation. I can't—it's just too far from the fenced-off pen that I grew up in.

"What changed things?" I eventually wonder out loud.

"One word," says Aunt Miranda with a melancholy smile. "I saw a word above a set of boarded-up doors. The building was derelict—it looked like nothing. But the word, the fact that *you* had said it? I broke a window, climbed inside, and discovered a miracle. Supplies stacked to the roof—food, water, clothes, gas, batteries. All that we needed to keep us alive. To start a Settlement, for real this time."

Laertes. Laertes Health Club. I said that word, back at Number 11.

"We divided everything up among those who were left," continues Miranda. "We avoided anything that reminded us of that terrible chapter. And we built the Wall."

Trauma. *Pain.* They didn't deal with it. They *hid* from it.

Just like me, with my story.

....

38

Ellis

2081

The world around me resolves into focus after the jump. The Control Room has disappeared—we are somewhere different. I recognize it: this is the hallway just outside Romeo's hospital room. Jules opens the door a crack, and I see who is lying in the bed. Not Romeo, this time. Not me either. *It is Jules.* Jules with waist-long hair, younger than I have ever seen her.

"I'm sixteen years old," whispers the middle-aged Jules by my side as she stares at her younger self. "I've just tried to take my own life."

I study the girl in the bed—the bandages, the monitors. She looks so fragile. It is hard to believe that she grew into the woman I arrived here with, and all that it took was time.

Jules's gaze travels to the end of the bed, where her father is praying. He is younger than when we last saw him—at a guess,

I would say late thirties. Almost the same age that Jules herself is now.

"Wait here," says Jules. Then she steps into the room, careful to stand where a monitor blocks her face, presumably so that she cannot be recognized by her younger self.

"Hello, Dad," she whispers as she hands him my book, disguised as a Bible.

"It's impossible," says her father, face-to-face with his daughter as a grown woman. He glances back at the teenage Jules, double-checking, then says it again. "Impossible."

"It's safe to come in now," Jules says to me. "She's asleep. She won't wake until morning."

"How do you know?" I ask from the doorway.

"Because I remember," says Jules. Then she turns to her father, who is still in a state of wide-eyed shock. "Here, let me hold onto that so you don't drop it."

Shaking his head in disbelief, Jules's father dutifully hands the book back. Jules tucks it into her sling. Then, without warning, she clamps a spare cuff around his wrist—

* * *

—and we are now in the Rocky Mountains; the Kimberley; Moscow, back when the Kremlin was still made of wood. But I am not watching the landscape change like a slideshow—I am watching Jules's father, Lucian. He grabs his head, screaming in pain. Of course, there is no one to hear it. Every moment we jump to is empty of people, except for us three.

"What is wrong with him?" I yell as we travel from Niagara Falls to the Sahara Desert in a matter of seconds.

Jules does not answer.

"Why do we keep jumping?" I ask in a panic, worried there has been a malfunction.

"To distract him from the pain," says Jules as we jump through farmlands in ancient Egypt. She gently rests a hand on her father's shoulder. "It's okay. The worst will pass soon."

Jules is correct. After a few minutes—and multiple continents, not to mention centuries—her father stops screaming. He slowly rights himself, except he is different somehow. There is emptiness to his expression—a *boredom*, almost—as he gazes upon Atlantis sinking, then Stonehenge under construction.

"It's done," says Jules, almost a whisper. She grabs the cuff around her wrist again, the flicking through centuries stops—

* * *

—and we are back in the hospital room, in the same moment we just left. Sixteen-year-old Jules is still wrapped in bandages, fast asleep on the bed.

The older Jules solemnly hands her father my book again, hidden inside the dust jacket of a Bible.

"It doesn't matter what I say right now," she says quietly. "We've run every scenario, and the words that I use don't matter. That first jump is what did it. A tiny aneurysm. Something in your brain was just . . . *damaged*."

And then, almost to herself, Jules adds, "Time can break."

That is what Frogs used to say—he even said it right before the "wake Romeo" mission. I always put it down to quirky AI humor. That he meant *time itself* could break like a teapot if we—the Deadenders—were not sufficiently careful. Not that time had the *power* to break . . . including things like a mind. Or a heart. Or, frankly, a world.

Jules is watching her father, who is focused on my book—*Wuthering Heights,* disguised as a Bible. He opens it to the first page with "H. ELLIS" written in the corner and starts muttering, "Hell is?" He is reading it wrong. Not realizing it is my name—Heathcliff Ellis—instead of a question. But a name, a question? It matters not. His brain is clearly grasping for something, anything.

"It's like Shakespeare said: *Hell is empty, and all the devils are here,*" says Jules. "Only it's all twisted now. Hell is . . . empty, and all the devils are *here.*" She tenderly touches the side of her father's head. "It was nine years before Frogs could operate. Dad spent nine years in hell because of this moment."

Jules's father stares at her blankly . . . and then, briefly, he appears to focus. He gazes at her intently. Then he strokes her hair, strokes her face.

"Hell is . . ." he says again, like he is trying to say more, yet cannot.

Jules answers him with a gentle, "I love you."

And then something seems to dawn on her.

"Hell is . . . *I love you,*" says Jules again to her father. "In the foyer that day. When you noticed my hair—short, like you're seeing it now—you said, '*Hell is . . . I love you.*' You touched my hair and then my face, like you did just now. I thought you were adding insult to injury. But you were replaying this moment between us. Recalling it as best as your damaged brain would let you."

Tears are streaming down Jules's face, although her father is oblivious. He is looking at my book, muttering, "Hell is . . ."

"You heard it," says Jules, managing a smile through the tears. "You heard my 'I love you.'"

She turns to me, opting to explain. "He struggled to remember. After the operation, Dad struggled to remember much of the in-between years. There were pages missing from his life completely."

Like the Travelers—how they jump over time.

"I never knew what manner of hell he was stuck in for those nine years," says Jules.

Though he heard her "I love you." It reached him.

This feels very much like a private moment—an *important* moment. And yet Jules chose to have *me* here with her, not Romeo. It makes me wonder whether I was perhaps more than naught to her after all.

"Why did you bring me?" I ask, daring to hope. "Why did you want *me* here, by your side, for this moment?"

Silence.

"Your memories of these jumps helped us piece it together, years later," she says at last. "You're here now, because that's what happened."

I was a part of her puzzle, and naught more.

"That is bollocks." I turn the tricky hurt into something harder. "Your father's brain was damaged, ergo it *had* to happen? No, I do not accept that. The past is not entirely fixed— that is the whole *point* of the Deadenders. Saying it had to happen because it did happen is circular logic."

Hearing my own words, I realize I am a hypocrite. Because I argued the exact opposite, back at Number 11: *The die is cast*. I feel at sea . . . like I no longer know what the rules are.

Jules locks eyes with me, perhaps deciding how to answer.

Then she nods at her younger self, who is still unconscious on the bed.

"I thought that the nurse with short hair told my dad a secret. One that not even *I* knew in this moment. I thought *that's* what changed him. For years I believed that truth. And thinking that my own father might choose not to love me? That he could turn his back, like Lord Capulet did in my play? Well, some wounds run deep. So deep you don't even notice they're there, eating away at things, making you compensate."

And, staring at Jules, at the obvious pain in her, I understand.

Right before we jumped here, Jules's aunt reminded her that this terrible moment *had* to happen. That without it setting things in motion, everything unraveled. Though it was more than that. What happened to Jules's father did not simply shape future events or the timeline. *It shaped Jules herself.* Without this moment—without this pain—she would have been a different person.

"Heartbreak forms our character just as much as love does," I say quietly, thinking suddenly of Emily and her tragic story. And of *me*, for that matter—my mother, my past.

Jules gives a humorless laugh. As she reaches for the cuff around her wrist, she mutters, "You have *no* idea."

* * *

One moment we are in the hospital, the next we are returned to the Control Room. Someone solemnly dims the "hospital" window—a bright light going out. The Web is mostly dark now—almost every moment hit, according to plan.

Jules's eyes find her father in real time—he is standing by the far wall, side by side with Miranda.

She nods at him, presumably letting him know that it is done. Then her focus shifts, and she seems to sadden even further. I follow her line of sight to a man in his forties. He is standing against the far wall, hands thrust deep in his pockets, staring back at Jules with a look of unmistakable intensity.

That other man is me.

....

39

Jules

2083

ONE DAY AFTER WAKING ROMEO

It's midmorning and pissing down rain as I drop my bike into a clump of daffodils. The Montague mansion was always strictly out of bounds to me, so I've only ever been here one time. I don't have a clue how I'll get in to see Romeo. If this were fiction, I'd use a costume, like Shakespeare was prone to. But in real life, disguises won't fool anyone. Eventually, you can't even fool yourself.

Staring at the House of Montague now, I can't help thinking about my story. Damn, I wish I had my time again. I'd write about whether the world is *"to be or not to be"* instead of penning some tribute to love. I'd make it all some clever metaphor, comparing death to sleep. Because that's been the theme, right? And not just with Romeo—or with me, for that matter—but with everyone. We've all been closing our eyes, letting the world go.

Now it's time to wake up.

I take a few steps back, considering all the windows, trying to remember which one was his.

"Romeo? Romeo?" I shout louder than I thought I'd dare. "Where the *hell* is Romeo?"

I scour the ground for something hard to peg in his general direction.

"I had a feeling you'd come anyway," says a voice as I'm scuffing around in the mud. It's Romeo's mum—Trudy. She's standing in the doorway, watching me. For a moment, I imagine her as Lady Montague from my story—all formal robes and rich disapproval. Then I remember her as the impish teen from back at Number 11. Both quickly fade into the lines and slump of what's real.

My hair's short now, just like it was when she first met me, all those years in the past. I wait to see if realization dawns, but it doesn't. Aunt Miranda was right—sometimes people only see what they want to. Besides, you can forget a lot, courtesy of time. To Trudy, I'm not that girl from her past. I'm that girl from her *son's* past.

The one who ruined his life.

I try to think of the right thing to say—the right kind of demands that will convince her to let me speak to Romeo. It's wasted. Trudy smiles—almost kindly—and says, "You're soaking wet, dear. Please, come inside."

It couldn't possibly be *that* easy. The Montagues hate me—they moved heaven and earth to keep Romeo and me apart the last time. I was expecting barricades or lectures or threats. *Something*. Instead, Trudy leads me into the house as though I was never *really* her archenemy. I don't get it. Why is my almost-mother-in-law being . . . nice?

Inside, party preparations are in full swing. The Montagues are well-off in terms of supplies, and they haven't held back. It's going to be lovely—the kind of happy, joyous event you'd throw if the "welcome home" was actually heartfelt.

Trudy finds me a towel, then shows me through to the parlor. When she gets to the door she says, "Darling, there's someone here for you."

It's Romeo's dad: Claude Montague. I try to picture him as he was in his teens—the wild king, high on drugs. I can't. There's simply too much distance between them. Now I can only see him as Romeo's father. He seems older than how I remember him in that role. Less threatening, too, like time has sucked the fight right out of him. As if to prove it, he doesn't scream and shout when he sees me. He just exchanges a look with his wife, then calmly gets up and walks over. As he approaches, I try to imagine him as Lord Montague from my story—*mine enemy, my foe.* But I just can't get past the cardigan and slippers.

As he reaches me, I'm half expecting some late onset anger, but it never happens—he walks right on by. As he passes me, he puts his hand on my shoulder. Not a warning, or a threat. The gesture seems almost *paternal.* Sympathetic, even?

I don't get it. Why bring me here to Montague if the old man's going to leave without saying a word? And then I realize: *Romeo.* The high-backed chair that's facing away from me—Romeo's sitting in it. *He's* the one who Trudy brought me here to see. They're just giving me access to Romeo, no fight, no drama?

What is this, some kind of trick? Did they decide that, given how badly things turned out the last time, they should do *everything* differently?

Taking a deep breath, I head toward the chair. The back of it's too high for me to glimpse him, but I sense that he's there. Some things you just feel in your gut, like love. Or its absence.

It's not until I'm all the way around the chair that I get my first look at Romeo . . . *and he really is exactly the same.* It's the boy that I fell for and the boy from the hospital, all rolled into one. Two versions existing in the same time and place, with no discernible rift whatsoever. I don't know why that throws me, but it does. I guess I figured that, with Romeo awake, *something* would have changed.

He stares up at me. "Hi, Juliet." His voice is exactly the way I remember it—melodic, although now it's also raspy. Talking is clearly a strain for him, and the effort sends him coughing.

"Sorry," he says when the coughing subsides. "I haven't talked for so long." With that, he gives the same old smile— the one that always seemed for me and me alone.

He looks small in the huge leather chair. He's still hooked up to a drip, and there's a walking stick nearby.

"It'll take a few months for my muscles to build back up again," he says. "Until then, I'll be taking it slow."

"Smart move," I say, and then I do a double take. This is *definitely* the first conversation I've had with Romeo that involved the phrase "smart move." Or "taking it slow," for that matter.

Romeo is ogling me—running his eyes from top to bottom as if he's making an appraisal—the hair, the arm, the body. Not so long ago I'd be blushing, feeling embarrassed or apologetic.

Today, I'm neither. Instead I take the opportunity to do exactly the same—to openly stare at my once-was husband.

His skin is still pale and soft. His eyes are still the unnatural green that made the girls swoon, me included. He's still pretty, just like I remember. But at the same time, I no longer catch my breath when I gaze upon him. There's no hiding from the truth: my sixteen-year-old heart no longer speaks for me.

"I'm a modern medical miracle," says Romeo when the gawk-filled silence gets too much. "One of the nurses had been giving me this special herbal tea, which is what they think must have cured me. You should talk to her. Maybe she can help with . . . you know, your arm."

I give a small, dismissive nod, willing myself to hide that he's pissing me off. Was he always like this? Yes, I think that he must have been. I had my reasons for needing to remember him differently, but this all feels familiar.

Suddenly, I don't want to be here—I want to opt out and leave all this hard stuff behind me. I can't, though. Much as I hate to admit it, Mum's right—I have to grow up and buck up and whatever other peppy clichés there are that basically mean I can't keep running away. Besides, despite everything else, Romeo deserves to know.

On the rare occasions when I was brave enough to imagine this moment, there was always a major lead-in. We would have talked about missing one another so much that, when I dropped the bombshell, it changed nothing between us. He would just hold me and stroke my hair and tell me, "It'll all be okay." I didn't imagine going into it cold like this, but I have to get it over with. I have to say my piece and then leave this place—this boy—for good.

"That night when we were together in my room . . . ," I say, my voice trailing off. How pathetic am I that I can't even say it? I didn't even put it in my story—I merely alluded to it as "*the love-performing night*," of all the childish cop-outs.

There's a long, drawn-out silence.

"I got pregnant," I finally say. "I didn't know it when I went to the crypt that night. When . . ." I leave that part unsaid. "The nurses didn't realize until after the third operation. By that point, they'd already pumped me full of every kind of drug to keep me breathing." I try to keep my voice clinical. "They said it was a miracle the baby wasn't gone already, but that if it survived, it would be . . . *different*." At the mention of "different," Romeo's eyes automatically travel to my arm—the numb one. I try to ignore it.

"Mum, Dad, and Aunt Miranda kept it a secret. I basically stayed in my room for a whole year. People thought I was grieving," I continue. "Or they thought my parents had locked me up because I was out of control."

I'm not looking at Romeo anymore—I'm focusing on his shoes. Those lovely loafers. I'm being a coward—I should be looking him in the eyes for this next part. When I forced myself to imagine how this moment would play out, we were always eye to eye. And he was always holding my hand for comfort. He'd encourage me to keep talking with gentle, whispered "Go on's" and cheesy platitudes. His eyes would well with tears as I revealed what I lost. What we lost. The magnitude of what could have been.

In the real-life moment, it's not like that at all. When I force myself to look at Romeo, he's not crying, and the only person who's holding my hand is me—the right gripping the left so that it doesn't dangle. I can't see his dry eyes without getting angry. I have to look away.

"A boy." I sit down on the chair next to Romeo's. "Three minutes—that's how long he lived. I never got to see him or hold him." Trying not to cry is a total lost cause at this point— it's all I can do to keep pushing my words through the sobs.

When I finally pull myself together, I'm nervous. For years when I played this moment in my head, it was always Romeo's reaction that scared me. I was terrified that he'd blame me or hate me somehow. Now it's the opposite. Now I'm scared that I'll blame *him* and hate *him* for it. *Despise* him for it, with as much heat as I once thought I loved him.

Eventually I glance up, and Romeo's staring at me. He's still not crying; he's wearing the same sweet expression that always enticed me. The same angelic face that I was once so sure was heaven-sent. He takes my hand, but he chooses the wrong one. It flops in his grip, all heavy. He's embarrassed or revolted— both, I think. He lets it go, and my arm falls right back into me like a pound of flesh.

Romeo tries to fix the awkwardness by squeezing my knee. It doesn't work—the gesture's too juvenile, too pal-like for this moment.

"I know," he says, his hand still resting on my knee. "Your mum told my mum, and she told me. It was probably for the best. We were young, Juliet. Young and impulsive. But we've got another chance now."

His eyes wander down to my chest, but it hardly even registers. I'm numb. I'm in shock. I'm . . . I don't know what I am. I told Romeo that his son died, and he said it was *probably for the best*? A child—*our child*—died because of what we did, because of our choices, and all he cares about is that *we* have a second chance? Not our baby, just *us*?

"It's not our fault," he adds with total calm, like he wouldn't even *dream* of beating himself up over it.

His eyes are still too low. My T-shirt's wet from the rain—it's sticking to my skin. I can't tell if he's straining to see the scar or my breasts; both are new since he last saw me. Whatever he's thinking, it's not about our son. It's not about what I just told him. Who *is* this boy that I see before me? Who is this sleazy, selfish—

And then I remember. *This is Romeo.*

All at once, my mind is filling with bits and pieces that I had to write a whole make-believe story just to gloss over. How he was busy telling Rosaline that he loved her *one night* before we got together at that party. How I cried on his shoulder about Tybalt dying and, somehow, he parlayed my grief into a make-out session. How he always played the victim and blamed others for everything. How he was forever talking up how great he was. How he told me that he loved me, over and over, after only a couple of hours. How the whole marriage thing came about after I told him I wanted to wait. How the drugs were *his* idea.

He didn't force me into anything. They were *my* choices. *I* did those things. I was there, in the thick of it, loving every moment—for the most part. But there was a reason the Romeo in my story was so perfectly romantic—*I was compensating.*

I realize I'm not in love with Romeo anymore. Honestly, I wonder if perhaps I *never* was.

"Your eyes are like dark stars," says Romeo, which is sweet enough. Only, he's said it before. He said it to me two years ago, when he came to my balcony. I thought those words had occurred to him on the spot, right then and there. That they were *inspired* by me. No, it was just a line. Just a lie.

He reaches out for me—for the wet T-shirt part of me. I take his hand in mine, like I dreamed of doing so often, and I squeeze like I used to at the hospital. But this time I *keep* squeezing. I squeeze hard. My right hand is unusually strong—again, *from compensating*. For a moment he's not put off—he must think this is heading in an interesting direction. I squeeze even tighter—crushing his hand, aiming to break bone.

"That hurts!" he squeals, pulling his hand back. He's humiliated, and if memory serves correctly—if memory *finally* serves correctly—humiliation makes him angry. Good. Angry is better. Angry, I can get on board with.

Romeo's eyes narrow.

"Tut, tut," he says slowly as he rubs his hand. "That's hardly any way to treat *the prince of your heart.*"

The lost note. *That's what I called him in the note.*

"You read it?" I can hardly breathe.

"*Romeo, prince of my heart. Let's run away together,*" he says, mimicking my voice, mocking me. "Man, I laughed so hard."

"But . . . but the note went missing. When they found us in the crypt, it wasn't there."

Romeo shrugs. "I left to take a leak. When I came back, the note was gone."

I thought Romeo hadn't seen my note. I thought he genuinely believed that we couldn't be together. He'd told me that he couldn't live without me. He'd said it over and over, right from our very first kiss. When I saw his seemingly lifeless body in the crypt that night, I thought . . .

"And then what happened?" I ask. I need the truth.

"I was bored. I got high."

An overdose. *Not* intentional. It was never a *pair* of star-cross'd lovers.

It was only me.

Romeo is staring now, staring with a kind of detached interest. I've seen this coolness in him before, but only in glimpses.

"You tried to kill yourself because you thought I was dead."

He doesn't say it with concern. Romeo, O Romeo—so much charisma, so much charm, so little empathy. Not even back then, when we were together. Not even over Tybalt being dead, and me in a downward spiral.

"It wasn't just about you," I say honestly. "It was about a lot of things."

"No, it was because of me."

Seriously? He figures he knows my truth better than I do? Why the hell did I waste my time on this boy, year after miserable year?

But deep down, I know. I know exactly what it was that kept me showing up at his bedside. *Guilt*. I didn't write poems and sonnets and a whole glorified version of events for *him*. I was just desperately trying to make it mean something, because if it didn't, then my baby died for nothing. If it wasn't some epic love story, then it was just a tragedy.

"It wasn't all about you."

"Sure. If you say so," he says with a mean little smile. Then under his breath he mutters, "Goddamn *crazy*." That's exactly what he used to say about Rosaline after they broke up two years ago. Behind her back, it was suddenly all, *she's crazy, she's wrong*

in the head. Later, when Paris and Laurence started hurling that word at me too, they were parroting their master.

But I don't let it get to me this time—not anymore. Instead, I mull over the right thing to say in this moment, given all the sticky past between us. In the end I settle on, "Good-bye, Romeo."

He doesn't try to stop me or act like the rash seventeen-year-old that I once knew. He just nods his head in a way that's subtle and restrained and so *not* like the old Romeo, that hell— maybe he *has* changed. Maybe we both have. Thinking about our parents, maybe we *all* have.

And just like that, we're done.

Our tragic little story is finally curtains.

ACT V

....

40

Ellis

2107

He is on the other side of the Control Room—*me, in my forties*. I study him—gray T-shirt, gray flecks in his hair. He looks fit and strong. His expression, on the other hand, is anything but fine. He is staring at Jules, and in his face, I see it—*love*.

Jules married Romeo, yet decades later I still love her.

"This next loose end is yours alone to handle," says Jules, suddenly avoiding eye contact. I have a million questions, but there is no time. She grabs the cuff around her wrist—

* * *

—and I am suddenly standing in a dingy alley that smells of fish. The older Jules is nowhere to be seen. Out on the street, there is a painted lady trying to catch the eye of a dandy in a top hat. There are horses and carts, a chimney sweep and his climbing boy. This is London in the 1800s. More specifically, it is the alley that intersects with Dorset Street, not more than a block from where I was born. This is right near where the kind Mr. Eyre saw me living on the streets and took pity.

A few meters away, I see them. It is Emily and me, both six years old. I am in a moment from my own past, and I know instantly *which* moment. This is when I got spooked. The idea of a new life on the moors was suddenly terrifying, so when Mr. Eyre stopped the cart, I snuck off. Emily caught up to me in this alley and somehow convinced me to stay.

As I'm watching the scene from my own past play out right in front of me, I realize this is my chance. When I fantasized about saving Emily from the pain that I caused her, it was by altering a moment like this one. By changing events so that our lives were never entwined. This is clearly the time for it. But should I? *Could* I, despite the untold ripple effects on the timeline? It goes against everything I have been taught as a Deadender.

I hesitate a moment too long, and Emily sees me. The incongruous clothes, the way that I am clearly staring. *The fact that there are two of me, at different ages.* She is scared. My poor little Emily, already with such a vivid imagination—what in the world must she be thinking? I open my mouth to try to fix what I have done, but it is too late—

* * *

—I am gone, jumped in time and space again. Now I am atop that cliff by the ocean, from all those years ago. The exact place where I fell and *should* have died. I look down at the breaking waves, trying to make sense of what just happened. I thought I knew everything about that alleyway crossroads moment back when I was six years old. I remembered every word that Emily said to me, yet I had somehow forgotten that her words were not what swayed me. It was not anything she *said* that convinced me to go with her and Mr. Eyre to the moors and leave my street urchin life behind me. It was the fact that she was scared. I could tell she was scared—*that* is why I returned to the cart and traded in my old life for a new one. It had naught to do with Emily's powers of persuasion.

It was not until years later that Emily admitted she thought she had seen a ghost that day. A strange disappearing man in the alley behind us, which is what had her quaking. There is symmetry in that, I suppose. That just like in her book, a ghost is what set it all in motion. Only, it was not really a ghost at all—the stranger was *me.*

"*Time brought resignation, and a melancholy sweeter than common joy,*" I say to the ocean below as a line from Emily's heartbreak book springs to mind.

There is a small thud. *I am not alone.*

I turn. Emily is standing behind me—she has clearly been here the whole time. At a guess, I would say she is about thirteen years old, the age she was when I fell off the cliff and—as far as *she* knew—drowned. She is wearing her Sunday best and bonnet, both dyed black. She is in mourning for me.

The thud I heard was a notebook dropping from her hand to the rocks upon which we are standing. Her eyes are rimmed red and her cheeks are wet—she has been crying. There are no tears at present, though. Now she is staring at me in wide-eyed, absolute shock. I open my mouth to say something, to try to explain. Yet there is no time. I am gone again—

* * *

—The world resolves around me, and I find myself inside a milliner's shop. Bonnets and top hats are being made by hand with hat blocks instead of machinery. I quickly duck behind a bolt of cloth so that I shall not be seen. Peering out the window, I am clearly in London during the gaslight era. Judging by the fashion, it is maybe the 1830s in the grand part of town. I see girls in white with colored aprons, boys in knee-length tunics, men in frock coats and full-length trousers, women in belted day dresses. Their florid clothes suddenly seem so elaborate in contrast to the plain black T-shirt and jeans that I am wearing.

I stare longingly at a happy family that is walking down the street outside . . . and then there she is, walking in the other direction. It is Emily, older than I have ever seen her. She is at least sixteen. She spies me through the glass, although the moment our eyes meet, everything changes—

* * *

—I am suddenly back on the moors that once were home. It is a stormy day; dark clouds gather overhead. I can smell the heather and the gorse, cold but fresh compared to the stink of London Town. This was Emily's and my rough yet vital world. I turn my head and sure enough, I see her. Standing alone across the moors, she looks to be about the same age as I am—

nineteen. In her typical fashion, she is ignoring the gathering storm. Instead of finding shelter, she has taken her bonnet off, letting the wind whip hair about her face. The bottom of her skirts are wet from the mud of the moors, not that she ever cared about such matters.

Emily pivots and sees me. A beat, then she picks up her skirts and starts running.

"Heathcliff!" she cries, her voice echoing across the rugged landscape. It is like a scene from her book, except that the girl is Emily herself, not some fictional creation. I start running toward her. I open my mouth to call out her name—

* * *

—and I almost crash into a pile of upturned cobblestones. Now I am in the village of Haworth, standing in front of the house that Emily grew up in. Through the upstairs window I can see her, writing by candlelight. She is older yet again—perhaps mid-twenties. Something catches her attention. She looks down and sees me—

* * *

—Things shift and I am at the edge of a beautiful park. There is a wooden bench with a woman sitting alone on it. Her back is to me, but the pale skin, the brown hair poking out from underneath the bonnet . . . it can only be one person.

"Emily," I whisper.

I hear a tiny intake of breath, but there is no other reaction.

Emily stays perfectly still on the park bench, keeping her back to me.

"I so very much hoped that you would find me again someday," she says evenly. "But if I turn around, you will disappear, will you not? That does seem to be the pattern."

She knows. She knows that it is me standing behind her, here in the 1800s.

"The alleyway. The cliff by the ocean. The milliner's shop. Out on the moors. Beneath my window," she lists. "Over and through the years—my whole life—you have been with me, even after you were gone."

For me, those jumps only just happened. Yet for Emily, I have been appearing like a constant throughout her life. It is somehow reassuring.

"You were there the whole . . . *time*," she adds, putting an obvious emphasis on the last word.

It finally dawns on me. "You knew," I say, incredulous. "All the lines that you put in your book. '*How many years do you mean to live after I have gone*' and '*time stagnates here . . .*' you knew. You knew that I had become a time traveler."

"I had other theories at first, but yes—that is what I settled on."

Another bulb lights up in my head. "Your book. You wrote it, *knowing* I would read it?"

I can feel her smile from here. "I *hoped* you would, yes."

"But the Heathcliff in your story—you made him the most ruinous version of me." I still do not understand why, and it has tormented me so.

She sighs. "I wanted to set you free. To *release* you. My whole life you have been appearing, haunting me. I wanted to show you what happens when you do not let go."

Though after my conversation with Jules, I have to wonder. Was it more than just that? Emily knew the gentler side of me. She loved me for it, I think. Yet in her book, such traits were mocked in a man.

"Why portray the feminine as weak?"

"Ah, yes," says Emily. "I made that a theme *precisely* so that readers might think on the matter. That they might challenge the thesis, I hope."

By "readers," I suspect she means me; that *I* might challenge it.

And then I ask the question that has plagued me for half a lifetime. "Did I ruin your life, Emily? Did loving me steal your happiness?"

A short, sharp bark of a laugh. "Ruin my life? Dearheart, you *gave* my life to me. I have had a whole, thrilling existence all because of you. Knowing that you somehow remained even after what happened on the cliff? It fueled my imagination. But for that spark, I fear my world would have been small, inside and out. Because of you I have lived . . . *fully*."

As if on cue, Emily coughs into a handkerchief.

"Now this is good-bye," she says, without any hint of sadness.

"No. Your disease—in the future, they cure it. If I can just get you to the future—"

"Dearheart, the future is not the answer," says Emily softly, speaking to a deeper truth, like she always did. "Besides, it is my time."

My instinct is to resist. I want to fight it. I want to rail against the loss, like the Heathcliff of her story. But *because* of Emily, I know better. No, because of Emily, I *am* better.

And perhaps *that* is what love is.

So instead of focusing on the future or on the past, I stay in the moment. I appreciate the precious "now" that I have been given. And here in my present, I pluck up the courage to speak my greatest shame.

"On the cliff that day," I say slowly, carefully. "I know that I could not say the words, but . . ." my voice trails off. On the third page of her novel, Emily wrote the line "*I never told my love.*" She was quoting Shakespeare, yet those words were quite clearly for me.

"Hush," says Emily gently. "I understood. Your mother said that she loved you, and then left. *Of course* I understood."

She reaches up and touches something that is hanging around her neck. It is a piece of wood on a strip of leather—the one that she made for me all those years ago.

"You kept it," I whisper.

"Close to my heart, at all *times,*" says Emily, clearly enjoying the play on words. Then she adds, "You have to let go of the past and let go of the pain . . . and let go of me, too. You have to let love in again."

I shake my head. The only girl I could imagine that with has already chosen another. She married and lived happily ever after. Mine was a love . . . unrequited.

"Promise me," says Emily when I fail to answer. "Do you promise me that you will let yourself love again? That you will trust it?"

"Of course," I say—a lie, though it shall not matter. And

then I reach over and lightly stroke her cheek with my finger. It is the most intimate we have ever been, despite worlds of tenderness between us. But love is what happens on the inside; there need not be even a touch to steal a heart.

I feel the wetness of her tears on my fingers.

"Good-bye, Heathcliff Ellis," she says, barely a whisper.

"Good-bye, Emily Brontë."

Emily turns her head toward me. Our eyes meet for one final moment. Then, like a ghost in time, I am gone.

Our story, sweet as it was, is over.

....

41

Jules

2083

ONE DAY AFTER WAKING ROMEO

After I leave Romeo's house, I ride around in the rain, going aimlessly up and down streets that are practically empty. Everywhere I look, there are tributes to all our yesterdays—the bank where Mrs. Dorian keeps our accounts, even though money's pointless. The police station that's manned 24/7 despite there being no real cops and no real crimes. A letterbox carefully wiped clean of bird shit, even though there's no mail. Our whole Settlement's facing the wrong direction—backward, not forward. Everyone's hanging onto the past with all their hearts, too afraid to move on . . . just like I was.

But good-bye has to happen eventually.

First things first, I ride out to the old theater. I drop my bike near the steps, though I don't go inside. I don't feel the need to risk my life, or to test whether forces above determine my fate. I simply stand on the road, staring at the place where Tybalt died. And then I do something that's badly overdue. I let myself remember my cousin.

I picture him as a kid—aged five, wearing red overalls—my very first memory of us playing together. Looking to my right, I see him at age nine—the day we made the rocket-ship fort. And as I slowly turn, like a hand on a clock, he keeps appearing in my mind: Tybalt at every age, exactly how he was, right by my side, my whole entire life.

And then, finally, I face the *last* Tybalt—eighteen years old.

Tybalt's death really was a sinking pebble, with ripple effects aplenty. It was the messy thread of my not-so-delicate unraveling. Because I didn't deal with it. And so death became this unspoken theme in me—one that I refused to think about or talk about. But it wasn't a case of "rest in peace." In my heart, there was a kind of fighting. There was *noise* inside me.

Now the rest is silence.

I stare at the eighteen-year-old Tybalt—a life cut short like an unfinished stanza, all jagged and lonely. As I watch, the kid in red overalls reaches up and takes his hand. Then they *all* join hands—Tybalt at every age, as he lives in my mind, surrounding me always.

Time is non-linear. There's no beginning, no end.

A circle.

As I pick up my bike to leave, I remember the theater stage. The half-painted bird—a sparrow, never finished because of the Fall. *The fall of a sparrow* . . . And I decide, maybe I got it backward. Maybe it's not half painted after all. Maybe someone was painting *over* the sparrow when the world went to shit.

Maybe it's been whole all along, underneath the layers. Maybe what I was *really* seeing was the start of a fresh canvas.

I get back on my bike. Cold and wet, I do one last lap of the block. I know exactly where I'm going; I'm just taking my sweet time getting there. I figure I've been on my way for years now, so what's a few more minutes? What's a bit more time in the scheme of something like death?

But I end up at the crypt eventually.

After so much avoidance, it seems only fitting that I come here now. I don't hover at the threshold like I thought I might—action versus inaction again. I walk straight on into the shadows and the cold. When my eyes adjust, it's not the same as I remember—all of the tombs have been pushed to the sides. There's a big, open space in the middle, just like an empty heart. My eyes find the tomb where Romeo overdosed and I tried to end my life. That's not what kept me from this place. I avoided it because of its *proper* purpose—the fact that it's our family crypt. At least, I thought it was—turns out we were never *really* Capulets. But whatever's in a name, this is still where they put him. This is where they laid my son to rest.

I stand in the empty middle and slowly spin around again so that I'll face him at some point, wherever he is. I feel like I should say something, except nothing in the realm of "sorry" will ever come close. Instead, I tell him the truest thing I can think of: "I love you."

I've been a fool about so many things, but love is clearly the standout. I mean, all that obsessing and second-guessing about Romeo and me? Whether we had true love and whether it was real and how it measured up and what constituted perfect? And then, whatever had begun with Ellis . . .

All that fuss about *romance*. How did I miss the fact that I knew exactly what real love was the whole time? I knew the way it was constant and never dwindled or altered or faded with time because I'd had that in my heart for years. And all for a boy that I never met, never held, and who barely lived three minutes.

Eventually, I leave. I sit on the grass outside, take off my backpack, open it up, and retrieve the notebook. In my story, I made Juliet thirteen instead of sixteen. I wonder what it says about me that I felt like her choices were better suited to someone younger. And the fact that I made her fall in love on the spot, without that critical factor—time.

I wonder what *a lot* of it says about me.

I look back over at the crypt, where his little life is grounded with a sleep. Shakespeare's only son died young too—his name was Hamnet. But the Bard didn't write some tragic play to deal with the loss. No, that special privilege is mine, all mine.

I'd planned to just leave my story here, except it doesn't feel right that it's still not finished. Part of that's about my son and part of that's about me. Truth be told, I want *The Love Story of Juliet & Romeo* out of my head once and for all. I want to *end* the blasted thing.

And there, right there—*that's* my answer.

I flick through page after page. There's so much work and worry about how to construct a happy ending. So much agonizing about what would happen *after* that night in the crypt and how Act VI would play out. Well, no more. I find where the fifth act ends, and I rip out every page that comes after.

It's months and months of work—*years,* even. Draft after draft of how Romeo woke and the world turned to roses—all of it goes. I tear away the hospital years and the messy, bloody night they brought us both back from the brink. I don't stop until I've rewound to the moment we effectively died in the crypt, and that's where I end it. I can't help but smile because, truly, it's perfect. Our love *should* have died that night. It *would* have, too—it would have died a natural death, except for the fact that I was so hell-bent on reviving it.

Taking my notebook, I kneel at the threshold of the crypt. I close my eyes and imagine myself in full period costume one last time. Me as the idealized Juliet, the girl I've been hiding behind. Except I'm not *quite* her. Underneath the long white dress, I'm wearing my regular black combat boots. And after a moment, my arm falls down to my side, numb again. My hair is short again. The wound on my arm—the one that Ellis bandaged with such care—starts bleeding. Bright red blood, seeping through the fabric of the virginal dress.

The real me is finally overwriting the fantasy.

"This story is for you, my son," I say with perfect composure. "Deep down, I think it was always for you that I clung to the idyllic version. Because I needed to believe that you came from something that wasn't ordinary."

As more and more of the truth bleeds through, my composure starts to crack. There are tears and snot and sobs. I'm the opposite of a performer in a play. I am the messy draft before the rhyming couplets. I am the ugly pain inside the pretty words. I am *real* heartbreak, which has *never* been poetic.

The kind that, for so long, I couldn't let myself feel.

All remnants of Juliet are finally gone. The words and the frills have been stripped back until I'm nothing but me. The *whole* me.

I make one final amendment—crossing out the words "*Love Story*" and replacing them with "*Tragedy.*" Then I lay the notebook on the ground in front of the crypt as my raw yet honest self. The cover now reads: *The Tragedy of Juliet & Romeo.*

Puffy-eyed, I pick the backpack up off the grass. Only the zipper's undone, so Dad's Bible falls out. It opens to the first page, where "HELL IS" has been scrawled in the top corner. As always, it just hangs there without an answer. Perhaps *this* is where Dad got it from—the eternal question he's been wrapping his head around ever since.

"Hell is . . . ," I say to myself, reading the words aloud. Then, looking back at the crypt where my son was laid to rest, I finish the sentence the same way Dad did.

"Hell is . . . I love you."

And you're gone.

Staring at Dad's Bible, I can't help thinking about the moment it came into his possession. I'd just come out of my third operation and they thought I was still unconscious. I wasn't—I was watching Dad as he stood at the foot of my bed. I don't remember him being religious back then, though I'm sure he was praying. Praying for me, his darling girl, who may or may not pull through.

As I watched, a nurse came in and whispered something before handing him this Bible. Dad said, "It's impossible." I remember that quite clearly. He looked over at me, then back at the nurse, and then said it again: "Impossible."

I drifted off to sleep after that. When I woke, the closest thing that we had to a doctor told me I was pregnant. Dad wasn't surprised—the God-bothering nurse had clearly already told him about the shame I'd brought upon our family. Dad never spoke to me after that. Other than his "Hell is . . ." mantra, he never said another word. He handled his little girl trying to take her own life with aplomb, but her getting knocked up at age sixteen? Well, that was a bridge too far. *That's* what broke him.

I'm about to shut the Bible, then something about the "HELL IS" gets my attention—a dot. It's so faded and small it almost looks like a mistake, a speck of dirt, a spot of dust. I try to get the damned spot out, à la Lady Macbeth. But no. It's a definitive, deliberate dot. I need no reminder of how much can turn on the tiniest of things. That one small change really *can* mean everything.

I put my thumb over the "H." The words now read "ELL IS."

Ellis said his first name was Heathcliff—that Ellis was his last name. *Heathcliff Ellis.* The dot. The old-fashioned handwriting doesn't say "HELL IS," it says "H. ELLIS." It wasn't a question about the nature of hell, *it was a name.* The book I'm holding in my hands—*this actual book*—belonged to Ellis.

I take off the dust jacket and underneath, it's not a Bible. It's a copy of *Wuthering Heights.* Not a modernish copy, like the one I read, with its bright orange cover. This is old. I run my hand over the cover—soft leather. It's such an early edition that it's written under the pen name Ellis Bell, not Emily Brontë.

This is the book that Ellis inspired.

I flick through the pages, trying to recall the story. It's been years since I read it, so I only remember bits and pieces. Vague recollections of a young man, all wild passion and hell-bent on destruction—masculine in the extreme. That's not the Ellis I knew. It wasn't the truth of him any more than I was the Juliet in my love story.

But no—it doesn't make sense. The nurse gave this book to Dad *long* before Ellis ever showed up here. What the *hell is* going on?

Chapter after chapter. Nothing, nothing, nothing . . . until I get to the very end. There's a note written straight onto one of the blank last pages. I know who wrote it. I recognize the handwriting.

Mine.

. . . .

42

Ellis

2107

"Why did you send me to her?" I burst out, unable to keep the emotion from my voice. I am back in the Control Room now, though my good-bye with Emily is still fresh, still raw. "Why did you send me to moments in her life?"

No answer.

I glance across at the "me" in my forties. He clearly loves Jules, yet she married another. It reminds me of Emily's book—fierce pain, tragic ending.

"Well?" I demand.

"You inspired *Wuthering Heights*," says Jules eventually. "It was *for* you. If I didn't send you back, the book would never have been written. The timeline would have changed."

"So?"

"*Wuthering Heights* is important," she says. "Removing its

existence would have impacted the Deadenders, and all that we're trying to achieve."

She means her—that it would have impacted *her*, and Romeo.

"Wonderful." I do not even bother trying to keep the bitterness from my voice. "So was *every* aspect of my life manipulated by you? By you and *your* love story?"

Jules does not reply—clearly a yes, then. She is avoiding eye contact too. She might be older, and she might have beaten the habit of pinching her arm when under stress, yet I still know how to read her.

"There is something you are leaving out," I realize.

"Ellis, my love story . . ." Jules does not finish that sentence. Instead, she says, "Follow me," and leads me out of the Control Room. I fall into step as she programs something into the cuff on her wrist—

* * *

—and then we are somewhere else entirely. Jules does not even break her stride, but I halt in my tracks so fast that I almost trip. Where *are* we? There is a putting green with fake grass and a Coke vending machine that is lit up and appears to be working. There is a banana lounge, a foosball table, and a jukebox. Above us there are stars, yet the smell is wrong. It is musty and metallic, like a confined space, as opposed to beneath the night's sky.

"What *is* this place?" I am thoroughly confused.

"Underground," says Jules. "We needed somewhere soundproof and free of interruptions."

I take a closer look: The stars in the sky are not real. They are some kind of light, but not akin to anything I have ever seen before. I know my history. In my line of work, it is rather a given. I am fairly sure the technology that I am currently eyeing does not exist in the timeline.

I hurry to catch up with Jules—she is walking toward an old train that is rusted dead on its tracks. Jules did not just mean underground in general, I realize—this is *the* London Underground. A whole little world has been created here in an abandoned Tube stop.

Jules enters the nearest train carriage, and I dutifully follow. The inside has been gutted and repurposed to function as some kind of home. It is filled with curios from across the ages. There are comics, 1950s TV sets, cassette tapes. There is even old electrical equipment rigged up to function again.

The walls are covered in mathematical formulas, historical quotes, photos of how pods ruined the world, and posters—Sex Pistols, the Cure, the Rolling Stones. I notice a pair of blood-soaked pajamas balled up on the floor, then I see something even more perturbing. There is a bank of monitors in the far corner. Only one of them is switched on, but it is showing a very familiar image: *the bus in the wasteland.*

"What the blazes is going on?!"

"I'll let *him* explain," says Jules. With that, she leaves the train carriage.

"*Who?*" I call after her.

"Hello, Ellis," says a voice from behind me.

I turn, and there he is—one dark eye, one green. It is the man who built Frogs and created the Deadenders. *Jules and*

Romeo's son. Only, he is younger than when I fell off the cliff and he saved my life—mid-twenties as opposed to late fifties. I only saw him for a short while that fateful day—just long enough for him to pull me out of the freezing water, inject the transmitter, and leave me on the bus in the wasteland. He spoke not a single word to me, though I shall never forget that face.

The man flicks a hidden switch and the other TV monitors light up. Dozens and dozens of them . . . and all are showing the bus. Hidden surveillance cameras, trained on the bus from every angle. Some of the monitors show the interior—our bunks, the ugly plaid couch. Some show the outside—the wash drying on the clothesline. One of the monitors even shows the mess where Frogs's mainframe was ripped out so that it could be stuffed into Beth's purse.

I look at the man with absolute confusion.

"That doesn't explain it? Huh, I thought that would explain it. Hang on a second." He picks up a microphone headset and speaks into it.

HOW ABOUT NOW?

His voice sounds mechanical. *Exactly* like Frogs.

It does not need saying, but I say it regardless. "You are Frogs."

He inclines his head. "It's a nickname my grandma gave me."

I look from him back to the monitors. "Frogs was never a machine." It all sinks in. "The voice on the bus. It was always . . . you?"

He sighs and rubs the back of his neck. "I tried to do it differently. To find paths that didn't mean I had to leave you on that bus for so many years with me keeping the truth from you.

But none of them worked. There was only one delicate thread. One chance. One tiny, fragile sequence of events that led to a future. It *had* to be this way."

"Why?" is all I can manage. My hands clench, and a sharp pain builds in my head.

"Fate. Chance. A confluence of statistical probability." The young man with the mismatched eyes—*Frogs*—shrugs. "All I know is there will be over four trillion meaningful options when you fall off the cliff and I jump you out of the water. And only five that lead us this far."

"*When* I fall off the cliff?"

"For you it's in the past, but for me it hasn't happened yet," he explains. "I won't go back in time and save your life for decades."

"How do you know all of this?" I ask. "These *probabilities, options . . .*"

"I am . . . unique," he says with a shy smile.

Frogs is a man, not a machine. I feel like my head is going to explode.

"But the circuitry in the backpack. The thing Beth crushed at the department store—"

"Just a voice recorder. I've been here in this room the whole time."

"Did something actually go wrong on the Romeo mission? Did you ever even lose contact with me?" I need to know the truth.

A pause. Then: "No."

"*Why?*" I demand. "What was the point?"

"Time," Frogs says quietly. "You needed time to fall in love with my mother."

I reel at this revelation. He *wanted* me to start falling in love with Jules? For me to have a glimpse of the possibility of love, and then lose it? The one thing I feared most, he *engineered* to happen.

It is too much to take in. I sit on the bed and run my fingers through my hair, struggling to process.

TIME TO BUCK UP, SOLDIER

Frogs says it through the microphone, so his voice sounds familiar. I glare at him. He puts the microphone down and, in his normal human voice, mutters a sheepish, "Sorry. Too soon?"

....

43

Jules

2083

ONE DAY AFTER WAKING ROMEO

Storming into the house, I pass Dad and Aunt Miranda—she's reading to him by the fire, just like she used to read to Tybalt and me. Mum's in the back room when I find her. The page that I ripped from *Wuthering Heights* is balled up tight in my hand, and I'm shaking, but not from the cold.

Mum takes one look at me and sighs. "I tried to warn you it wouldn't go well. That he wasn't how you remembered him."

She thinks this is about Romeo—that I'm crying over *him*.

"What happened to *my son*?" I demand, no lead-in whatsoever. Mum's face drops, the fake concern gone in an instant.

"How did you find out?" she says at last. I can't answer that question. I can't explain about a note written in the back of Dad's Bible, which was never really a Bible. A note written by me, but not yet. A note that said, *Ask Mum what actually happened to William.*

Instead, I sniff up the snot. "*Tell* me!"

"You weren't ready to be a mother," she says, tears starting to stream down her face. "You'd tried to end your life. And after that, in the months when you were pregnant, you were still recovering. I was worried you couldn't handle it. I was worried . . ." Her voice trails off, implying so many things.

"She couldn't bear the whips and scorns of time, so she took the easy way out?" I repeat Mum's words from back then. "You weren't worried, you were angry. You *blamed* me."

"I blamed *myself*," Mum says. "And yes, I didn't handle it perfectly, or say the right thing at the time. *Of course* it's not taking the easy way out. But I was *scared*. I wanted to help you. I wanted to fix things. So I . . ."

I'm numb. Inside my head I'm screaming, *What have you done? What have you done?* But I remain silent. I make *her* keep talking. Make her say it.

"I'm sorry that you never got to see him," says Mum, wiping at her face without much success. "I thought it would be for the best. That if you got to hold him, you'd never let him go."

I give her nothing—not a comfort, not a word.

"Come with me." She reaches out to take my hand. I snatch it away; I won't let her touch me. But I follow as she leads me outside, back the way I've just come.

Back to the crypt.

My story's still on the threshold. In order to enter the darkness, I literally have to step on it. Once, I would have appreciated the metaphor of that. Not anymore.

With the coffins all pushed back against the walls, the middle of the crypt is nothingness. And that's where Mum stands—right in the empty heart of it.

"It was hidden over there, behind the statues," she says.

"What was?" I ask, because clearly I'm meant to.

"Our pod."

A day ago I wouldn't have believed her—would never have believed that *we* had a pod. Now I know that the supposed "founding families" were really Travelers. Not to mention reckless teens, just like Romeo and me.

"Your father, Aunt Miranda, and I jumped here from 2056. When we decided to stay, we sabotaged two of the pods that we arrived in," she explains. *The rocket ships on the empty block.*

"But we kept one, just in case. All of the original families have at least one," says Mum, as if she can read my mind. The mantra about "staying put no matter what" was a lie. Those with the means were always hedging their bets.

"We hid them somewhere safe," continues Mum. "Ours was here because it had to be in a place that was usually clear of people." *A safe place to jump.*

Mum's silent for a moment, and then she says, "I brought him here, wrapped in a blanket. He was still covered in blood and goo. Only minutes old. Everything was ready. The space was cleared. The pod was right where I'm standing."

I gape.

"You weren't mature enough," she says, "and after what happened with Romeo, I was terrified you wouldn't cope. You needed a chance to heal." Mum stares me dead in the eyes.

"You needed *time* . . . and I could give it to you. *I could give you more time.*"

I don't believe it.

She put him in a pod.

She sent my son forward in time.

"William . . . he's *alive?*"

....

44

Ellis
2107

I was *meant* to fall in love with Jules. To love her and then lose her—that was all part of the morbid plan. Thrusting my hands deep into my pockets, I glance around the converted train carriage. But I am not taking stock of my surroundings, pursuant to Deadender training. I just cannot bring myself to look at Frogs—this feels like a betrayal.

As I'm turning away from him, my eyes stop on the notebook that is resting atop an old computer. It is Jules's story, except that the title has been changed—now it is called *The Tragedy of Romeo & Juliet*.

"Mum wrote it in the style of Shakespeare," says Frogs, following my line of sight. "I've been toying with the idea of trying to send it back. Add it to the canon, you know?"

It takes a moment for the implication of that to sink in.

"You want to pass off Jules's story as a play *actually* penned by Shakespeare?"

"It'd be incredible, right?" Frogs has a cheeky grin. "The idea that one of Shakespeare's plays was really written by a teenage girl from the future." Then he adds, "Mum says that one day she might finally finish her *second* story. So perhaps *two* plays, even."

"By all means, go ahead and manipulate Shakespeare," I say bitterly. *Hearts* apparently were not sacrosanct, so why the blazes not?

Frogs ignores my jibe. "Won't work. Too many ripples. Maybe in some parallel world I manage it, but I doubt it'll be in *this* one."

He continues, happily nattering away. "I think you'd like her next story, actually. It's about a prince this time. Starts with a ghost, just like in *Wuthering Heights*, and opens with the same first line as the myth of Narcissus."

I am no longer focused on Jules or her stories. I am staring at a concert poster that is taped above one of the monitors—it is advertising something called Woodstock. I notice the words "Creedence," "Cocker," and "Santana." They were the random things that Frogs said when he pretended that his circuitry was fried. Only, apparently, they were not random words at all— they were the names of musical acts.

It was all a performance.

"So was it *you* talking to me on the bus, pretending to be a computer? Or was it some *future* version of you?" I ask.

"Me. I won't save your life until I'm older, when you fall off that cliff. But the one who talked to you on the bus—that was me."

"When I was on the bus, you were never *not* there," I say. "How? How did you live your life and still talk to me the entire time?"

"I didn't," confesses Frogs. "While you and the others were on the bus, I stayed on this train, tracking your missions. Monitoring. Talking to you. Making sure you were all okay." He gestures at the wall of monitors.

I examine the footage of the empty bus.

"Were they in on it? Henry and Iggy and Beth?"

"No," says Frogs, looking uncomfortable. "Statistically, it had a higher chance of playing out correctly if none of you knew."

I take in my surroundings a little more closely—tiny kitchen, single bed, toilet, shower. It is effectively a bunker.

"I was on the bus for six years. You spent *six years* in this room, pretending to be a computer?"

"We've all had to make sacrifices," he says quietly.

I say naught.

"You're thinking about how we've both done the exact same time," says Frogs. "That for every day you were stuck on the bus, I was effectively trapped there too."

I am stunned. "How could you possibly know that?"

"Because you told me. You told me when I was ten." Frogs smiles, a little sadly. "I've known about this conversation for more than half my life."

Shaking my head, I say, "But I did not *know* you when you were ten."

"Actually, you did."

This fellow is disconnected from reality. I *definitely* did not.

"Other than now, I have only met you once in my life," I insist. "The day I fell off the cliff and you jumped me out of the water." *The day I was recruited as a Deadender. The day I was meant to die.*

The corner of his mouth twitches. "Remember how you once said that I practically raised you?"

It is so strange to hear him say that—right now he is only a handful of years older than I am. And yet it is true—those years on the bus, he *did* practically raise me.

"Well," continues Frogs, "you're about to repay the favor."

I just blink at him.

"Romeo's my *biological* father," he says, "but *you* are my dad."

It takes a moment for the hugeness of that to sink in. "I thought Jules *had* to be with Romeo."

Frogs laughs. "I barely even *know* Romeo." He sweeps his hand around the small room. "*You* created all of this. I built the technology, but *you* built the Deadenders. You and Mum did it together. My parents created the Deadenders. And my parents are Mum and *you*."

There is a long pause while I grapple with the concept. In the end, all I can manage is, "Why did you not tell me before?"

"Delicate thread," he says. And softly adds, "There were only a finite number of specific paths where ... *where it all worked out*."

He is getting choked up.

"But why make me think that I could not be with Jules if we end up together?"

"Time," says Frogs, as though that explains all. "You were young—way too young. You both needed more time."

"We needed more time . . . *and we got it,*" I say, marveling at my reversal of fortune.

"Dead . . . certainty," says Frogs, somewhat woodenly.

I laugh, for the comment is clearly intended as ironic humor. Dead certainty. On the bus, that is what Frogs would say when something was *not* guaranteed.

....

45

Jules

2083

ONE DAY AFTER WAKING ROMEO

The crypt is deathly quiet. Mum doesn't answer, so I ask her again. "My son. *Is he alive?*"

She nods. "I set it for a year. I figured that you'd be ready by then. That you could handle it, that you'd have given up on the obsession. And sweetheart, you *were* obsessed. First with Romeo, and then with the baby. There was no . . . no *moderation*," she says. "And in that year, you didn't change—you just became obsessed with Romeo all over again. You visited him every day. You wrote fantasies about how *perfect* he was."

She read my story. Somehow, it doesn't surprise me.

"I came out here at the end of that first year," she says, gazing around the crypt. "I'd meant to bring him back to you. When the pod arrived, he was still minutes old. He wasn't crying. I was going to bring him to you, I honestly was. Except you were still so young. And you were so far from okay." Her eyes find mine again and I see tears welling in them. "Sweetheart, you spent all your time down at the hospital or writing that play of yours. You refused to make friends or do anything except moon over Romeo."

The silence is heavy.

"I should have brought him back to you," she says again, almost a whisper. "I really did mean to. But it was so easy to just push the button once more, sending him forward another year. Just one more year, until you were ready . . ."

Suddenly her constant mantra about me needing to grow up makes sense. She needed me to show that I was responsible. That I wasn't suicidal or reckless anymore. She needed me to prove that I was ready *to be a mother*.

Mum looks at me with a kind of raw desperation. I still give her nothing.

"He hasn't suffered," she says, suddenly talking fast, "not one bit. When he arrives, no time has passed for him. He hasn't missed you—he hasn't even had the chance to feel that you're gone."

But I've felt *him* gone.

I remember Mum's rule about the crypt being off-limits. It wasn't about what was buried here. It was about what was *alive* here. She couldn't have people wandering about in the crypt when the pod reappeared—everyone knows what happens when two things try to occupy the same space at the same time. So she made up a rule about staying away. Still, she crept in here herself on his birthday. It wasn't to pay her respects, like I'd thought; it was to send the pod—and my son—forward another twelve months.

"Please, you have to remember that you'd tried to kill yourself, and your father couldn't help me," says Mum, desperately trying to justify her actions. "Miranda was still reeling from losing Tybalt. There was no one else to ask, no one else to talk to. So I did what I thought was best. To protect you. I did it out of *love*, Juliet."

There it is, that word again. *Love*.

Only, her calling me Juliet? It doesn't feel like a slap in the face this time. It suddenly reminds me of being a kid, and her being "Mummy." Of the way she's always tried to protect me. *Don't climb too high. Don't talk to Travelers. Don't go beyond the Wall. Don't get involved with Romeo.*

Misguided, perhaps, but it was always to protect me. And then I realize . . . is it possible that rather *a lot* of what Mum's done lately has been about protecting me? All her silly "keeping up appearances" antics—was it really for her benefit, or for mine? For some reason, my mind goes to this story from Greek mythology, about how Persephone gets stuck in hell after picking a narcissus. How her mother never gives up on her . . .

And I think about the teenage Mum, in the past. The one who was tough and brave and totally unflinching. Who risked her life to protect her sister. Who would have perhaps done *anything* for the people in her heart.

Then I remember what Mum was like before everything happened with Romeo. She never used to give a crap what people thought. She never used to seem so tired and defeated either. And I wonder: Is it possible that all the polite morning-tea crap and social schmoozing was for me all along? So that one day I might find a place in this ever-shrinking world, so that I wouldn't be the total social outcast I seemed hell-bent on making myself? Was she trying to smooth things over for me? I've been so focused on "Juliet and Romeo" that I never saw it—never saw anything else. Our love story was so goddamn bright in my mind that the rest of the world was in shadow.

"He's beautiful," says Mum, filling the silence. "One dark eye like yours, one light. The nurses said that the drugs they gave you to save your life would make him . . . different. But he's perfect. *Unique.*"

"The last time—it was set for a year again?" I croak. Mum nods.

William was born on the 28th of September. That gives me nine months. Nine months until I can finally hold him in my arms.

It's just a matter of time.

"When you meet him, you'll see that there's nothing a mother wouldn't do out of love for her child." Mum is openly crying again. "I hope that *then* you'll understand why I did what I did. That then you'll forgive me."

"You made me believe that my child was dead," I say, totally steady. I'm expecting Mum to defend herself—more justifications, explanations, the works.

Instead, she looks right at me and simply says, "Ditto."

46

Ellis

2107

"Here, let me show you something," says Frogs while I am still trying to process the fact that I am apparently *his father*. He clips a cuff around his wrist—it is thick, like the one that Jules was wearing.

"A *manual* cuff?" I ask—that is what she had called it.

Frogs nods. "When you were on the bus, I had to control your jumps. That's what *those* are for." He indicates the much thinner cuff of metal around my wrist. "Provided you were wearing one, I could move you in time and space using one of *these*." He holds up his wrist, displaying the thick cuff that is clamped around it. With his free hand, he grabs the cuff—

* * *

—and we are suddenly not in the underground train carriage anymore. We are both outside, beneath a sky that is threatening to storm. This is the Settlement again, yet I still cannot fathom how different it is from when I was first here, to wake Romeo. What was once a row of empty houses has been cleared to plant vegetables. They are living off the land, not off the past.

The buildings—they have integrated greenery. Vertical gardens, grass, and plants coexisting with the structure itself. Over by a well, I see the same solar panels that we had on the roof of the bus. Beyond the tree line, there are wind turbines too, and large pumps that I have never encountered before. I know not their purpose, though it appears to be connected to the soil?

"We've recruited over a hundred Deadenders now," says Frogs, "plus the people from the original Settlement, and a few that we found beyond the Wall. We've got skill sets from almost every single era of humankind."

Then, with a grin, "Your collective noun has become a bit of an ethos."

Family. A *family* of Deadenders.

I find myself staring at a young Chinese woman dressed in a tunic. She is showing a lad in slick, ultramodern clothes how to plant sweet potatoes. She seems to know a lot about farming. I am about to inquire as to crop yields when I am practically levelled by a collie barking with excitement. I kneel and give her a big, rough belly scratch, which is clearly how she likes it. I have always loved collies—my kind of dog.

As I am getting to my feet again, my gaze falls to a nearby grove. There is a willow growing aslant a brook, dangling its leaves over the glassy water. Some manner of technology is suspending a thin wall of water, shaped like a disk. The disk is facing the willow, catching what little there is of the sun. Jules's father is there, painting the reflections.

"He holds a mirror up to nature," says Frogs with obvious affection. "It's beautiful, don't you think?"

"Yes," I say honestly. The circles of light that Lucian paints have unexpected depth. It is reality, yet through a different filter. "Utterly extraordinary."

Only then do I notice the small device attached to Lucian's head, where the skull meets the spine. Back in the Control Room he was facing me, which is why I did not see it before. Returning my gaze to the painting, I recall the difficulty that Lucian had with his speech.

"He is not the same as before the aneurysm?"

Frogs shakes his head. "I made the device that he's wearing to help him communicate. I wanted to *ask* if he wanted my help. If he wanted me to try to return him to how he was. He didn't."

"With talent like that, perhaps it is no wonder."

"He made the choice *before* he started painting," clarifies Frogs. "And now he seems content using the device and continuing with physical therapy." Then, switching tones: "There is nothing either perfect or imperfect, but thinking makes it so."

And, in his regular voice: "Mum drilled that into me."

I remember how Jules struggled to see her own beauty—the way she referred to her arm as dead and the shyness about her scar.

"She has changed."

"So I'm told," says Frogs. "According to Mum, learning to love *herself* was at the heart of everything."

"Perhaps . . . perhaps we are *all* a work in progress," I say in earnest as the concept occurs to me. "Perhaps the capacity for change lives within *everyone*."

I am being heartfelt, yet Frogs grins. I suspect I know why.

"In the future I say that often, don't I?"

"Like there's no tomorrow!" says Frogs with an easy laugh.

His sense of humor—it is the same as it was on the bus. Our rapport is still there, I realize. My son, the young man who practically raised me; *we are already friends*.

Turning onto a new street, I notice supplies piled high. Box upon box of canned food and bright new clothes, their tags still on. Gas, batteries, make-up, high-heeled shoes—it all seems so incongruous against the backdrop of this eco-settlement. As I watch, a young Asian boy picks up a box of canned peaches, disappears, then reappears empty-handed. I give Frogs a questioning look.

"Sometimes it's the *mistakes* of one generation that prompt the next generation to act," he says cryptically. I am about to ask what he means when my eyes fall to a separate, much smaller pile: *books*. I see heavy tomes penned by all the greats, slimmer volumes on farming, several picture books of Danish castles, a stack on dealing with grief and trauma, plus the golden spines of encyclopedias.

"For the Supermarket," says Frogs. I have questions about this Supermarket, yet I do not ask them. For atop the nearest pile, I have spied it—Emily's novel. The cover is bright orange, not at all akin to my leather-bound copy. Yet there is a comfort in seeing her book here. In knowing that a piece of her remains in the world and always shall.

Emily's words tormented me for years. Now, for the first

time, I am truly glad they were written. Perhaps Frogs is right.
Perhaps sometimes it is the mistakes—

I never finish the thought, because there it is in front of
me—the bus from the wasteland. It is parked on a patch of
grass, in the process of being dismantled.

Frogs follows my gaze. "Our tech can still only move *people*
in time and space, plus what they're wearing and carrying. We
have to pull the bus apart so we can take it to the wasteland,
one piece at a time."

"Why?"

"So that when I save your life on the cliff that day, you'll
have somewhere to live," says Frogs, like that much should be
obvious.

"But the bus is *already* in the wasteland. I lived on it. Hell,
I saw it on your monitors."

"All this fluid nature of time shite—does your bloody head
in," he says with a wide grin, mimicking my accent.

"Whoever said that is clearly a very wise man." I stop to give
the dog another rough pat. "So, this delicate thread of yours.
Did it fix what went wrong?"

And of course, I am thinking about the wasteland. The place
where all life on earth ended in nothingness and pods.

Frogs shakes his head. "All that stuff we put you through
was just about making sure the Deadenders *even existed*. Everything else . . . well, it's complicated."

"It appears you have your work cut out for you."

"Nobody said that saving the world was easy, but some poor
bastard has got to do it," says Frogs, mimicking my accent again.
"You told me that when I was five. You sat me down and told

me that we have to be the best there ever was, by a landslide. Because if people don't change, then the world won't either."

"That is a fairly serious talk to have with a five-year-old," I mutter, still grappling with the idea that Jules and I—together—will be the ones who raise him.

Frogs laughs. "I'd just used revised quantum theory to warp and fold time. You felt I was ready."

I cannot suppress my grin—parenthood shall not be *dull*, apparently. And then I stare at him again. *The first time I met my son, he was older than me.* But we are a family of time travelers; there is clearly no normal.

Besides, I have always considered "normal" much overrated.

"So, the future remains a mess, though perhaps one day it shall not be?" I say, getting back to the bigger question. I am remembering the chalkboard on the bus. The one which showed that, even after years of tweaking the timeline, there was still but a tiny prospect of saving the world.

"Everything's already happened," says Frogs. "But time isn't linear. There are . . . *loopholes*. I think I maybe have a plan," he adds, a little shyly.

"And what is the plan for me? What now?"

Silence for a moment, then: "The time of your life."

"Ha!" I add, "A house, a vegetable patch, a dog, maybe a horse—"

"—A family of your own, and love that you can count on. You'd rather have that than all the time in the world," Frogs finishes. I give him a curious look. "You said *that* a lot too. Like, *all* the time."

"Well, I was probably pleased with myself. From what you have told me, I got everything I ever wanted."

"You did," says Frogs, although for a moment he almost seems sad instead of happy. Turning away from me, he stares off into the distance. Then, softly, "You once told me that the amount of time you have isn't important. What matters is how you use it. Do you really believe that?"

I think about all those dragged-out years that I spent on the bus, as opposed to how much I have lived these past couple of days. And it is true—all the things that actually matter are immune to the passage of time. Love, life, purpose, meaning— they can pack themselves into seconds or minutes, and then skip over years completely. Lifetimes, even, if you are not careful.

"The amount you have does not matter," I say with absolute conviction. It is a statement that my young, street-brat self could never have believed. Though *times change* . . . and apparently, so do people.

"A life of unbridled bliss awaits?" I am still grappling with the fact that it is destined. That my happily-ever-after is literally guaranteed. "Well then, what are we waiting for?"

"Dad, aren't you forgetting something?"

The "Dad" pulls me up short—hearing him say it out loud, so naturally.

"The ring," he says. "You've got to get Mum's wedding ring."

Jules told me that her husband found the ring. I thought she meant Romeo.

"*I* was the husband who found it for her," I say as it all sinks in.

"In a manner of speaking."

I give the dog one last scruff of the ears, which she clearly adores. Then Frogs grabs the cuff around his wrist—

* * *

—and the Settlement is gone. Now we are in some kind of derelict kitchen.

No, this is wrong. "Jules cannot have lost her wedding ring *here*," I say. "We never *came* here."

Frogs puts his finger to his lips, indicating quiet. Then he points at the kitchen door, which is wedged open. Through the door, I see a familiar set of stairs. A moment later, the "earlier" version of me heads up them.

This is the Chinese restaurant from before. Jules is in the next room with her back to me. I take a few steps in her direction. I am not going to interact—I just want a proper look at her as she is now, in her late teens.

Then fate happens—I step on an ancient fortune cookie. It crunches underfoot, and Jules hears it. *She sees me.* I look exactly the same as the other "me" who is currently upstairs—same clothes, same everything. *She thinks that I am he.* I should make an excuse and pretend to go directly back up there. I should not interfere. Except Jules seems scared, and I cannot just leave her like this. Not when I do not have to. *There is time.*

I take another step toward Jules, smiling at the symmetry. Back in the alleyway, I could not just leave Emily, precisely because she was quaking. That one decision changed my entire life; I regretted it for years. And yet here I am, making the same choice, again.

"I know that it feels like everything is moving terribly fast right now, but just trust your heart," I say gently. And then, with conviction: "It will be all right."

"Will you quit pretending you like me?" she says, defensive.

I hear the first chime of the broken clock tower. By the last chime, I will have been shot.

"Who is pretending?" I say, taking her right hand in mine. Then I carefully take her other hand too—the numb one. Jules flinches. She does not know that we have touched like this before.

For her, this is our first time.

I want to pull her into an embrace, like the Heathcliff in Emily's story. To lay my lips roughly on hers, kissing with fiery passion. *She is my wife; she is going to be my wife.* Yet time is out of order. Here in this moment, Jules barely knows me. It would not be right. It would be taking liberties, taking advantage. So instead, I lean down and kiss her gently on the hand. My breath catches as my lips press softly against the skin. Other than kissing her forehead in the music room, this is the most intimate I have ever been with a woman. The vulnerability of it is terrifying. But I have seen the future. I can finally trust in love because I know for a fact that it happened.

"You're a fool," says Jules, pulling her hand away.

Only I know her, now. I can read her lines and feel the precious beats of her complicated heart.

"And *you* are smart and brave and beautiful and strong," I say, speaking words that have never felt truer. Then I clear my throat and take a step back. "But I really do have to go upstairs now. Quickly see if the man in the gas mask is coming."

I am still holding her numb hand—when she pulled her other hand away, this one stayed limp in my grip. I give it one last squeeze, and that is when I feel it. The wedding ring—it is still on her finger. And I realize . . . the reason it was gone is because *I* took it. I took it from her, right here, right now.

I release Jules's numb hand, sliding her wedding ring off in the process. She does not feel it—*cannot* feel it. Later, when she notices it is gone, she will not suspect that the thief was me.

Then I remember there was one more thing. Something that Jules told me I'd said, but which I forgot to tell her when I was here, before.

"Check your book. Page forty-nine," I say as I leave the room.

When I have turned the corner, out of view, I do not go upstairs. Instead, I quietly return to the kitchen, where Frogs is waiting. A moment later, the other me comes back downstairs. He has no idea that I was ever there.

It all clicks into place—the image that I saw in the Control Room; *me kissing Jules's hand.* I assumed that moment never quite happened. In truth, it happened now.

Back in the kitchen, I hold the wedding ring up, revealing to Frogs that I have it. Now that the deed is done, I am expecting him to jump us out of here. He does not. Instead, he waits. After the thirteenth chime I hear a thud, then Jules screams. On instinct I try to rush to her, but Frogs grabs me by the shoulders. He holds me back for one beat, two beats, three. He checks his watch, counting down the seconds until he finally lets me go.

I hurry back into the room just in time to catch Jules clipping the cuff around her wrist and disappearing. She was facing the other way—she did not see me. It is just the man in the gas mask now, holding the gun, standing over my wounded body from before. He takes off the mask and . . .

It is Romeo, in his forties.

I suppose I should be surprised, but after today, surprise

takes rather a lot to accomplish. Besides, Jules explained that it was all a performance . . . and there is poetry in casting Romeo as the fake antagonist. Indeed, it seems almost fitting that everyone had a role to play in this orchestrated series of events, Romeo included.

Then I notice that Frogs is white as a ghost. He stares at his biological father and says, "Oh God . . . *What have you done?*"

. . . .

47

Jules

2084

ONE MONTH AFTER WAKING ROMEO

I wash my hands in the girls' bathroom. The faucets don't work, but every morning someone fills the sinks with a few inches of rainwater so we can sort of pretend that the plumbing still functions. Just like the toilets are actually buckets in stalls, placed right alongside the yesteryear loos. It occurs to me that we should be digging *new* toilets, outside. It stinks in here.

I gaze at myself in the mirror—short hair, school uniform. No black hoodie this time, marking me as different. Mum made me a sling instead. It means that my numb arm's always front and center, but these days that suits me fine.

Looking at my hair, I can't help thinking about when I first cut it short, back at Number 11. At the time, I imagined that Romeo was in the mirror with me, whispering words of love. Now, for a moment, I imagine *her* sharing the reflection:

me from before. Greasy fringe to hide behind, baggy hoodie to cover the body she hated. We just stare at each other, across the glass, across the month, across the divide between fantasy and real. And in my head—in *my* voice—I hear the same words as before.

"Did my heart love till now? Forswear it, sight, for I ne'er saw true beauty . . ."

I give a humorless snort at the sappiness of it. If life really was a story, I'd make this a poignant the-wheel-is-come-full-circle moment. It would be all "the true beauty that I needed to see was in me" and "the love that I journeyed to find had nothing to do with a boy," et cetera.

Well, corny or not, maybe it's true. Either way, when I look in the mirror, I know—and am even starting to *like*—who's there . . . which actually strikes me as a pretty good beginning.

The bathroom door slams open suddenly, and I start from the fright. I've been doing that a bit this past month—constantly checking my back, getting all jumpy. But no, it's not the man in the gas mask—he never *did* show up again. It's Rosaline.

"Hi," I say, because it feels like I should say something.

"Hi," she says back, like there's an echo.

And that's it—awkward exchange officially over.

Rosaline disappears into the middle stall, which used to boast graffiti about yours truly. Maybe it still does; I honestly don't care. Because words? Tales told about a teenage girl and her "drama"? *Not* the big-ticket item.

I check my watch—*Ellis's* watch. The one that used to give the measure of his day and now counts the minutes and the hours of my new life without him. For a tiny moment, I lose myself in the *tick-tick-tick* of time and the pain it's digesting.

The past, which sits sharp in the gut, as it chews through the "now."

Then I rein it in and focus on practicalities—I'm late.

By the time I get to the chapel, assembly is already underway. I take a seat near the front and wait while Mr. Marcellus drones on about "appropriate length of school skirts." When he's finally done, Headmistress Cisco says, "And now we'll hear a special address from Juliet."

I take the stage, weirdly not nervous. A few weeks ago, I'd have been mortified to stand up here in front of everyone. I would have felt like all eyes were on my arm, and that no one could see past the Romeo drama. But I'm choosing to put that behind me.

Looking out across the chapel, pretty much every kid in the whole Settlement is here, together in one place. My eyes drift to the back bench, where the cool kids are sitting. Laurence, Paris, Rosaline . . . and of course Romeo, the prodigal son, returned.

Paris is grinning, ostensibly giving me the two thumbs up. Except that he's gotten Laurence to prop up his left arm, like it's not working. Subtle.

I remember them on their bikes, before. Me choosing to stand still and do nothing, despite the collision course. *Inaction.*

Turns out, I'm done with that approach.

"We can't keep living off the past," I begin, in a steady voice. "We're going to run out of food."

There's a murmur—clearly *not* what people were expecting right after Marcellus's reminder about school uniform modesty. People shift in their seats, because the fact that our cans and jars and cereals are dwindling? That what we have is finite? It's a very uncomfortable truth—one that nobody mentions.

"I'm going to learn how to grow vegetables. Try to become self-sufficient," I continue, as though it's a radical concept. "Anyone who wants to help, find me after assembly."

"Yes, let's just magic up our own food, shall we?" says Paris, mocking me from the back row. Laurence obliges him with a snigger. Romeo and his goons kind of rule the roost these days; none of the teachers intervene. General apathy, I guess.

"We don't need magic," I reply, loud enough for everyone to hear. "I've been going to the Supermarket a lot this past month, looking for answers. The toiletries aisle—it has *all kinds* of books on this stuff."

Hardly anyone from my generation goes to the Supermarket. Or if they do, they don't venture beyond the sweet escape of romance and science fiction.

"All we need is hard work. And resources."

"Yeah, resources *that we don't have*," says Paris, shaking his head at me, like I'm the one living in a fantasy. Romeo stays silent, but that's nothing new—he always *did* let others do his bidding.

"You're right, we don't," I agree. "Not here, anyway. We'll have to go beyond the Wall."

"That is *not* appropriate, Juliet," warns the headmistress, as if I've just suggested a spot of hard drugs and binge-drinking. "There could be *Travelers* out there."

I remember her from Number 11. She was the kid with the shaved head and a penchant for violence. I stare, marveling at how much people can change. Ironic, because the idea that people can change?

It's exactly what I'm counting on.

With that, I address my true audience—my peers. They're all just sitting there, killing time, hanging on to the past like I did. But we have to let go of the old ways. Besides, I need their help, and I'm ready to ask for it.

"This Settlement was *founded* by Travelers." I drop my bombshell. "All of our parents used to be Travelers."

Another murmur, except this time it's peppered with laughter—they don't believe me. Paris starts doing that finger-circling-the-ear thing. Just in case the implication isn't obvious, Laurence fake-coughs a loud, "Crazy." I ignore them both, focusing on all the *other* faces—teenagers like me, or younger. If I'm going to try to turn this place around, I can't do it by myself. My previous status of "loner" quite simply won't cut it.

And nor do I want it to.

"That means *we're* the first generation," I push onward. "*We're* the first generation of true Settlers. It's us. It's up to *us* to shape our future. To *save* our future. To make a difference."

I think of what Ellis told me: *It is never too late to change.* And I have faith.

Nobody says a word, but several kids are staring just off to my left. I see that Headmistress Cisco is more or less standing beside me—she must have come up on stage to force my exit. Now she's hovering there, ashen. I've told the truth, revealed the big secret . . . and she looks like she might puke.

"I've been beyond the Wall," I say, putting it out there. "There's nothing to be scared of."

"Juliet Capulet, still completely bonkers," says Laurence, though he sounds a bit less sure. From the smell, I think that

Rosaline's mum might have *actually* vomited, but I don't let myself get distracted. I need to keep everyone's attention.

"Look around," I say, becoming more desperate. "We have to fix the now, or there won't *be* a future. We have to think of the next generation."

And yes, I'm thinking of one member of the next generation in particular: *my son*. He'll be here in eight months. I won't stand by and do nothing. I won't let him inherit some doomed world—not if I can do something about it. Because yes, it's *always* been about more than just one generation. Even Shakespeare got that right, with his plays.

"We live in a world that was brought to its knees because everyone thought that the 'now' was someone else's problem." I wonder if I'm getting through to anyone. "Nobody put the effort in. Nobody took responsibility. But everything's connected . . ."

Deathly silence.

"We know what we are, but know not what we may be!" I say, slipping into some old-fashioned language in pure desperation.

Suddenly, Paris starts up a slow clap. "Great story," he says, mocking me.

He looks like he's about to continue with the insults when one of the younger kids says, "Let her talk. I want to hear it."

And then it happens.

Rosaline stands and says, "Me too."

....

48

Ellis

2083

The man behind the gas mask is Romeo in his forties ... and he has just shot "me" from before in the chest. He is still standing over the body, holding the gun.

"No, no, it can't be *you* behind the mask ..." Frogs is in a panic.

What does he mean? Why on earth not?

"One man in his *time* plays many parts," says Romeo coolly. "See what I did there, quoting Shakespeare?"

"Omelia," says Frogs. "The person behind the mask is meant to be *Omelia*!"

"Omelia became ... *indisposed* ... after the car chase," says Romeo. "The understudy stepped in." With that, he takes a dramatic bow, adding a flourish with the hand that is holding the gun.

"Grandma—" Frogs looks stricken. "You didn't . . . ?"

"Oh, relax," says Romeo, dismissively. "I slipped her a seda-tive. She's *sleeping*. Ironic, no?"

Romeo is wearing boots with a splatter of blood on them—*my* blood. Before, it was sneakers. The person behind the gas mask—it was two different people all along, playing the same role.

Frogs keeps shaking his head, like he cannot comprehend this. "But . . . but . . . even the smallest deviation could—"

"—change everything? Oh, I'm counting on it," says Romeo.

"It was *you*," says Frogs slowly. "The splinter—it was you. It . . . it was *now* . . ."

Romeo catches my confusion and turns to me with a smile that is decidedly fake.

"What they neglected to mention, Heathcliff Ellis, is that the ending of this story's not a given. Every time our clever boy here sized up the future, *you weren't in it*."

I turn to Frogs to see if that is a lie—his face tells me it is not.

"In almost every version, the timeline splinters," says Frogs quietly. "Everything changes. You disappear from the future. We never knew how or why. You were just . . . *gone*."

That is why the older Jules was strange and standoffish with me; why *everyone* was a little odd with me. Why I caught glimpses of Frogs and Jules both looking so sad.

"The Deadenders survive, so mission accomplished," says Romeo. "Everyone else survives too. Just little old you who misses out, I'm afraid."

"I ran the scenarios a million times," says Frogs, tears well-ing. "But there was always something I was missing."

"The famous Ellis conundrum," quips Romeo. "That's what gave me the idea in the first place, actually." And then, to Frogs, "Guess you're not the only one in the family with a flair for cause and effect."

Without taking his eyes off Frogs, Romeo puts his boot on the earlier version of me—the one who has just been shot and is lying unconscious at his feet.

"What are you going to do?" I ask, expecting something dramatic.

"Absolutely nothing."

"Inaction," says Frogs, as it dawns on him. "Time. *Time* is all it takes to change things."

The earlier version of "me"—his breathing is shallow.

"But I cannot die down there on the carpet," I say, putting my hand up to my chest. The bandage is still there from where they successfully stitched up the gunshot wound. "If I died then, I would not be standing here now. Besides, I saw myself in the Control Room—I was in my forties. I married Jules. *It has already happened.*"

"A self-fulfilling prophecy?" Romeo is clearly amused. "You're alive now, ergo you didn't kick the bucket then? The die is *necessarily* cast?"

I shrug—that is more or less where I was heading.

"If it was as simple as that, do you think everyone would have gone to so much trouble making sure everything played out *just right* with you and Jules?"

"No, I suppose not," I admit.

"Everything's already happened, but time isn't linear," explains Frogs. "If something goes wrong—if a mark isn't hit *exactly* according to plan—then the timeline can splinter. That's ... *not good.* Time can unravel. Our existing thread can break."

Time can break. Frogs was warning me all along, right from the very start. I simply did not know it yet.

"Everything unwinds," says Romeo. "This reality gets overwritten, like an obsolete draft. And you, Heathcliff Ellis, get deleted."

Romeo is reminding me of his father, now—the bully king, brandishing a weapon.

"You are a coward," I say—a timeless truth that bullies so often are.

Romeo considers me, with obvious loathing.

"They *knew,*" he says eventually, with a heartless smile. "Your so-called loving family knew that you'd probably die. They knew that your happy future would be wiped from existence. *And they did it anyway.*"

The anguish on Frogs's face is writ clear.

"Even if the timeline splinters, the Deadenders still happen," he says in a soft voice. "Mum does it without you. She does it alone. You made us promise that we'd go through with the plan, even if it meant sacrificing your life. You said the future was bigger than just a love story."

"The boy dies in Jules's ridiculous story too, so I guess it's a case of life imitating art," says Romeo. Then he turns to me and says, "Only *this* time, the dead lover will be *you.*"

He is smiling again. One can smile and smile and be a villain, apparently.

"But why?" asks Frogs, staring at his biological father with total incomprehension. "Why do this?"

Romeo glances at him. "I've spent the last twenty-four years living here in this supposed 'last Settlement.' Living at the arse-end of time, where everyone's obsessed with saving the goddamn world. With Jules and Ellis and the Deadenders and this one oh-so-critical day. Twenty-four years on the periphery, as nothing but a minor character."

When he looks at me, the hatred in his eyes is unmistakable.

"You stole my life," he says bluntly. "My wife, my son. *I* was meant to be the hero. It was meant to be *my* story, not yours. Romeo and Juliet—*that's* what was meant to happen."

"But that's *not* what happened," says Frogs. "That's not the life she chose."

"She wanted me. She was *obsessed* with me," insists Romeo. "Without Ellis, I would have stayed at the center of everything. I was meant to be important. I was *born* to be important. So really, this isn't even my fault. *Ellis* is to blame. I'm just putting things right."

As if on cue, the "me" on the floor gives a little splutter. And then his breathing stops. For a second everything goes black, then returns to normal.

"What the blazes is going on?" I say, in a panic. "For a moment everything became dark."

"You're flickering out of existence." Romeo laughs hollowly. "Because in *this* reality, you're going to be dead. Gunshot wound to the chest, I'm afraid, *which will prove to be fatal.*"

I hold my hand up—it is there, solid and real. Then, for a flash, it is not.

"In a few minutes, you'll disappear completely," says Romeo with fake concern. "Once you're gone, everything will unwind. We'll have a fresh start. A *new* story."

He gives a dramatic bow and adds, "Time to make my exit."
Then, grabbing the cuff around his wrist, he disappears.

Through his tears, Frogs's eyes are darting backward and
forward at lightning speed. He looks like he is in pain.

"Frogs, what is wrong?" I say, as everything flicks dark again.
"Are you all right?"

"I'm holding on to this reality," he says, with obvious difficulty. "As long as I can remember it, it will remain solid.
Can't . . . can't hold on much longer."

Frogs is almost doubled over with the strain of it, though he
manages to produce a spare cuff from his pocket. No explanation required. I clamp it around the wrist of the other "me"—the
one who has stopped breathing. Then I guide Frogs's hand to the
cuff around his own wrist—

* * *

—and we have jumped. The Chinese restaurant is gone—all
three of us are now in a room full of medical equipment. As
soon as we reappear, a burly male nurse picks the wounded "me"
up off the floor and lays him onto an operating table. There is
a doctor and monitors—everyone is moving in unison to save
my life.

Except it is too late.

Jules and Ellis are here too, both in their forties. They rush
over to Frogs, *their son*.

"There's no pulse!" says the doctor in a panic. "There's meant
to be a pulse!"

Everyone turns to Frogs; his eyes say it all.

"It is all right," says the middle-aged me, putting his hand on Jules's shoulder. "We knew that something like this would probably happen. That it would mean good-bye."

As I watch, he flashes in and out of existence. He will be gone before long. *Just like me.*

And once we are gone, everything will reset. History will be rewritten.

"How long?" asks Jules, fighting back the tears, but more or less failing.

"Only . . . moments . . ." Frogs struggles to respond.

The middle-aged me wraps Frogs and Jules in his arms. Soon he will lose them both. No, *far* worse than that. Soon he will never have even had them.

It was not a love story after all. It truly *was* a tragedy.

But then I look more closely—at the expression on his face. On my own face, as a grown man. He does not seem sad or full of regret. He is not railing against the slings and arrows of outrageous fortune or cursing his fate, like the fictional Heathcliff. He appears calm. *Proud*, almost. And, finally, I understand.

When I kissed Jules's hand before, I only trusted love because I thought I knew for a fact that it happened. Except love does not work like that; there are no guarantees. Watching myself as an adult, saying final good-byes? He clearly had love, even though he always knew that it could be taken away. He trusted it despite his greatest fear always looming large.

And seeing him, I realize . . . I *did* achieve the impossible feat which Emily asked of me. I opened my heart. *That* was the future I chose for myself.

That was my character.

And perhaps it matters not if in a few moments it never

even happened. Maybe time was *never* everything. Maybe, for me . . . in the end, it was nothing at all.

I take one final glance at myself as a father and a husband, which now will never come to pass.

And I change my mind one final time. It was a tragedy *and* a love story.

One which will never be read.

A love story lost in time, of which the world will never know.

....

49

Jules

2084

FOUR MONTHS AFTER WAKING ROMEO

Turning the soil at Number 11, I uncover a small, high-tech metal chip. It's another piece of the Deadender cuff that Ellis scattered here, all those years in the past. I toss it into the jar, like always. I don't even know why I bother—it'd take a certified genius to Humpty-Dumpty all the pieces back together again. So I guess they'll always be but scraps, filling a marmalade jar.

Changing the past will never again be possible.

That just leaves the now, which I'm currently working on. And I'm working on me too. I found some good books down at the Supermarket. *Trauma, Healing, Recovery*—title after title, all covered in dust. Mum's been pretty amazing, reading everything with me. What we've learned together so far? That pain and grief are like big black holes. There's no easy way out. But we're nailing baby steps in the right direction.

Looking down, I smile at the scar bursting through the top of my soil-stained T-shirt. It reminds me of a vine—tendrils growing up my chest wall, spreading out from the heart.

It takes no imagination to see it as beautiful.

Dripping with sweat, I walk across the road and around to the back of my house, where I've rigged up a bucket shower. Most people still bathe in the old bathrooms, even though there's no point. I mean, lugging water into a bygone space, only to have to carry it away again later? It's a relic of the past, which serves no purpose. I'm trying hard to change that way of thinking.

I kick off my shoes and am about to strip down when a voice from above me says, "*Romeo and Juliet.*"

I look up and see my once-was-husband dressed in all white, holding a single red rose. He's standing on my balcony—Dad must have let him up there.

"*Romeo and Juliet,*" he says again. "Has a certain ring about it, don't you think?"

With that, he throws the rose down. It lands gently at my feet, like some storybook moment—the perfect romantic gesture.

"But Rosaline . . . ," I say, because it's the first thing that comes to mind. They're dating again—he has a girlfriend.

"It was always meant to be *you*." Romeo gives me a charming smile. "Even my parents can see that now."

That part's true enough. Maybe it's the fact that the Montagues know that their grandson will be arriving in five months, so suddenly it's all "bury the strife." Or maybe time *really does* heal all wounds. Either way, now it's like the opposite of last time. Instead of being kept apart, Romeo and I are being pushed together.

"The past is the past," says Romeo for the umpteenth time. "We both said things we didn't mean. But that's all behind us. Now it's about the future."

Yes, *the future;* tomorrow and tomorrow and tomorrow.

I gaze up at him—the father of my child, my one and only lover. He looks so shiny and *clean*. Most of us have been working at Number 11 all day—turning soil, planting seeds. We're smelly and sunburned and covered in dirt. And yet Romeo . . . is immaculate. Of course no one expects him to do anything beyond his physical limits—everyone in the Settlement helps in different ways, however they can. But Romeo *volunteered* to fill bottles with water from the well so that the kids who were doing the planting didn't get dehydrated. He made this big fuss about it and everything, like he was basically running the whole show. Only, staring at Romeo now? At the way he's casually leaning against my wall, with that indulgent cat-who-got-the-cream expression? I get the sense he hasn't done his task. He didn't do it yesterday either.

Running my fingers through my grotty hair, I'm suddenly rather *over* all this chitchat. Aunt Miranda and I harvested our first batch of tomatoes today. The plan is to try to make chutney—we're both pretty excited. *That's* where I want to be, not waylaid with this lover-boy nonsense.

"Look, I need to clean up," I say, hoping that Romeo gets the hint.

"Well, don't stop on *my* account." He nods at the bucket shower.

"Excuse me?"

"Come on, it's not like we haven't seen each other naked

before," he says with something akin to a leer. Romeo clearly remembers our one night together differently than me.

"You should probably go now," I say bluntly.

"Should I go . . . or should I *stay*?" He has a confident smile, like he assumes he's winning me over. What, does he think I'm just playing hard to get? Does he genuinely believe this is some kind of viable courtship?

"Go," I clarify.

"Why fight it?" says Romeo, still smiling, still smug. "You know we're going to end up together anyway. It was *written in the stars*."

That's a line from my play. He must have taken my notebook from the crypt and read it without asking.

When Ellis read my words, it felt like a connection. But with Romeo?

"You should have asked before reading my story."

"*Our* story," he corrects.

"No, *I'm* the one who gets to decide—"

"We'll be like royalty," he says, cutting me off. "Montagues and Capulets, united at last. I'll make you my queen. *Officially*, this time."

With that, he places something on the ledge of the balcony. It's a ring box.

You've got to be kidding me.

"You want to marry me?" I'm incredulous. "*Again*?" Has time seriously taught him nothing?

"Indeed, fair maiden," says Romeo, channeling old-fashioned valor in a way that, I'm ashamed to admit, once would have worked on me. "I will make you my wife."

"Listen . . ." I trail off, taking a moment to choose my words.

I'm actually kind of annoyed that I'm having this conversation from down here, looking up at him. Then it occurs to me: *That might not be a coincidence.* These past few months, people have started treating me differently. They come to me for advice, for leadership. And when the truth got out about how I sort of inadvertently *founded* the Settlement, years before I was technically even born? It gave me a bit of celebrity status, especially with the younger kids. I get the sense that Romeo doesn't like it. That he'd prefer they were focused on him, not me. He's even started making noises about how *he's* the one who cares about the sorry state of our world so much, like it's some kind of trend to claim. Like he *owns* it somehow. So maybe he chose to be up there—above me—for this conversation, on purpose.

Well, I'm sure as hell not going to let a little thing like *being looked down on* throw me.

"Thank you, good sir," I say, chucking some old-fashioned language right back at him. "But I respectfully decline."

"It was always meant to be *our* love story," continues Romeo, as if "no" is simply a jumping-off point. "When are you going to realize it was just that the timing was wrong?"

"Romeo, when we made love . . ." I begin, but then I decide that, actually, I *don't* need to explain myself. Not to him, not to anyone. Instead, I go with an abundantly clear, "We are never getting back together."

That doesn't fit Romeo's narrative, so he ignores it. "We simply need a fresh start."

"You can't *have* a fresh start!" I finally lose my cool. "Don't you get it? There is no going back. *What's done cannot be undone.*"

And yes, I'm totally ripping off Shakespeare. But Romeo doesn't know that—he was never into other people's stories.

"Wake up, Juliet," he says. "This is how it's going to be. You and me, side by side, helming the Settlement. Besides, it's not like you're flush with *other* options."

Maybe he's referring to the fact that there aren't too many eligible bachelors hanging around here at the end of the world as we know it. Or maybe it's another dig at my arm—he's implying that others won't want me because of it. The latter's total bullshit, I know that now. But the former? He's not exactly wrong. This really could be my big moment of choice between a boy and a life without one.

Just to hammer it home, Romeo adds, "Marry me, Juliet, and you'll never have to be alone."

"I can cope with being alone," I reply, and mean it.

"What, you'd seriously choose that over being married to *the father of your child*?" he says, like it's the ultimate checkmate.

"Yes."

"Oh, grow up, Juliet."

"I *have* grown up. And that's *not* my name. Not anymore."

"Well, *I'm* still Romeo," he says through gritted teeth, "and I'm still the main attraction."

Holy shit, *that's* what this is really about! Romeo always acted like he was the king of our generation—totally entitled to everything he wanted. But now that people are listening to me instead? He just wants to stay at the heart of things.

"You're obsessed with me," he says, like he's just decided it's true. "Even in your silly story, it was all about me."

No. Romeo's *not* the hero of my story. He's merely a player.

"My story is a work of *fiction*," I say with confidence. "I'm not the lovestruck girl in those pages. I'm *real*."

He looks down at me. "More's the pity. At least the fictional you was *agreeable*."

I've finally got a billion things to say about all that "boys prefer agreeable" bullshit. Instead, I go with a simple: "Get out of my room."

Romeo doesn't budge, so I yell at him again: "*Leave!*"

When he *still* doesn't move, I storm toward the trellis under my balcony. I stomp on the rose for effect, and a thorn gets my foot. Serves me right for trying to be dramatic. It hurts, sure. But the prick doesn't pierce my sole. I have thicker skin than that. I keep on going. I start climbing the latticework, a total role reversal. Last time it was *me* up there, doing nothing, looking pretty.

I climb higher and higher. At one point I almost lose my footing, and a line from my play pops into my head: *Women may fall when there's no strength in men.* Not bloody likely.

"You want me. You're *obsessed* with me," repeats Romeo when I'm almost upon him. "You're making a big mistake. *You'll regret this.*"

He's dead wrong.

By the time I actually reach the balcony, Romeo has vanished. Coward. I go inside, and sure enough, my notebook's open on the desk—Romeo was in here reading it when he should have been outside helping. I close the cover and see that he's changed the order of our names—*Romeo & Juliet* instead of *Juliet & Romeo*. Self-centered jerk. I'm about to change it back, then I decide no—it's better that way. In my story I *did* put myself second.

But not anymore.

I lay my notebook back down alongside Ellis's novel. His story and mine, finally united . . . if only here, on my crummy old desk. For a moment I stare at *Wuthering Heights*, lauded by history as a tale of epic love. Then I look to my own play, *Romeo & Juliet*. And I decide, actually, they're both pretty crap examples as far as the *women* go. I mean, all-consuming love and passion? A focus on nothing but hearts?

No, there's a much bigger picture.

But contemplating fictional love stories just reminds me of the *real* one—*Juliet & Ellis*. Except, of course, it wasn't a love story. I wasn't "in love" with Ellis. Maybe—for a moment—I almost went there, because my head was so full of that thinking. Only, the instant love that I brewed in *Romeo & Juliet*? It's not real; I see that now. The truth is, love takes time. And Ellis and me? We simply didn't have enough of it. I can live with that.

Because love isn't everything.

The old me probably would have dreamed up some larger-than-life romance. Got myself all caught up on the idea that, in some alternative universe, Ellis and I *did* have more time. That we got to have a life together, to grow old together. But that's not what happened. That wasn't my story, and dwelling on the idea of alternative worlds is as pointless as hiding in made-up ones.

Ellis is gone. The Deadenders are gone too. And yes, without them, there's no going "back." All we have left is the "now," though maybe that's all we *ever* had. And maybe that's enough.

No, screw that—I'm *making* it enough. I'm going to *fight* for the future.

....

50

Ellis

2107

This is the end. I am flickering in and out of existence.

Jules abruptly breaks from the embrace with her son and the older version of me. She starts pacing the room, lost in concentration, then stops short—an idea has clearly taken hold.

"Everything's connected," she mutters, mostly to herself.

Quickly turning to Frogs, she says, "You studied anatomy *for years* to reach Dad's mind safely, to find a way to communicate without being invasive. You learned about all the medical procedures, the drugs, the equipment. You know *way* more than a doctor or a surgeon. Don't you see? *Everything's connected.* Because of what happened to Dad, you can save Ellis now. I *know* that you can."

But Frogs is in no state to help anyone. His eyes keep darting backward and forward too fast—it is clearly taking everything he has just to keep hold of this reality.

"Sweetheart?" says the middle-aged me to Jules. "You have to let me go."

It is what Emily said—her advice, serving twofold.

Jules stares at her husband with a stubborn look that really rather suits her. Then she turns to a young Buddhist nun who is monitoring the equipment.

"Get Frogs in real time," she orders.

"We can't," says the nun. "It's started. He's in the middle of—"

"I am *not* giving up," says Jules, fierce as anything. "Call Frogs."

The nun nods.

"Complete quiet!" yells Jules in a booming voice. She is clearly in charge; everyone is instantly silent. A moment later a *second* Frogs appears out of nowhere. He is wearing pajamas and the headset that I saw before in the converted train carriage.

"Me . . . from this morning . . ." says my Frogs—the one that I arrived here with. It is almost like a question, like he is struggling to keep hold of even the most basic information.

The "other" Frogs does not respond. He is mid-conversation with someone else, talking into the headset's microphone. His voice sounds mechanical through the speaker, just like it did on the bus.

IF YOU DON'T WAKE ROMEO, I'LL NEVER EXIST. THE DEADENDERS WILL NEVER EXIST . . .

I have heard these words before. This is the conversation Frogs and I had right before I left on the "wake Romeo" mission. Everything is coming full circle.

... NEVER BE A CHANCE OF FIXING WHAT HAPPENED WHEN PODS WENT TO MARKET ...

His voice is measured and calm, in contrast to his actions. He is working at lightning speed to try to patch up the gunshot wound and bring the "me" who is lying on the operating table back to life.

... INCIDENTALLY, YOU'LL BE DEAD, HUNDREDS OF YEARS IN THE PAST

With a bloody hand, the pajama-clad Frogs flicks a switch on his headset, muting the microphone. Then he yells to the doctors, "Up the levels of thalopena!"

He switches the microphone back on and continues in a calm voice, made mechanical through the speaker again.

FOUR STEPS TO YOUR LEFT

Muting the microphone, he barks a panicked, "Swap out the rethurex. The stitching has to happen from the inside!"

Another flick of the switch.

THAT'S THE PROBLEM. I DON'T KNOW. SOMETHING WEIRD IS GOING ON WITH THIS MISSION. SOMETHING ... UNSTABLE

He is holding two conversations. By flicking the speaker on and off, he is trying to revive me in this room ... and talking to me, from before, in the wasteland. He is doing both simultaneously. It is incredible.

But then the "other" Frogs stops. He stares down at the gunshot wound, except it is like he is not really *seeing* it. His eyes dart backward and forward like he, too, is getting lost in something. Then he pulls himself together, focuses again.

CAN'T. THE DIE IS CAST. THIS IS OUR WINDOW. IT HAS TO BE NOW

One of the monitors emits a loud beep. I realize—it is the strange beeping sound that I heard through the comms when I was in the wasteland.

DO TRY TO BE CAREFUL. AND DON'T FORGET THAT TIME CAN BREAK. IF ANYTHING GOES WRONG, THERE'S A RATHER HIGH CHANCE I WON'T EXIST ANYMORE TO CORRECT IT

The Frogs wearing pajamas flicks the microphone switch with bloody fingers and yells, "Maintain that level!"

MUST BE A MISTAKE

Last time around, those were the final words that I heard from Frogs before the radio silence. Sure enough, this Frogs mutes the microphone, then rips the headset off. The moment he does, the "quiet" spell is broken—now there is the din of panic and chaos.

But I am only half seeing it.

More and more, reality is being replaced with the black of oblivion. Through the void, I catch flashes of the other, older me. He flickers in and out of existence too. I start to go. *Everything* starts to go.

From somewhere in the darkness I hear someone yell, "It's too late!"

And as I slip away, I hear Jules say, "It's never too late. I am *not* giving up."

Words for her to live by.

And for me to die by.

·······

51

Jules

2084

NINE MONTHS AFTER WAKING ROMEO

Mum, Dad, Aunt Miranda, and I walk up the grim rose path in silence. Romeo and his parents are standing outside the crypt, waiting. It suddenly feels like a scene from my play: *Montagues versus Capulets.* Even the full moon and the gas lamp that Romeo's holding feel like part of it—props to set the mood as opposed to celestial bodies and real-life necessities. Except this isn't some dramatic ambush or unexpected plot twist. I invited them to be here.

"You came." I state the obvious.

"Of course," says Trudy. She's smiling, like everything's dandy. But the smile's too wide. She's nervous—maybe a bit uncomfortable, even. I'm guessing we all are, since this is the first time that the seven of us have ever been together in one place. And yes, I can't help picturing all the messy threads between us.

The children of Trudy and Aunt Miranda were secretly half brothers. The children of Trudy and Mum got secretly "married." Trudy loved my dad, but Mum married him. Trudy married Claude, the father of Aunt Miranda's child. I "married" Claude's other son, my cousin's brother. We had a son . . .

Shakespeare would love it.

I glance across at Aunt Miranda—she's looking anywhere but at Claude.

I guess time doesn't heal *all* wounds.

"Thanks for coming," I say, since bringing this tangle of hearts together was my idea. Then I stop—suddenly unsure what should come next.

"What are the voices in your head saying?" says Romeo when the silence drags on.

The question is slurred. He's drunk again. Just like he was the night before last, when he showed up outside my window, yelling rage in lieu of sonnets.

"What did you just say to my daughter?" snaps Mum, already on the offensive. She's reminding me more and more of that gutsy teen back at Number 11.

"It's okay Mum, ignore it," I urge her quietly. I've learned from experience—that's the best method.

After that balcony scene months ago, Romeo turned brutal. He went all-in on the theme of madness, telling anyone who'd listen that I'm crazy—and that the Deadenders are all in my head.

"Actually, it's *not* okay," says Mum, glaring at my once-husband.

"I don't appreciate your *tone*, Omelia," says Claude, putting himself in the mix.

I marvel at how much can change in so little time. Only

months ago, the Montagues were hell-bent on a teenage wedding, and the old folks wished us well. But when I said no? When the Capulet girl rejected the Montague boy? It stirred up all the old strife. History got rewritten, along with my mental state and overall character. Now we're right back to where we started—feuding houses.

And yes, this feels like a powder-keg moment. Like the tensions flaring dynamic at the start of my play, when the families at odds just couldn't keep their shit together. I can't have that—not again, especially not now. I need a new start, a *different* beginning.

In my play it was all *"naught but their children's end could remove the parents' rage."* Tonight, I'm banking on the exact opposite. That a child *being alive* is what will change things.

"Everything's connected," I say, heartfelt. "And maybe it sounds silly, but lately I've been thinking that . . . that there are more things in earth than are dreamed of in—"

That's as far as I get before Romeo cuts me off with a bark of laughter.

Mum fumes, but it's Dad who has the outburst. He yells an abrupt, "Hell is!", which really isn't like him. Not the words—they're all he has—the fact that he yelled.

"Hush," Aunt Miranda gently soothes, just like she always did with Tybalt and me, in the business of scraped knees. Except Dad doesn't want to calm down. He's agitated—struggling to say more, yet he can't.

And he's refusing to let it go.

"Hell is!" says Dad again.

"Hell is . . . a broken brain?" says Romeo, mocking him. "Hell is . . . no method in the madness?"

Trudy puts her hand on Romeo's arm, urging him to stop, but he swats her away.

"This was a mistake. You all need to leave," says Mum. With that, she stands in front of Dad, exactly like she did back at Number 11. And seeing them together like that, united against a Montague boy, again? It's like history repeating.

Except that *this* time, it's a different Romeo in the mix.

"Deadenders? Traveling back in time?" says my Romeo to me. "You've got serious problems, you know that, right? Frankly, I'm not even sure you're *fit* to be a mother."

"Hell is, he llis, he llis!" says Dad with increasing urgency. Then he finally blurts out a very loud, "He *lies!*"

It's a jumble of the letters in his two-word repertoire.

And hell . . . is it not perfect? Romeo *does* lie. But I'm the one who gets to frame my story now, and there's no way I'm casting him as the villain. Because really, he's nothing more than a small character. Besides, I refuse to let hate chew up my attention, like love once did. I've got *far* better things to do with my precious time.

"We don't have to bury our child," I say bluntly. "I propose that, instead, we bury the hatchet. I know there's a lot of past between us, but we're family now."

"We're not family," sneers Claude. "A bastard son does *not* a Montague make."

It's a dig at Tybalt as much as it is at William, and I flush with shame—I *asked* Aunt Miranda to be here. Begged her, even. Mum was right—this was a terrible mistake.

I open my mouth to say so, but Aunt Miranda gets there first.

"Tybalt was a Capulet," she says quietly, staring at her shoes.

"Though really, what's in a name? That which we call a rose by any other name would smell as sweet."

She's quoting my play—it's her way of letting me know that she's on my side, as always. But Claude doesn't know that. He shakes his head and delivers a cutting, "Smelling the roses, Miranda? You truly are a document in madness."

A document in madness—that's pretty much what he said when Aunt Miranda left him, back at Number 11. Basically the same thing Romeo said about Rosaline, too, after they broke up. And then about me, in turn. It's a pattern, I realize. *History repeating.*

Aunt Miranda doesn't meet Claude's gaze. She doesn't look up and finally face him in some clichéd, full-circle moment. Yet her voice is firm when she says, "Your words are weak."

Claude just glares at her, then barks, "We're leaving." And yes, I can see the bully king in him again—proud and unkind. I can see the temper, too, from years ago. Time hasn't *really* changed him at all—not where it counts. Underneath the cardigan and wrinkles, the hate lines are deep as ever.

The Montagues start walking away. I failed. I tried to bring this knotted family together, except it didn't work. I tried to unite the Montagues and the Capulets so that it wouldn't be all "new mutiny" and "parents' rage" for my son, but ...

The thought trails off, because *one* of the Montagues isn't moving. Claude sees it too and snaps, "Gertrude. *Now.*"

Trudy doesn't budge. She holds her ground. "I want to stay."

"No, you *don't*," says Claude with a sickening calm. "You're confused. What you *want* to do is leave."

I get chills, because that's what Romeo used to say, back when we were together. If ever we disagreed, he'd smile—*smile ever so sweetly*—and tell me that I was confused or mistaken. How could I have forgotten about that? How could I have glossed over how he tried to dictate what was real? How it was all "doubt truth to be a liar," or worse?

I turn to Romeo now. It's getting dark, but I can see him by gaslight. And I realize ... the stuff that Romeo used to say to me, what his own dad just said to his mother—it's connected. All the focus I've been giving to how one generation impacts the next? It doesn't only apply on a global level, or to the world at large. It applies at *every* level.

Even to families.

"*Now*, Gertrude," says Claude again, and he really is a bit intimidating.

Trudy shakes her head. "No. I'm staying to meet my grandson."

Claude considers her coolly, though I catch the anger bubbling beneath. It's the same brand that I've been copping from Romeo lately. *Like father, like son.*

"You'll regret this," says Claude. Trudy doesn't say another word, so the comment just hangs there. It gets kind of awkward—like the scene was meant to have ended, but didn't. Eventually Claude walks off, a total anticlimax.

"Romeo, please stay," begs Trudy. "We have to make peace."

Romeo ignores his mother. Instead, he turns to me and delivers a very blunt, "I regret the time that we spent together. I regret *all* of it."

He means our son—that having him wasn't a price worth paying.

I could hurl something sharp right back at him—words, truth, whatever. But that's what he wants—the all-consuming passion of old, only this time with hate as the new flavor. He's got a nasty taste for drama, and I'm the supply.

The *test* is silence.

"You're still obsessed with me," he says again. "It's kind of pathetic that you just can't accept that it's over."

I don't respond. Maybe I've built a wall, or drawn a line, or conjured up some other breed of magic. Whatever the case, the sticks and stones of his *words, words, words* can't hurt me. Because I won't let them.

"You know, I actually feel sorry for you," adds Romeo.

I still don't react. I'm silent as the crypt, cool as its gray rock, giving him zilch. Because yes, you *do* have to take action. But sometimes the powerful move is not playing the game.

"Nobody even *likes* you," he says, really grasping at straws with the insults. But I've learned this nifty trick: *What he says to me is what's actually true of himself.* And yes, Romeo's the social outcast now. Other than Paris, no one bothers with him.

"I *know* you," he adds, glaring. "Everything you're doing? It's all just to get back at me. You're doing it purely out of *spite*."

And the sad part is, he believes it. We were lovers once; I'm the mother of his son. Yet he cannot see the *real* me at all. And sure, I was guilty of some rose-colored fantasies. I imagined the best in him, even though it didn't exist.

He is the opposite; all *he* sees is the worst in me.

And that worst is fantasy also.

Romeo finally leaves, taking his dim lamp with him. We're left in the dark, but that's no tragedy—the moon is full and the stars are bright. Besides, I brought a flashlight with me. It's the same one that I dropped last year, with Ellis. I found it again, fixed the parts that were broken.

One click and we're lit—an unlikely circle of women, plus Dad.

Aunt Miranda puts a hand gently on Trudy's shoulder. It's a gesture of empathy—like she understands. Which, in a way, I guess she does. Though it's the expression on Mum's face that really gets my attention. She's staring at Dad with the kind of passion that I haven't seen between them in years.

"You were wonderful," says Mum, looking Dad right in the eyes, bold and vital. Dad stares back at her blankly—his moment of clarity must be over. Mum's expression turns complicated. Maybe a bit *angry*, even.

But underneath it all, I still see love.

Unlikely as their match is, I'd say it's a true one. It humbles me. I once felt like the tragic love sat squarely with me. But maybe, on that particular score, it was their story too.

Dad looks away from Mum and out into the middle distance. He seems confused, like the universe has turned into a mighty stranger.

"Go inside, get warm," says Mum, her expression softening. With that, she takes Dad by the shoulders and gently points him in the right direction. He's facing the house—there's a fire in the hearth, so the downstairs windows are lit up like a beacon. Dad follows the light until he's safely inside.

Now it's just Mum, Aunt Miranda, Trudy, and me. And boy, there's so much complicated drama between us—through our men, by our hearts, in our past, on the page. But somehow, none of that touches this moment. There's a feeling of peace, of resolution.

In my story, right before Tybalt dies, there's this line: *A plague o' both your houses.* I meant it as a curse on both families.

Turns out, it's not a plague that precedes this next chapter. Instead, it's a calming sense of balance. Tybalt was half Capulet, half Montague—a child from *forth the fatal loins of these two foes.*

My son is the same, closing the circle.

I check Ellis's watch, just like I have a million times these past months, always counting down to this exact moment. And finally . . . "It's time."

We enter the crypt in silence. Even with the flashlight, it's dark and cold. The heart of it's still empty . . . but it won't be for long.

William will be here soon.

Inside, I find myself staring at the two angel statues. I remember them well from that night with Romeo: *an angel apiece, to watch us die.* Now their stony eyes will bear witness to the bringing of life, not the taking of it.

My son—he disappeared from this stone tomb, as if by some modern-day miracle . . . and now he will return. It's kind of surreal. I mean, there was no conception nine months ago, and yet here I am, about to be delivered my child. It's almost like he's being resurrected, a second coming.

One light eye, one dark, they tell me. He's special; *unique* . . . which I'm seeing the beauty in more and more lately.

I wonder what it's been like for him these past couple of years—a king of infinite space, no crib for a bed. But mostly, I just can't wait to welcome him back into the world again.

"The last time the four of us were together in one place, there was gunfire," says Aunt Miranda, her voice crisp and clear—there used to be an echo, but it's gone now.

"Not to mention *actual* fire," adds Trudy.

"Times have changed," says Mum with a quiet calm.

For a moment I remember who they were, back at Number 11. Then I try to imagine who they became in that first, desperate year of the Settlement, when things got so bad. And finally, I consider them now—who they've grown into. Coming together like this can't have been easy, given all the past between them. And yet here they are, with kindness. They really have transformed from reckless teens into three wise women.

Humanity can be so beautiful.

"I brought a gift for your son," says Trudy, handing me a polyester baby's blanket that's covered in a garish frog print.

"Frogs?" Mum raises an eyebrow—the blanket's definitely not Trudy's usual style.

"He's been jumping through time and we thought that he'd croaked," deadpans Trudy. "Frogs seemed appropriate."

There's a moment of silence, then all of us burst into laughter. It feels good. Because, sure—there's history and tragedy, but there's comedy too. Three genres, all of them important—even the Bard knew that.

And if I had my time again, I wouldn't change a thing. Not even to rewrite the heartache chapters. Because our past is connected to who we are. And lately I've been thinking that maybe . . . well, maybe the pain is part of what shapes us.

Maybe Ellis was right.

Maybe everything *is* connected.

....

52

Ellis

2107

It is blacker than the bits between stars, and twice as still. Time passes. Perhaps a lot of time passes, though who can say, really.

And then, with a gasp of air, I return.

I hear the steady beep of medical equipment beneath the hubbub of excited chatter. In a daze, I look around the room—relief, smiles. The patient on the operating table is breathing again. I check the version of me in my forties—he has returned too.

"I remember this happening," says the older me to no one in particular. "I remember being here, in this room, when I was nineteen years old. I remember standing right over there."

He points to where he was standing . . . and of course, he is pointing at me.

"The timeline is restoring. It is becoming solid again," he explains. "It is in the past. *It happened.*"

He lifts his T-shirt to reveal the white lines of an old scar. I pull the front of my own T-shirt down and peel the bandage away, just to be sure. Yes—my stitches are fresh, but matching.

Time can break . . . *yet time can also mend.*

Now that it is over, everyone springs into action—mopping up blood, moving the patient from the operating table onto the bed, wheeling equipment out, putting the room back to normal. Back to exactly how it was when I woke, after having been shot by the man in the gas mask.

The man in the gas mask—I must warn them that it was Romeo, that he was trying to sabotage the timeline. I open my mouth to do so, then stop short. If I tell them, it may change things—perhaps catastrophically. I dare not interfere, so instead, I watch.

The version of Frogs who was operating picks up his headset off the floor. Just before he grabs the cuff around his wrist and disappears, I notice the blood. *Pajamas covered in blood.*

That is what I saw on the floor of the train carriage.

A young Sikh boy puts a black T-shirt and my copy of *Wuthering Heights* on the antique chest of drawers. Both are exactly where I found them when I woke after the operation. I am marveling at the puzzle of it all when I catch something out of the corner of my eye.

It is Frogs—the original one who was "holding" this reality. He has collapsed into his father's arms.

"*My love for Linton is like the foliage in the woods: time will change it, I'm well aware, as winter changes the trees,*" says the older me urgently. "What comes next?"

Frogs says naught.

Jules rushes to her son and pulls his head up by the chin, forcing him to face her.

"Frogs, what comes next?" she says in a firm voice, with worry clearly sitting behind it. "What does Cathy say to Nelly?"

Frogs's eyes— one dark, one green—are still darting backward and forward much too fast. He looks *lost*, almost.

"*. . . time will change it, I'm well aware, as winter changes the trees,*" says the older me again as Jules holds Frogs even more tightly by the chin.

Frogs squints, like he is struggling to make out her features.

"Come on, *come on,*" urges Jules.

And slowly, his eyes stop darting back and forth. He focuses on his mother's face and says, "*My love for Heathcliff resembles the eternal rocks beneath: a source of little visible delight, but necessary.*"

Then Frogs turns to the older version of me. "Dad?"

"I am right here," he replies, breathing a sigh of relief. "Appears you are stuck with me."

"And the marmalade jar?" says Frogs, inexplicably. "I . . . I still pieced it all together? The Deadenders, Mum, and you together—nothing changed?"

"Nothing changed," confirms the older me. "You did it, my boy."

"*We* did it," says Frogs, his eyes welling with tears. Then his father pulls him into a hug, squeezing tight. In Emily's book, Heathcliff *despised* someone like this—the child that the woman he loved had with another man. Perhaps this is my final proof that I am not him—that I am *naught* like that brutish character.

Frogs is crying openly now, *unashamedly*. I feel suddenly proud that I raised a man like that—a man who can cry. He is so much more than the singular dimension to which I was once reduced on the page. He is masculine *and* feminine, most beautifully entwined. Ironic that I spent years believing he was a machine when he is so utterly—impressively—human.

The older me meets my gaze, like he knows what I am thinking. Though perhaps he does; perhaps he remembers. Giving his son—*our* son—another squeeze, he says "Time—"

"—to buck up, soldier," Frogs cuts him off. "I know, I know."

"I was going to say, *time was never everything*."

"Well, it's kind of the family business," says Frogs weakly.

"Doesn't that make it even funnier? Huh. I thought that made it even funnier." The older me is repeating the same line that Frogs used right before the "wake Romeo" mission. It is a joke. *Even now*, he is joking.

I decide I *like* that about myself. I silently determine to always make it so.

"No beginning, no end, remember?" says the older me, squeezing Frogs even tighter. But he is looking over Frogs's shoulder—*at me, his younger self*—when he says it.

"The Romeo chapter happened for a reason," says Jules quietly to me. "The drugs that they gave me to save my life? I was pregnant. They changed him; made him special."

She means Frogs—that the drugs did something to him in the womb.

"He can *see* time," she explains. "When there's a possible

splinter in the timeline, he can see all the infinite alternative paths, all the threads. He lives them all—*experiences* them all—in that moment."

I stare at Frogs, registering the toll that it has taken. Then I think about what brought him back from the brink.

"Why *Wuthering Heights*?" I ask. That passage just now was from it.

"Because it is what you knew," says the older me. "What *we* knew."

I look at him blankly.

"*You* were the one who worked out how to help him," says Jules with tears in her eyes. "It was *his dad* who saved him. When he was young, when it got bad, you'd recite that whole entire book to him, over and over, from dusk till dawn if you had to. Chapter after chapter, until he came back to himself."

And then, more quietly: "In my entire life, I have never witnessed *anything* more beautiful."

She smiles at Frogs, who seems to be somewhat recovered. "He probably has the greatest mind that's ever existed. But the one who worked out how to bring that mind back to us was *you*, Ellis. You and *Wuthering Heights*."

"Let's not forget the *physical* dimension," says Frogs. "You distracted my mind with the book, but when that wasn't enough, we planted potatoes. Or re-shoed horses at three in the morning. Once, we fished the Thames for twenty hours straight, you reciting that book the entire time."

Reciting Wuthering Heights. *Honest, physical work.* I commit it to memory. That is what I will do. I shall not disappoint him.

Then something else occurs to me.

"Emily," I say to Jules. "You said that without sending me

back in time to cross paths with Emily, *Wuthering Heights* would never have been written. You said that it *needed* to be written. Is this why?"

"*What's past is prologue*," says Jules cryptically. "Shakespeare wrote that."

"I do not understand."

"Emily Brontë, *Wuthering Heights*—they are your past," says the older version of me. "And the past sets the stage for the future. We are meant to learn from it. Everything is connected."

Is *that* not the truth.

"*All* our yesterdays matter," says Jules. Then she adds an emphatic, "The pain is part of what shapes us."

I think about my pain, my history—so much hate for no good reason. Then I think about the future right outside that window. The one where all kinds of people work side by side. It is a future that I helped create. And I decide that yes, the pain probably *did* shape me. Perhaps *drove* me, even. But I shall not let it hold me back—not ever again.

"Waking Ellis!" announces a doctor, pulling me out of my thoughts.

And I cannot help but smile, given all the drama we had "waking Romeo."

The doctor injects the patient with something. I examine my left arm—there is a needle mark.

"Three minutes, everyone," announces Jules, checking her watch, suddenly all business again. "Dolores, some music to cover the packing-up sounds in the hallway?"

A moment later, "Disco 2000" starts playing—it is the same song that I heard when I woke up here in this room, after the gunshot wound. Staring at Jules, I notice that her T-shirt has a fresh smudge of blood on it—the same as when I first laid eyes on her as a grown woman. For me, that moment is in the past. For her, it has not happened yet.

"You will spend the next month here being briefed and recovering," says the middle-aged me. "After that, a handsome lad from Jules's past is due to make his reappearance."

I must appear confused, because Frogs says, "I'll send you back to Mum. When I do, she'll be nineteen. A year will have passed. That year she spent without you was important. It helped her become who she needed to be. Not as your wife or as a leader or a mum. But as her own person."

I glance at Jules, who is now across the room, supervising the pack-up.

"And then what?" I ask. "What happens when I get there?"

"Darling?" the older version of me calls out to Jules, his wife. "Remind me what happened when I showed up again, back from the dead, a year later?"

Jules raises an eyebrow and deadpans, "You knelt to the ground and pulled out a ring." But she cannot quite suppress the mischievous grin, and he cannot take his eyes off her. For a moment, they just stare at each other across the room, stare with expressions of mirth and something deeper. Despite the chaos and the drama and the many years of marriage, they are . . . *flirting*?

"You two are incorrigible," says Frogs, shaking his head in mock disapproval. Except I catch his smile.

I watch them—my family and me. It is a universe—and centuries—away from the life that I once imagined for myself on the windswept moors. Yet the world can change, and clearly people can too. Looking at them now, I remember my private wish list for the future: *a house, a vegetable patch, a dog, maybe a horse . . . a family of my own . . . a love that I can count on.* I decide that the first and the last parts are blessings to have and to hold.

But all I truly *need* . . . is the middle.

....

53

Jules
2084
ONE YEAR AFTER WAKING ROMEO

"When we reach the city ruins, we'll head north-northwest," I say to the others. There are twenty of us out scavenging today, mostly kids and teens. A few more steps and I add, "Also, we could probably make use of these."

I'm referring to the old love letters. When we pulled the Wall down and cleared up the rubbish, the letters were just left out here, still wrapped in plastic. We're currently stepping on them.

"I'll do it," says Laurence, practically falling over himself to scoop them up. Poor kid. I've told him a dozen times that it's all in the past between us. I guess he still feels bad about the taunting years. He compensates.

"Collecting words of love? Don't tell me you're regressing," says Rosaline to me with a familiar look of wide-eyed innocence.

Only, now that we're friends, I catch the subtle undertones of sarcasm.

"No, paper is simply hard to come by," I say, playing it straight. "I figure that on the flip side, there might be a blank page."

Rosaline smiles, clocking the double meaning. Because yes, that's basically what happened with us. On the flip side of all the Romeo drama, we started afresh. Turns out, without a boy in the middle—

I sense there's suddenly someone *right* behind us. In a loud, very dramatic voice, he says, "This . . . *is how it started.*"

I spin around . . . *and it's Iggy.* He's holding an ancient video recorder, filming us. Beth and Henry are with him.

Closing the gap in two steps, I hug them as best I can with William strapped to my chest. There's an excited murmur from the other scavengers—everyone's heard my stories about the Deadenders. And with Beth's 1950s skirt, Iggy's punk attire, and Henry's Georgian britches? Not to mention the fact that they're all wearing cuffs around their wrists and clearly "jumped" here just now? There's no doubting who they are.

"The music room. What happened?" I say.

"A Viking came to our rescue," says Henry.

"She didn't *rescue* us," says Beth, indignant. "I don't do being *rescued,* thank you very much. Estrid merely showed up . . . at a most convenient juncture."

"Estrid?" I ask. Beth shrugs, like there's really no story to tell. But the smirk on Iggy's face says otherwise, as does Beth's blush.

Looking at them all more closely, I register the small differences. Like how Henry's hair is shorter and slicked back—more modern styling than before.

"How long ago was the music room, from your perspective?"

"A month," says Henry.

I just stare, waiting for the sense of that to sink in. It doesn't.

"To quote a dear friend of mine," says Iggy, pointing the recorder at William for some reason, "*all this fluid nature of time shite—does your bloody head in.*"

"But what are you doing here, now?" I wonder aloud.

"Where else would we be?" says Henry. "This is where it all begins. *Began?*"

"Everything was to bring us to here, to *now*, darling," adds Beth. "The Settlers and us, together. *We're* the seed. We're what will one day become the Deadenders."

And of course, my mind goes to Ellis—the one Deadender who's missing.

Beth must guess where my head's at, because she says, "Give it time."

Time to what? Time to mend? Time to forget?

Then Beth adds, "Not *much,* though."

Iggy winks at me and turns his recorder toward the old fountain. Checking his watch, he announces, "Two o'clock. Folks—counting down now. *Five. Four . . .*"

There's a flash.

White light, followed by afterimage colors. I squeeze my eyes shut, waiting for the dancing bright to fade. When I open them, there it is . . . again. A pod, resting on the grass by the fountain down the road. I realize it's the same pod as last time, in the exact same spot as before.

A year ago, when that pod appeared by the fountain, then disappeared again? It clearly jumped to here, to now. Whoever's inside, it's the same person. For them it's only been seconds since Ellis tackled me to the ground, setting everything in motion . . .

Last time, I rushed in. Now I stand my ground; I wait.

The hatch of the pod opens, and a Traveler gets out.

Only it's not a Traveler.

It's Ellis.

I don't say anything or do anything—there's just this moment of total inaction, like time *really is* standing still.

"Cinematic gold!" says Iggy, zooming in on my face for a close-up.

Henry gently pushes the recorder down, stopping him from filming.

"But it's the epic meet-cute!" protests Iggy.

"Let's just *live* the moments, shall we?" says Beth.

"But . . . ," says Iggy. Then he sighs and adds, "Fine," before switching off the video recorder.

A line from Shakespeare's *All's Well That Ends Well* pops into my head: *They say miracles are past.* Turns out miracles are alive and well, right here in the now. And with that in mind, I tighten my arm around William . . . and start walking toward Ellis.

The others hang back, giving us the best that they can in terms of privacy; everyone's heard the story of Heathcliff Ellis. It feels like we're on a stage—performers, with an audience at our back. But hell, maybe *all* the world's a stage, just like Shakespeare figured.

"You're not dead," I say when I'm close enough that only Ellis can hear me.

"No." He grins. "You refused to give up. *It worked.*"

He lifts his shirt. There is a scar where he got shot—still pink, still fresh.

He didn't die. Wait, *I* refused to give up? None of this makes sense.

"The Chinese restaurant," I say, struggling to keep up. "How long ago was that, from your perspective?"

"A month, same as them." Ellis nods over my shoulder at the other Deadenders. "We were together at headquarters—being briefed while I did some mending."

A month. For me, it's been a year.

I stare at him—dark skin, dark eyes, so many yesteryear scars. Time has passed, but not for him. He hasn't aged or changed—not really. He's exactly the same—like he's been lifted straight from memory's page without edit.

"The man in the gas mask. Who was he?" I finally ask.

Ellis pauses a moment, then says, "Just some chap."

"Just some chap?" I am incredulous. "He *shot you*, Ellis. That's kind of a big deal. I mean, is he still out there? Is he still posing some kind of, I don't know, *threat*?"

"He is no longer a threat," reassures Ellis. "In the future, his ill deeds all catch up with him. He is currently serving out his time on a bus, in a wasteland."

The man in the gas mask is gone. More to the point, Ellis is back. The last time we were together, he kissed my forehead like it meant something. He told me . . .

"So Deadenders use pods now?" I say, banishing my thoughts from all that.

"No, but this one is the exception," says Ellis. "We reassembled it back in the past so that I could jump here." He smiles. "Made one quick stop along the way."

A year ago—the pod that appeared by the fountain. It was Ellis all along.

"*You* set everything in motion," I say as it fully sinks in.

"Yes, I was as surprised as you on *that* score," he says.

"But *why*? Why you in the pod? Why any of it?"

"Askim," he says.

"Huh?"

"Ask *him*," says Ellis, nodding at William. "Something to do with a delicate thread and a robust love story."

I look down at my son—he's only three months old. He can't talk yet.

"That makes no sense."

"Give it *time*," says Ellis, echoing Beth, and smirking at the pun.

I roll my eyes, saying nothing. Ellis says nothing too, and then the whole "not talking" stretches into this weird self-conscious silence. A year ago, I didn't fall in love with Ellis. I know that now. I did have feelings for him, though—it felt like the start of something. But so much has happened since then—everything's changed, including me. And Heathcliff Ellis? The truth is, I hardly even know him.

"Well, *now* what?" I say when he just keeps staring.

There's this pause, like a beat that builds the drama. And then Ellis bends down on one knee. He produces my wedding ring, the one that I lost, all that time ago. I hear gasps and excited whispers from behind us. A warm gust of wind blows petals into the air, as if even Mother Nature is marking the moment.

"Oh, you have *got* to be kidding me." I am deeply unimpressed. "Of all the ridiculous moves. Hell, it's not even *original*."

"But this is our storybook moment," says Ellis with a barely suppressed grin. "A scene befitting a truly timeless romance." Then he raises an eyebrow and adds, "Do not tell me we are both *finally* done with all that shite?"

"Stop *smiling*," I snap, irritated.

"I cannot," says Ellis, getting back to his feet. Then he looks at William and his demeanor changes. Instead of mucking around, Ellis softens. Reaching out, he gently touches William's cheek and is rewarded with a giggle.

"This no-nonsense mother of yours?" says Ellis quietly to my son. "The one who is messy and real, as opposed to some scripted ideal? *I am going to be her husband.*"

That snaps me out of it.

"Like hell you are!" I say with a snort. Because marrying a near-total stranger?

No longer my thing.

"Maybe it will take some time to win her over," says Ellis, ostensibly still talking to William, but looking at me now. "Judging by that scowl, perhaps rather a lot of it. Yet time is finally on my side. This is just *the start* of our story."

And in my head, I hear the clichéd beginning to all the fairy tales.

Once upon a time . . .

Nope, no way. I've got bigger things to do than fuss over some storybook romance.

All the world's not a stage—*the stage is all the world*. Our planet, as a whole? *That's* the story. It's where the action—as opposed to inaction—needs to happen. And I've got a part to play that's bigger than wife.

"I don't need a husband," I say—same thing I told Romeo.

Ellis doesn't fight me on it. He just nods. "Yes, I know."

"Love isn't everything," I say, feeling weirdly defensive. Like I have to justify myself, even though I don't. But hell, hasn't that always been the theme for me? Love is everything . . . love *isn't* everything . . . love is somewhere in the middle. *Love, love, love . . .*

"Love isn't everything," I say again, more forceful.

Ellis says nothing.

On instinct, I gaze down at my son. Then I look back at my friends, my family. They suddenly don't strike me as an audience anymore. Audiences are bad as tourists—watching things go south, but doing nothing. No, they resemble *an army*. Not soldiers, like in Ellis's "buck up" mantra. Not troops; *a troupe*. Every single person a key player in the new narrative. Everyone—big and small—with an important role in the fight to turn the tide. *We still have time, and time can mend.* I stare at them and decide they really *are* the seed: the past, the now, and the future. Then I look beyond them . . .

. . . and I *feel* it.

I feel it in the fight and in the hope and in the will-not-give-up way of thinking. I feel it in the rough beginnings and in the bitter end. But most of all, I feel it in the messy middle of me. The *heart* of me.

Love.

Everything worth dying for, and worth living for, and worth *changing* for . . . is underpinned by love. Love is the ultimate theme, the timeless factor. It's the stage that we set and the characters we become and the only true lines we deliver. It's the bravest thing we can do with our tiny breath of time. It's the delicate thread that holds it all together. It's the why and the how of saving our broken world. It's the story *and* the answer. It's the connector, the everything . . . *everything is connected.*

I turn back to Ellis.

And I come full circle.

ACKNOWLEDGMENTS

Thank you to my wonderful agent, Sarah Burnes, who not only believed in this story, but also helped shape it.

Thank you to my American editor, Sarah Barley. Sarah, your thoughtful insights, unfailing instincts, and deft guidance have lifted this story in so many ways. Working with you has been my absolute privilege.

Thank you to my Australian editor, Nicola Santilli. Nicola, finding the heart of this story wasn't always easy, and I am so grateful for the care, skill, and patience that you showed in helping us bring it into the light, together. You are an extraordinary talent, and I am enormously lucky to have worked with you so closely.

Thank you to Anna McFarlane and Susannah Chambers for all of your input and support. This book is stronger because of you both. Thank you to Amy Daoud for your gorgeous cover and internal design, to Vanessa Lanaway for your wonderful proofread, and to everyone at Allen & Unwin who has championed *Waking Romeo* behind the scenes.

Thank you to my unofficial editor, Ian Barker. Dad, I'd hate to think how many times you read (and reread) this manuscript for me, always with such insightful feedback and encouragement. Mum, thanks equally for the deal that you did with the universe to ensure that my books (eventually) get finished. I doubt there are two more supportive parents in all of existence, and I know exactly how lucky I am to have you.

Thank you to Justine Larbalestier, Melina Marchetta, and Lili Wilkinson for the beautiful stories that you put into the world and for your incredibly kind words.

Thank you to William Shakespeare, Emily Brontë, Jessica Walton, and Trae Hawkins—I learned from you all.

Thank you to Adam Barker for being the most wonderful brother, role model, and man. Thanks also to Sian Denning, whose extraordinary heart (and skills) I have benefited from so often.

Thank you to Kate Armstrong-Smith, my advisor, co-conspirator, counselor . . . not to mention best friend. Kate, our friendship is one of my things most treasured.

Thank you to Austin, Ethan, Ivy, Harrison, Elizabeth, the Bhandari family, my cousins, aunts, uncles, nieces, nephews, brothers-in-law, sisters-in-law . . . and the eternally impressive Diana Barker, aka Nanna.

Thank you to Polly Staniford, MJ Nolan, Joanna Houghton, Lynn Furniss, Helen Dallimore, Sophia Rahmani, Anne Maniquis, Anna Metzger, Zara Dempsey, and Harriet Hood— the world is so lucky to have such wonderful women.

Thank you to Pulp, Dire Straits, Chuck Berry, Taylor Swift, and David Bowie for the songs that were playing while I wrote this book. I tried to include a little nod to you all, in homage.

Thank you to Danny. Our story started when we were just five years old, and the magic of it has been weaving through our lives ever since. How fitting that the most epic, seemingly destined love story that I know . . . is ours.

And thank you to our children. You fill my days with more meaning and joy than I will ever have words for. You are the song in my heart, and my love for you is bigger than universes.

ABOUT THE AUTHOR

KATHRYN BARKER lives in Sydney, Australia, with her family. She has spent a lifetime exploring the magic of the universe through storytelling. Her first novel, *In the Skin of a Monster*, was published to high acclaim in Australia, winning the Aurealis Award for Best Young Adult Novel. *Waking Romeo* is Kathryn's second novel, and the first to be published in the United States.

www.kathrynbarker.com
@kathryntbarker